STAR TREK NOVELS

STAR TREK GIANT NOVELS

A *STAR TREK*® NOVEL

THE RIFT
PETER DAVID

TITAN BOOKS
LONDON

STAR TREK 52: **THE RIFT**
ISBN 1 85286 389 7

Published by
Titan Books Ltd
42–44 Dolben Street
London SE1 0UP

First Titan Edition November 1991
10 9 8 7 6 5 4 3 2

British edition by arrangement with Pocket Books, a division of Simon
and Schuster, Inc., Under Exclusive Licence from Paramount Pictures
Corporation, The Trademark Owner.

British Library Cataloguing-in-Publication Data. A catalogue record
for this book is available from the British Library.

Printed and bound in Great Britain by Cox and Wyman Ltd, Reading,
Berkshire.

THE RIFT

Dedicated to Shana, Guinevere, Emily,
Michael, and Bun-in-the-Oven . . .
the genuine "Next Generation."

The original manuscript for this book was printed entirely on recycled paper. And if that prompts any comments about recycled ideas going with paper, kindly keep them to yourself.

PLEASE REMEMBER: No smoking, no talking, and crying babies should be deposited in the receptacle in the lobby.

—Thank You
The Management

FIRST CONTACT

"Most people are on the world, not in it—have no conscious sympathy or relationship to anything about them—undiffused, separate, and rigidly alone like marbles of polished stone, touching but separate."

—JOHN MUIR

Chapter One

THE CAPTAIN OF THE *Enterprise* stared up at the shimmering viewscreen and said thoughtfully, "Opinion, Number One."

After a moment of consideration the first officer replied, "I'm not altogether certain, Captain. Mr. Spock . . . what do you think?"

Mr. Spock had not even looked up from his science station. "Difficult to be precise without completed computer analysis, Lieutenant . . . wait. It's coming through now."

Smoothly, noiselessly, the thin piece of paper slid out from the dispenser and into Spock's hands. He held it up and studied it for a moment.

He started to frown and then caught himself before the others noticed it. Silently he scolded himself—his mental discipline had been exceptionally sloppy of late, and he was going to have to pay much closer attention if he had any hope of conducting himself in a manner befitting a Vulcan . . . especially a Vulcan in

3

the highest position of Starfleet command that anyone from that planet had ever achieved.

"Computer analysis indicates a variety of readings that are an agglomeration of several different energy patterns already known to us," he said.

Number One looked at him with her dark, snapping eyes. "Specify," she said.

"It shares the spatial displacement traits of a wormhole," Spock said, studying the readout. "However, it is giving off subspace flux that is surprisingly similar to that created by the time warp generators of our own hyperdrive."

"Time warp?" said the captain.

Number One leaned on her console at the helm, studying the image on the screen. "Fascinating."

"A most appropriate term," Spock couldn't help but note. "It is indeed . . . fascinating." He rolled the word around in his mouth. A simple, elegant word. Descriptive, indicating the attractiveness of a puzzle in human terms without going overboard into emotionality. *Fascinating*. He'd have to remember that.

The fascinating object of their attention was directly ahead of them as the starship hovered in space several thousand kilometers away.

The crew of the *Enterprise* had encountered many different types of space phenomena before, from quarks to quasars, black holes to wormholes to any kind of hole that could be imagined. But this was something . . . unique.

In relation to the starship, it was on a vertical axis. It seemed to resemble nothing so much as a large crack, but it was not stable; its length varied from two to five miles, but no matter how much it seemed to fluctuate, its length was always greater than its width. Its center was narrow and dark—so dark that no light seemed to issue from it. Its outer edges were thinner, stars shining through. Whether it was artificial or had grown as a result of some physical anomaly was something that none of the observers could guess.

"A rip," said Spock after a moment's further consideration. "A rip in the fabric of space. The manner in which reality is being distorted around it is making it impossible for our sensors to probe more deeply. A rip or—"

"Or what?" The captain spoke with a sharpness that seemed to scream of impatience. For someone who was an explorer, Spock mused, the captain was tremendously irritable if he did not know all the answers immediately.

"A portal," finished Spock.

This brought silence to the bridge for a long moment, and the steady if irritating sounding of the red-alert klaxon filled the air, as it had been doing for several minutes since the *Enterprise* had first encountered this . . . this whatever-it-was.

Clearly it was getting on the captain's nerves, because he snapped, "Navigator, shut that damned noise off."

José Tyler reached over without a word and snapped it off. The red-alert triangle in front of him went out immediately, and the bridge settled into blissful quiet.

The captain leaned back in his chair, looking thoughtful. "A portal," he said slowly. "To where?" He turned his piercing blue eyes on Spock. "Well, Science Officer?"

"Unknown with present data," said Spock.

"Take a guess." From another captain it might have sounded like a gentle gibe, but with the captain of the *Enterprise* it came across quite clearly as a direct order.

Spock fought down the human urge to shrug and said simply, "It leads to the other side."

The captain sighed and turned back to Number One

in a manner that seemed so dismissive of Spock that the Vulcan might have taken offense were he capable of doing so. "Number One, you're the most experienced officer here. What's your guess?"

Number One flashed a glance at Spock, drummed her green fingernails a moment, and then said, "Mr. Spock is correct. It leads to the other side. Further speculation would be pointless."

"Unless we go through," said the captain.

"Yes, sir."

"Is it possible?"

Spock, studying his readouts, now spoke up. "It would be possible, sir. However, it would be extremely hazardous. The physical makeup of the space rip is in flux. It ranges from two miles in width to as little as five meters. We could be sheared in half just by the act of passing through it, if it should happen to close at the wrong time."

The captain rose from his chair and circled it slowly, thoughtfully. "Open a subspace hailing frequency."

"Open," said Communications Officer Vincent.

The captain squared his shoulders even more than usual and spoke in a slightly raised voice. Spock speculated on what an odd human trait that was, as if talking more loudly over subspace made one easier to hear.

"This is Captain Christopher Pike of the United Space Ship *Enterprise,*" said the captain. "If there is anyone hearing this transmission, we are positioned directly outside what appears to be some sort of interspatial rift. The fluctuating nature of the rift makes it impossible for us to pass through. We wish to know if there is any sentient life on the other side of this spatial distortion. If you are hearing this, please reply." He paused and then added, "Send that out on all frequencies, Lieutenant."

"Yes, sir," said Vincent.

He sat back down in his command chair and rubbed his chin thoughtfully. "There have been ships in this area before, haven't there?"

Spock began to call up the computer records, but Number One spoke before Spock could access the information. "Two science vessels and the *Potemkin* have traveled this sector in the past three years. There has been no mention of any similar spatial rifts in their reports," said Number One.

Pike looked at her with just the vaguest hint of amusement, which was the most he ever allowed. "You carry around in your head the findings of all ships in any given sector for the past three years, Lieutenant?"

"No, sir," Number One told him coolly. "The past five years."

"I see," Pike said. If this struck him as particularly odd, he nevertheless said nothing. "So it wasn't here before?"

"Either that," said Spock, "or it was in existence but slightly out of temporal synch with our universe."

"What?" asked Pike.

"Essentially, it existed a few seconds before or after the natural time flow of our own universe. As a result, normal instrumentation would never have been able to pick it up. But some occurrence, natural or otherwise, may have caused it to slow down or speed up and thus be detectable."

They waited there, hanging in space for long moments, but no reply was forthcoming, and slowly Pike shook his head. "All right," he said. "Let's summarize here: We have a temporal rift that may or may not have been here before. There may or may not be someone on the other side, and we may or may not survive trying to pass through. Is that about accurate?"

7

Spock and Number One both nodded silent assent.

Pike rubbed the bridge of his nose with thumb and forefinger. Then he looked up and sighed. "As intriguing as all this is," he said, "we were on our way to Vega IX to attend to our injured and wounded. We've already had one significant delay in that respect, and for a lot of 'mays' and 'may nots' there is no way in hell I'm going to delay that mission any further. Helm, resume course for Vega. Go to hyperdrive, time warp factor five."

"Course computed and laid in, sir," said Number One.

He nodded and said briskly, "Engage."

The *Enterprise* angled away from the rift and shot off toward Vega IX.

Pike watched the rift recede as he headed for the turbolift door. As he was about to step into the lift Yeoman Colt stepped off, apparently wrapped up in thoughts of her own, and Pike stopped just short of knocking her over.

"Yeoman," he said in exasperation, "how many—"

"Fuel consumption report, sir," she said quickly, holding the clipboard up in front of her as if it were a shield. "You said that you wanted—"

"Yes, yes," he overlapped her impatiently. He barely glanced at her as he flipped through it. He took note of the fact that he should speak to the engineer about the speed with which they were depleting dilithium— it seemed the energy curve was a tad high. Perhaps there was a warped baffle plate somewhere. If that was the case, there could be a serious hazard in the making—Pike had once seen a crewman devastated by leaking delta rays from a warped baffle plate and had no intention of such an unpleasant fate befalling any member of his crew.

He signed the report, checking off the box that read "Consult with captain," and handed it back to Colt.

She smiled briefly at him and then looked down as if embarrassed, and Pike sighed inwardly.

"Strong female drives." The phrase echoed in his head, and she stepped aside as he entered the open turbolift. He made a conscious effort not to look at her as the doors hissed shut.

And as the *Enterprise* shot off into space the rift began to pulse a bit more steadily. . . .

Chapter Two

PIKE'S FISTS WERE a flurry of rights and lefts as he pounded the punching bag. He grunted softly every time he made contact, and he remembered a time when he could have kept up such a volley for half an hour without letup. Now, after a mere ten minutes, he felt his breath coming hard in his lungs.

There were several crewmen in the gym concentrating on fencing or weight lifting or other fitness pursuits, but they were surreptitiously sneaking glances at Pike, watching admiringly.

The captain never spoke to anyone when he came down to work out. Perhaps an acknowledging nod here or there, but that was all. He was always totally focused on whatever he was setting out to do, and he never did the same thing twice in a row. Fencing, swimming, running, self-defense—whatever it was, he went about it with an intensity that was unmatched by anyone in the crew.

Now, as he pounded on the bag, the volley speeding up with each passing moment, he seemed so locked in to his target that anyone who happened to step between Pike and the bag would likely run into the captain's fist.

After another three minutes of punching Pike stepped back, his face covered with sweat and his thin shirt plastered against his chest. He tapped his boxing gloves together a couple of times and shook out his muscles, but his heart was still pounding.

He turned and glanced around, the adrenaline racing through him. There was no one else with boxing gloves on, though, and he had started to turn away when José Tyler entered, gloves on his hands, glancing in the direction of the punching bag. Tyler stopped when he saw Pike standing nearby and then cast an involuntary look over his shoulder, apparently trying to decide whether he could get out without being noticed.

"Mr. Tyler," said Pike with a wave of his gloved hand, "I could use a sparring partner."

"Oh, well, sir," said Tyler, and he quickly looked to the other crewmen for help. None seemed forthcoming. "I—uhm—actually wasn't planning on boxing. . . ."

Pike inclined his chin slightly in the direction of Tyler's hands. "Why the gloves then?"

"My hands are cold, sir."

"Come on, Tyler," said Pike, and he gestured to the mats in the center of the gym. There was no boxing ring set up, but that was the area used for any type of hand-to-hand combat. "It'll be good for both of us."

Tyler sighed, trying to ignore the smirks from the crewmates around him. "If you say so, sir."

They moved to the center mats, and now the rest of the crewmen gave up any pretense of ignoring what was going on. From the supply cabinet one of the crewmen stepped forward with mouthpieces that were quickly inserted into Pike's and Tyler's mouths. Protective headgear was strapped on moments later.

Pike's appraising gaze flickered over Tyler, assessing the young, lithe Latin navigator—not as a crewman, but as a potential foe. Tyler was balanced lightly on the balls of his feet, and Pike saw genuine concern in his eyes.

"All right, Tyler," he said, working to make himself understood through the mouthpiece. "Just relax. Watch your footing. We're just having a workout, just two guys in the gym. Happens every day. No need to worry, just so long as you remember . . . I'm your captain."

It was difficult to tell if Pike was joking, since he did it so rarely. Even when he was joking he tended to keep his face deadly serious. Tyler sighed once more and started toward Pike, trying to move lightly from side to side, keeping his guard up.

The tactical computer that was Pike's mind quickly processed information about Tyler. He was more limber than Pike, and younger, of course. He was already hopping around a good deal more than the captain was capable of doing—Pike tended to take a stance and just start pummeling. He had the edge on Tyler in experience, and he also had a devastating right cross. He could take him.

Pike brought his guard up as Tyler suddenly launched an attack, a couple of quick rights followed by a left. Pike hardly felt them. "Come on, Mr. Tyler," he said in annoyance, and he drove a quick uppercut to Tyler's chin that rocked him. "You can do better than that."

Tyler stepped back out of Pike's reach and moved along the perimeter, watching his captain carefully. He did not resume his attack, however, and after thirty seconds of pussyfooting around, Pike began to get annoyed. He came in quickly, landing several fast, powerful blows on Tyler's body, each accompanied by a satisfying thud, and Pike said, "For crying out loud, Mr. Tyler, this is sparring, not a square dan—"

Pike never even saw the shot that snapped his head around. He wasn't even aware that he was falling. All he knew was that the world seemed to shift at a forty-five-degree angle, and then he was on his back.

He found to his surprise that he hated the color of the ceiling, and then José Tyler was looking down at him with sheer terror in his eyes. "Capped in!" Tyler seemed to be saying, and Pike was wondering what was capped in what.

Then the world hazed out for a moment, and when it returned Dr. Phil Boyce was standing over him, shaking his head. The middle-aged man with the thin blond hair did not seem particularly sympathetic to the fact that Pike was moving his mouth and nothing was coming out. An agitated Tyler was next to him. "What was it again?" Boyce asked.

"A left hook," said Tyler. "Doctor . . . what should I do?"

"Offhand, I'd say work on your right hook. I doubt your left needs any improvement." Boyce shook his head, and then he raised his fist and extended his thumb, index finger, and middle finger. "Chris . . . how many fingers do you see?"

"I'm not sure," said Pike thickly. "Does the thumb count as a finger?"

"You'll be fine," Boyce said. He put an arm under Pike's forearm and, with the help of Tyler and another crewman, hauled the woozy captain to his feet. Pike was surprised at the amount of strength in the doctor's grip.

"Captain, I'm so sorry—" began Tyler.

Pike shook his head and then had to remind himself not to do so again, as the swaying motion made him dizzy. "That's quite all right, Mr. Tyler. Quite all

13

right. It's comforting to know you're on our side." He held his jaw for a moment and moved it from side to side. "I'd hate to have you as an enemy."

"Yes, sir," said Tyler, breathing a visible sigh of relief.

Leaning a bit more heavily on Boyce than he would have liked to let on, Pike allowed himself to be helped into the hallway and to his cabin. Boyce had the tact not to say anything to his captain until the door of Pike's quarters had closed behind him.

"You want to tell me what that was all about?" asked Boyce.

Pike was studying himself in the mirror and already saw the beginnings of a bruise on his jaw. "Sparring, Doctor. A way of keeping in shape."

Boyce folded his arms and looked at Pike skeptically. "Most ways of keeping in shape," he noted, "don't entail almost losing consciousness."

"It was just a lucky punch."

"Lucky punch my butt," snorted Boyce. "From what I heard, he tagged you good. The one who's lucky is you—lucky that he didn't dislocate your jaw."

"Ah"—he waved off Boyce's concerns—"you worry too much, Phil. Tyler's ten years younger than I am. He couldn't have hurt me too badly."

"If you were thinking straight, Chris," said Boyce, "you'd realize that the ten years' difference actually makes it damned lucky that he didn't take your head off." Still shaking his head, Boyce opened up his bag and started pulling out his mixes.

Pike turned and eyed the quickly assembled minibar without comment. Boyce didn't even look at Pike but simply said, "The usual?"

"Someday," said Pike, "you'll pull a hypo out of there and give me a heart attack."

"Thank God you'll have a doctor nearby in that

14

case." He proceeded to mix a martini for Pike. "That's not like you, Chris. Sparring with your junior officers. Mixing it up. You've always been . . ."

"Aloof?" Pike finished for him.

"I was going to say 'reserved,' " said Boyce, and he handed the drink to Pike.

"Rooms are reserved," said Pike. "Library books are reserved. I'm aloof. Removed from my people. From their feelings. Maybe from my own."

"Oh, nonsense," said Boyce. "A few days ago you sat right on that bed and told me that you were thinking of quitting. That you were tired, worn out, sick of making decisions. And now you're saying that you're unfeeling, when before you were feeling too much. You're concerned about how you deal with your crew? Different captains have different approaches, Chris. What works for you—and your crew—is for you to possess a great deal of formality and 'aloofness,' if that's what you wish to call it. Have you noticed that, particularly on the bridge, you tend to address your crewmen by their positions far more frequently than by their names?"

Pike frowned slightly. "No. I hadn't noticed."

"Everyone else you address by Mister followed by surname, with the exception of my humble self," continued Boyce with a slight, modest inclination of his head. "And some people not even that. Since Number One is your first officer, naturally she can be addressed by the title of Number One. But you never call her anything else. Why is that?"

"I can't pronounce her name."

"What? Why, it's . . ." His voice trailed off, and he frowned. He'd seen it written in records but never tried to say it out loud before. The woman hadn't engaged in small talk on the occasions of her physicals —simple nods had sufficed. He tried to frame the syllables. "Son of a gun."

15

"You see? Not everything has deep meaning," said Pike. Then he stared down at his boots. "You want to know how in touch with my crew I am?"

"Sure."

"We were just discussing Number One. Well, she"— he took a sip of his martini, as if steeling himself for an ordeal—"she has sexual fantasies about me."

Boyce went slack-jawed, and it took him a moment to realize that some of his drink was trickling down his chin. He quickly wiped it away as he said, "May I ask . . . uh . . . how you know?"

"The Talosians said so."

"I see. And what was your response to this?"

"To her? Nothing. I was threatening the Talosians at the time."

"And since you've come back, have you spoken to her about it?"

Pike pursed his lips. "No."

"How . . . uh . . . how do you feel about it? Do you have . . . uhm . . . reciprocal feelings in this matter?"

"I don't know," admitted Pike. "It goes back to what I was saying before. I feel removed from my crew's feelings, and from my own. I thought of Number One as cold, methodical, even utterly passionless. The ideal woman."

"Oh, really?" said Boyce in amusement.

"Of course. The trouble with most women is that they let their hearts rule them instead of their heads. Decision making is an intellectual process. Women are—"

"A distraction?" offered Boyce.

Pike pointed in triumph. "Yes! Exactly. They distract you with their emotional reactions and—"

"The way they look? And smell?"

"There's that."

Boyce leaned back thoughtfully. "The curve of a

16

woman's neck if she's wearing her hair up? Or the way her hair cascades around her shoulders if her hair is down?" His voice softened, and he smiled. "The way the very air can seemed to be charged when a woman enters a room? The way just hearing her take a deep breath can make you lose your train of thought?"

Pike was staring off into space. "The way her eyes could sparkle when she looked at me, when her whole world consisted of wanting . . ."

Then he caught himself and saw Boyce looking at him, not unsympathetically. He looked down into his drink, staring at the olive floating there.

"Vina was quite a woman, wasn't she?" said Boyce.

Pike shrugged. "You read my log entries."

"And it's all there? Everything you experienced? Everything you felt?"

"Everything that was important," said Pike firmly.

"Ah, now that's the debatable part, isn't it?" Boyce replied. "What's important, that is. And what arc you going to do about Number One?"

"Nothing. If she wanted me to know her feelings about me, she would have told me. The Talosians invaded her privacy. I'm hardly going to capitalize on that." Abruptly there came a beep from the small viewscreen on Pike's desk. He rose and went to it, pushing a button. A small image of Number One appeared, and she said, "Captain, we're getting a transmission."

"From Starfleet?"

"No, sir. From the rift."

This snapped Pike completely to attention. "The rift?"

"Yes, sir. The temporal rift in space."

"I'll be right up."

He turned toward the door, and Boyce began to put away his portable bar. "Duty calls?"

"Very loudly."

"Try not to let yourself be too distracted by Number One."

"I'll try."

He exited his quarters and started toward the turbolift. He got there and stepped through, but before the doors could shut he heard a voice call, "Hold, please!"

Pike turned and saw his Vulcan science officer hurrying down the hallway, presumably also in response to a summons from Number One. He was still favoring the one leg, a result of their encounter with the hostiles on Rigel. God, were they *ever* going to get to Vega to tend to their wounded?

"Bridge," said Pike. Then, after a moment of thought, he turned to Spock and said, "Tell me, Sci—Mr. Spock. Lately you seem to be spending much more time by yourself."

"Sir?"

"You don't fraternize with the rest of the crew as much as you used to."

Spock seemed to look straight through him. "There's no regulation against that, sir."

"No. No, of course not. But as your commanding officer, I would like to be kept informed if you were having any problems. I'm interested in the well-being of my crew."

"You are, sir?"

"Of course I am," Pike said a bit testily. "I'm always concerned. Concern is my middle name."

"No, sir, your middle name is—"

"It's an expression, Mr. Spock. I was just . . . curious. That's all."

"Curiosity. Ah, yes," said Spock, as if he had just noticed an interesting specimen in a zoo. "A human emotion. Perhaps, Captain, I am simply a bit . . .

18

overwhelmed by human emotions. The air can be a bit thick with them at times."

At that moment the turbolift hissed open onto the bridge, and Pike immediately stopped talking, now all business.

"All right," he said briskly as he stepped down to his command chair. "What have we got?"

"Transmission directly from the rift," Number One said, turning in her chair to face the captain. She held up a paper display of the message. "It says, 'Seventy-two-hour window of contact. What do you want?'"

"That's it?"

Number One nodded.

Pike leaned on one of the arms of his command chair. "There is someone on the other side."

"So it would appear," agreed Spock.

"But the other side of what? Another part of our galaxy? Another galaxy entirely? Perhaps even another universe?"

"We won't know unless we try to find out," Number One pointed out.

"And if we go on to Vega, as originally intended, we'll never get back within the seventy-two hours that whoever's on the other side of the rift claims we have." He thought about it a moment, but his mind was already made up. "Address intracraft," he said briskly.

"You're on, Captain," Number One replied.

"This is the captain," he announced. Throughout the *Enterprise* crewmen stopped in their tracks to attend to the announcement. "I regret that we will have to delay our needed downtime a short while longer. The sort of rare opportunity that we're out here for has presented itself unexpectedly. This is what we signed up to do, and I expect that you will be able to put your personal needs aside for as long as is required to complete our latest mission. And that mission is contact with a new species accessible only through a previously undiscovered rift in space. You will be kept apprised of mission progress. Bridge out."

He turned to Tyler at navigation, who, if he was thinking about how he had earlier laid out his captain, was far too professional to let on. "Mr. Tyler, take us back to the rift. Hyperdrive, time warp factor seven."

"Laid in, sir."

"Engage."

Pike settled back in his chair and noticed the way that Number One's hair fell around her shoulders. With sensitivity that bordered on the psychic, Number One turned and looked at him curiously with her luminous eyes. "Sir?"

He frowned and shook his head. "Yes, Number One?"

She gave a small shrug of her shoulders. "Nothing, sir." And she went on about her business.

Pike felt the great gulf of his command separating them but refused to dwell on it. Instead he stared intently at the screen as the stars hurtled by them, and he couldn't help but notice that the stars, as they streaked past, seemed like a woman's tears. . . .

Chapter Three

"IT'S OPEN, SIR."

Spock turned from his science station and concentrated on keeping surprise from his voice. "The readings are unmistakable. The rift is now stable. The dangerous fluctuations that could have destroyed the ship have ceased, making passage possible."

Pike stared at the spatial aberration that hung before them. There was no hint of what, if anything, was on the other side. Instead there was only inky blackness. "You're saying we should go in?"

"No, sir," said Spock. "I'm saying that it is possible."

Pike nodded and stood. "Recommendation, Number One?"

"Caution, sir."

"You always recommend that."

"It's always a good idea," she said primly.

"Send a communication," he said. "Tell them we're here, and that we await their advice."

The response came in short order. Spock read it in

surprise. "Captain, it says: 'Come on in. The water's fine.'"

The bridge crew exchanged glances.

"Now what are we supposed to get from that?" demanded Pike.

Number One drummed a moment on her console. "We can surmise that they are either a race with some degree of telepathic ability, or else they are capable of interfacing with our computer records without tripping any alarm systems that tell us we're being scanned. Therefore they are either mentally or technologically advanced."

"Another race of telepaths," said Pike sourly. "I've had a bellyful of them lately."

"They would seem to be somewhat more aboveboard than the Talosians," Spock observed. "They offer no false images, no prevarications. They simply invite us to enter, stating in old earth vernacular that the conditions are suitable for our existence."

"Tell them they should come out here," Pike said after a moment.

The message was duly sent, and this time a much shorter period of time passed before the response came back.

"They said, 'That is not our way.'"

"Perfect," said Pike. "Science Officer, arm a probe and prepare to launch on my order."

Spock nodded and quickly entered the instructions into the computer. On the nod from Pike he checked the telemetry one more time and then fired the probe off into the rift.

The probe appeared as nothing so much as a ball of light as it spiraled toward the temporal opening, down, down, and then was completely swallowed up.

They waited.

"Any readings, Science Officer?"

Spock studied his telemetry board, waiting for some

22

sort of response from the probe. "Nothing, sir," he said. "It . . . wait. Sensors are detecting something."

"Specify."

"Emerging from the rift, at 331 mark 20 . . ."

Pike swung his chair around and snapped, "Viewer on full magnification, to Mr. Spock's coordinates."

The viewscreen wavered a moment, and then it closed in tight on the lower right-hand corner of the rift. Something seemed to be floating out of it—metallic scrap.

"It's the probe," Spock announced. "It's been broken up into pieces."

"Incoming message," said Number One.

"What's it say?"

It only took the computer a second to spit out the printout. Spock picked it up and read two succinct words off it, which represented the entirety of the message.

"It says, 'Nice try.'"

In the conference room Pike and his officers surrounded the table as Spock placed the fragments of the probe on the table with a clank. Number One picked up one of the smaller pieces and held it between her fingers, staring at it with curiosity. "Is this what I think?"

"Yes, Number One," Spock told her. "I've run a full spectral analysis, and it confirms my original supposition and your current one. That piece of metal you're holding is approximately 33.4 years old."

Pike looked from Number One to Spock. "What? I thought it was part of our probe."

"It is. Was," amended Spock. He gestured to take in the rest of the pieces on the table. "As were these. They test out similarly, with minor variations of a year or two on some of the pieces that emerged first."

"We didn't launch that over thirty years ago, dammit," said Pike.

"Of course not, sir. I have a working theory, however."

"Don't keep it to yourself," said Dr. Boyce. "You're not going to get any brownie points by keeping us guessing."

Spock barely glanced at him. He and Boyce had never gotten on particularly well. Boyce's amateur psychology attempts at Spock's expense had been a continuing source of distraction. Spock, however, didn't worry about it overmuch. In a few years Boyce would be retiring, and whatever future ship's doctors Spock might encounter, he was quite certain they could not possibly be as acerbic or annoying as Boyce.

"The temporal shifts within the makeup of the rift," said Spock, "caused a field distortion around the probe as well. The rift is not simply a hole in space. It is a collapsed field of time travel, bending temporal waves around whatever enters it. The probe was subjected to year upon year of temporal stress. Perhaps it was sent into the future and aged backward—perhaps back into the past and aged forward. It's impossible to say."

"My head is starting to hurt," murmured Boyce.

"Essentially, the probe fell apart due to the stress of passing years," concluded Spock.

"And the same thing would happen to us if we passed through it," said Pike.

"Not necessarily." Number One spoke up. She looked at Spock, who was clearly already aware of what she was going to say and merely nodded his agreement. She continued, "If we enter using the hyperdrive, the time warp factor of our engines should protect us from the ravages of the temporal flux."

"*Should* protect us," said Pike.

"There is a ninety-eight-percent probability," Number One told him.

Pike slowly circled the table. "Meaning there's a two-percent possibility of failure. Correct?"

"Correct," she said, staring at Spock to see if he disagreed with her. Again he merely nodded slightly.

Pike crossed the room again, his hands behind his back. "If we went in at hyperdrive, we wouldn't even have the time to react to any danger that our sensors alerted us to. You're asking me to take a significant leap of faith here with the lives of this crew. Roll dice based on the odds."

"But," Spock pointed out, "it would seem that the odds are significantly in our favor, Captain."

Pike turned his cold gaze on Spock. "Then again, you're not the one who has to carry the weight of the decision, are you, Science Off—Mr. Spock?"

If Spock noticed the abrupt change in form of address, or cared particularly about it, he gave no indication. "No, sir. I'm not. But there is something else that should be brought to your attention, Captain." He held out his hand, and in his palm was what appeared to be a small triangular device, with delicately printed circuits on it. It was no larger than Spock's fingernail.

"What is it?" said Pike.

"It was mixed in with the debris," said Spock. "'Planted,' if you will."

"By whoever is on the other side?" asked Number One.

"It would be the logical surmise." Spock manipulated the small device. "It would appear, from my initial studies, to be a sort of energy conversion chip. But far more efficient than the one that currently powers our hyperdrive."

The chief engineer, Caitlin Barry, reached out a

25

hand, and Spock handed the device to her. She studied it in amazement. "Are you sure about this?"

"It is only one component of an infinitely more complicated propulsion system," said Spock. "We could not develop the complete system from this one piece any more than one could accurately replicate the entire human body by being given a kidney to study. It is an indicator, though, of the advanced nature of those on the other side of the rift."

"So what you're saying," said Pike, taking the piece from Barry, "is that this is bait."

"Or their way of letting us know that whatever risk we perceive in this contact is worth it," pointed out Number One.

Nothing more needed to be said. The command crew knew almost instinctively the expression that came across Pike's face when he had heard everything he needed to in order to render a decision.

There was total silence in the conference room as he weighed the options.

Then he became aware somehow, in the back of his head, of a very soft, steady sound.

It was Number One. Breathing.

He turned to Barry. "Ready the hyperdrive, Engineer," he said briskly. "We're going in."

Moments later the command crew had assembled on the bridge, and Pike was once again addressing the general crew over the intracraft. He was a strong believer in constantly apprising everyone of what was going on. With a crew this large he did not need rumors floating around.

"We are about to enter an unknown section of space," he was saying. "I want everyone at his or her post, in full readiness. This ship is now on yellow alert. I'm not anticipating a battle situation, but we must be prepared for whatever circumstances we face. I have the utmost faith that all of you will carry through with your duties. Bridge out." Then he turned to Number One and said, "All right, Helm. Bring us forward on rocket power only, to within two thousand kilometers of our anomaly there." Into his communicator he said, "Engine Room."

"Standing by, Captain," came Barry's voice.

"Prepare for hyperdrive, time warp factor . . ."

He paused, unsure of what to allow for in this new situation. Number One looked back at him and held up two fingers.

"Two," said Pike.

"Aye, sir. She'll be ready."

Slowly the *Enterprise* began to ease forward, drawing closer to the rift. Pike waited for a report that some sort of energy flux was pulling them in against their will, the slightest hint that this was a trap. But none was forthcoming. Come into my parlor, said the spider to the fly, he thought bleakly. "Sensor readings?"

"Unchanged from before," said Spock. "Still obscured."

"We are at two thousand kilometers," said Number One.

"Full stop."

"Full stop, Captain," Number One affirmed.

The rift was before them, seemingly part of normal space and yet part of something else. The surface rippled and flowed as if it were a thick porridge being heated to boiling.

And he was going to hurl himself and his ship and crew into the midst of it, in hopes of finding—

What?

Well, that was what they did every day, wasn't it? Blasted further and further into the depths of space, into the unknown. No one ever knew what they were going to find, did they? Or what the risks to life and limb might be.

It was just unusual to have the unknown facing one so bald-facedly.

"When you look long into an abyss, the abyss also looks into you," said Pike slowly. Then he took a deep breath and said, "Full ahead. Hyperdrive, time warp factor two." He paused a split second before he said, "Engage."

Tyler laid in the course, and Number One, taking a slight breath (which Pike heard), punched it in.

The *Enterprise* hurtled forward, powered by hyperdrive, and a moment later was enveloped by the rift.

The universe howled in Pike's head.

All around them the stars telescoped away and vanished, and what was left was nothingness filled with everything.

Pike screamed soundlessly, and the scream seemed to take up everything as the past and future collided around him. He saw images, bizarre and insane images that made no sense. Images of a reality gone mad, images from out of time, out of mind.

He looked to his left, and he was growing younger before his very eyes; and he looked to his right, and there was a bizarre creature staring at him, crouched in some sort of metal chair. The sight of it made his soul freeze.

On the screen was nothing but a vast miasma of undulating space, as if the cosmos had become a vast lake and someone had skipped a stone across it.

"Maintain power!" shouted Pike, and he wasn't sure if anyone had heard him. He wasn't sure if he'd even said it, or if he was going to say it, or if it had already been said and just infinitely repeated. . . .

The ship seemed to vibrate uncontrollably, and there was a shout from the engine room. It wasn't Barry but Lieutenant Scott, who usually communicated with the bridge on Barry's behalf if she was tied up. In an alarmed brogue Scott shouted, "Captain! The engines canna take much more of this!" There was more than just concern about machinery in his voice—it was as if he were being forced to stand by and watch his children being tortured.

And then the stars snapped into existence. And so did the ship.

Ahead of them was a vast ball of whiteness, and there was something surrounding it, and then the *Enterprise* flashed past at hyperspeed.

Pike's mouth was moving before he managed to get the words out. "Reduce speed!" he shouted. "Take us out of hyperdrive! Shut down the time warp field!"

Number One was paralyzed at helm, her eyes wide, and to her right was Tyler, his face contorted. He was muttering something over and over, something like "Ma, Ma." Great. Pike needed the ship stopped, and Tyler was calling for his mother.

Pike leapt forward, shoving his way to the helm control, pushing Tyler aside as he reached in front of Number One. Tyler lashed out with a quick left, but this time Pike saw it coming and managed to knock it aside even as he shut down the ship's forward thrust at helm.

The captain's arm in front of her shook Number One from her momentary paralysis, and she seemed to register for the first time that the captain had made a request of her. She started to reach for the controls to slow the ship but then hesitated when she saw that the command had already been carried out. She turned and looked with surprise into Pike's eyes.

She licked her lips and said, "Sorry, sir."

Relieved to have some degree of normalcy on the bridge once more, he said, "It's all right. Navigator?"

Tyler was still staring off into space as if fixated on something very, very specific. His lower lip was

29

trembling. "Mr. Tyler," said Pike firmly, and still there was no response. For a moment he considered summoning Boyce to the bridge, but then without even really thinking about the overt familiarity it suggested, he rested a hand on Tyler's shoulder and said, "José. You with us?"

Tyler blinked several times and then looked up at Pike. "Captain?" His eyes took a moment to focus, and then, more firmly, he said, "Captain."

"At ease, Mr. Tyler. Tell us where we are, if you please."

Tyler quickly called up his navigational charts and ran an analysis on the stars that hovered in front of their viewscreen. Pike didn't even need the report to know that he had never seen this particular array of stars before. Nevertheless, he waited patiently.

"As near as I can determine, sir," Tyler said finally, "we are somewhere in the outer reaches of the Gamma quadrant."

There was a momentary hush. "That's light-years beyond explored space," said Pike. "Are you sure?"

"Confirming Mr. Tyler's assessment," Spock said from the science station. "We are a significant distance from known space."

"How significant?"

Spock turned and looked at his captain. "At time warp factor seven—which we could not possibly maintain—it would take 21.3 years to reach the furthest Federation outpost. Furthermore, even at time warp factor one, we would drain our dilithium crystals dry years before we could return to known space."

"Meaning," said Pike slowly, "that the rift had better be our ticket back . . . or else we'll be able to tell our children and grandchildren stories of how they came to be the first children born on a starship."

"That is correct," said Spock.

"All right," Pike said with a no-nonsense tone. He went back to his chair and turned it to face the screen. "Bring us around. I saw something when we came through, and I want to get a closer look at it."

The *Enterprise* swung around and, at impulse power, retraced her steps. As she did so Pike ran a quick check with Engineering to make sure that all was well with the engines. Once satisfied, he turned to Spock and said, "Have we got a reading on the rift?" He was almost afraid to ask, because if the spatial aperture had vanished, there was a good chance they would never see home again.

So it was with great relief—not that he let on, of course—that he heard Spock say, "Yes, sir. At 213 mark 8. Same temporal readings as before. And . . . something else."

"I see it. Helm, magnification three."

The screen rippled, and when it snapped into focus Pike became aware that his mouth was hanging half-open. He closed it quickly, hoping that no one had noticed.

In front of them a planet was on fire.

Chapter Four

SPOCK AND NUMBER ONE spoke at the same time: "Fascinating."

It was an understatement.

It was a large planet, roughly the size of Jupiter, and it looked aflame. The entire surface was covered with a dark blue blaze, burning steadily and unceasingly. But that wasn't the only bizarre thing that faced them.

For around the planet was a series of satellites, linked with each other by an intricate system of connectors that gave the entire thing the look of a giant spider web. The satellites varied in circumference but shared a generally uniform look in that each of them had a vast, clear dome over it that encompassed what appeared to be a gleaming city.

Two satellites were exceptions, situated at the opposite poles of the planet. The one at the southern pole was the second-largest satellite of the group, with a single tower that seemed to reflect the steady fire of the planet.

The northern pole satellite was the largest by far,

and it did not appear to have gleaming towers on it in the manner of the others. Instead it sported buildings that were low and squat. Furthermore, in addition to the connectors that bonded that particular satellite to others nearby, there was a connector that plunged straight down into the planet below.

"Analysis?" said Pike when what they were seeing had had a chance to sink in.

"The 'fire' on the planet surface," said Spock after a moment, "would appear to be a type of self-regenerating energy plasma, supplying the satellite web around it with all its power needs on a perpetual basis."

"Self-regenerating?"

"Yes, sir."

It was a remarkable concept, right up there with the perpetual-motion machine. The energy needs of the *Enterprise* were met through the use of dilithium crystals, but each of them were precious and had a finite life. The idea of being able to regenerate an energy source was something of a dream.

"The satellites?"

"Interior atmospheres would appear to have a breathable oxygen/nitrogen balance, but the mix would be somewhat thinner than what we're accustomed to," said Spock. "Suggest any landing party members be administered a tri-ox compound to compensate."

"Noted. Forward the recommendation to Medical."

And then the screen shifted again, and to their shock, a face appeared.

It was clearly a male, but it was difficult to determine his age. His face was crimson, and his eyes seemed to shimmer with a vague iridescence. He had no hair on his head, but instead a delicate lined

33

pattern stretched from his forehead across the top of his head to the back of his skull—a pattern that was identical in shape to the network of connectors that linked the satellites. His nose consisted of two slits in the middle of his face over which thin layers of skin fluttered delicately as he breathed.

"Incoming message," said Tyler, somewhat unnecessarily.

Pike didn't comment on the obvious statement. Instead he took a step forward and said, "I am Captain Christopher Pike of the space vehicle *Enterprise*."

The alien inclined his head slightly. "So you are," he said. "I am Zyo, Master Builder of the Calligar."

"'Master Builder?'"

Zyo shrugged, a surprisingly human gesture. "An hereditary title, for my lifetime. A small honor among a people who give few such."

There was an uneasy silence for a moment, and then Pike said, "We are unfamiliar with your people."

"As we are unfamiliar with yours," replied Zyo. "Therefore, I suggest that we become better acquainted."

"If you tell us where to beam—"

But Zyo merely smiled. "Oh, I think not, Captain Christopher Pike. To be honest, you have absolutely no idea what a stir your presence has caused among the Calligar."

"Why? We mean you no harm."

"Oh, that is irrelevant." Zyo actually grimaced slightly at that. "It is the mere fact of your being here—of our letting you know that we existed—that has caused something of a sensation. I will be happy to apprise you of the situation, Captain, but I am afraid it will have to be on our terms."

Pike looked at Number One, who gave the slightest

shrug of her shoulders. It was her way of letting him know that she really didn't have much of anything in the way of advice to offer. And if there was one thing that Number One did not tend to do, it was to speak for the purpose of hearing herself talk.

"All right," said Pike. "Your terms, then . . . as long as they do not involve anything that I think would be dangerous to this ship or crew."

"You are the leader of your people. I can certainly respect that. Shall we say . . . one of your hours?"

"You're familiar with earth measurements?"

"Of course." Zyo smiled slightly. "We've thoroughly studied all your computer records."

"I can't say I appreciate that. If we're to establish any sort of relationship, it must be predicated on trust. If you wish information from us, I suggest you ask next time."

Zyo tilted his head slightly in acknowledgment. "As you wish, Captain Christopher Pike. One hour, then." And the screen returned to its image of the satellite cities that the *Enterprise* crew now knew belonged to the peoples known as the Calligar.

Pike immediately faced Spock. "Science Officer, would you care to tell me how in hell they scanned our computer system without tripping any alarms?"

Spock frowned and said, "It would seem to indicate a computer sophistication that is considerably beyond anything within the realm of our science."

"In other words, you don't know."

"That is correct, sir," said Spock.

"Well," said Pike, "in an hour we'll have them aboard, and then we can ask them."

Pike studied himself in the mirror, smoothing the front of his dress jacket. He nodded briskly, satisfied with his appearance. He did not often call for dress

35

uniforms among his crew, but this was a first contact on an extremely foreign turf. Top elements of decorum had to be adhered to.

There was a chime at his door, and he said, "Come."

The door hissed open, and José Tyler was standing there, looking uncomfortable. "Captain . . ."

"Yes, Mr. Tyler?"

Tyler took a deep breath and said, "I wish to apologize for my conduct on the bridge, sir. It was . . . inappropriate."

"Yes, it was." Pike was silent for a moment and then gestured for Tyler to enter. Tyler did so, the door hissing shut behind him. "Would you care to tell me what provoked such a strong reaction?"

Tyler looked down, hesitating, and Pike continued, "If there was anything you experienced that could be of help, I would like to know about it."

Tyler sighed and then said, "I saw . . . things. I saw . . . this female. She was . . . I don't know, there was just a flash of her, and she was calling to me, I thought. That's what it seemed like, at any rate. And it was as if I knew her and yet . . . didn't know her. You know? Captain, do you know what happened when we went through there?"

Pike turned and looked into the mirror. It seemed for just a moment that that bizarre apparition—that strange creature in that outlandish chair—was staring back at him.

"I'm not sure," he said. "I thought I saw something myself, but I wasn't sure . . . it happened so quickly. Now that I know you also saw . . . images, I'll want to confer more thoroughly with Mr. Spock. I would theorize, however, that what we experienced was some sort of time ripple as a result of passing through the rift. Time bent around us, and we each saw, briefly, people whose time lines are somehow going to cross with ours. That must be what you experienced when you saw that woman. You had a glimpse of your own future, Mr. Tyler. A rather disconcerting experience."

Tyler stared at Pike, the light starting to dawn. "It happened to you, too, didn't it, sir?"

Pike hesitated, but then he shrugged. "I saw something. I didn't understand at the time. I was concerned for a moment that I was seeing something out of my own future . . . and if that was the case, I don't think I would want to live to see that future. But I think we can safely assume, Mr. Tyler, that you will not be changing into a female anytime soon. That being the case, I don't think I need to worry too much about transforming into the rather unpleasant vision I saw."

"No, sir."

With a quick nod Pike checked himself once more in the mirror and said, "Come on. Let's greet our guests."

When Pike and Tyler arrived at the transporter room they found Number One, Spock, Boyce, Barry, and Chief Petty Officer Garison already waiting. Transporter Chief Pitcairn was glancing at Assistant Yamata as if to affirm that there was something they were missing. "Captain," said Pitcairn, "I understand we're to be bringing someone aboard?"

"That's correct, Chief," Pike told him. He was looking approvingly at his officers. Boyce was shifting in place, and Pike remembered that Boyce had complained from time to time about poorly fitting dress boots.

Number One's dress uniform, on the other hand, was extremely flattering. It was a long yellow dress with a scooped neck, belted, with a slit on the left side that went to just under the knee. It made her look surprisingly feminine. She looked at Pike, one eyebrow

raised, as if challenging him to say anything about it.
Trust Number One to make the concept of issuing a
compliment seem tantamount to throwing down a
gauntlet.

The transporter chief's questions brought him
around, though, as Pike turned and said, "I'm sorry,
Chief. What was that?"

"I was asking, sir," repeated Pitcairn evenly, "how
we're supposed to beam anyone aboard considering
that no one's given us any coordinates to lock on to."

"I wouldn't be overly concerned, Chief," said Pike.
"I suspect that our guests have that well in hand."

Yamata suddenly blinked in surprise. "Transporter
circuits have just been activated," he informed Pitcairn.

"Never doubt your captain," Pike told them serenely.

At that moment the transporter beams snapped on,
the pads glowing to life. Pike took his place at the
front of his officers and waited.

As the pads glowed four forms were slowly coming
into existence. Pitcairn was looking at his board
uncomprehendingly and saying, "I think you should
know, Captain, I'm not doing this. I can't take responsibility in the event—"

"So noted, Chief," Pike said with quiet confidence.

The hum reached a crescendo and then faded.
Standing on the transporter pad was the individual
who had identified himself as Zyo. There were two
other males beside him, one who seemed roughly the
same age as Zyo and one who, by the general lines of
his face, seemed younger. The younger male was
about a head taller than the tallest individual in the
room (namely Pike) and looked rather powerfully
built. There was also, to his right, what appeared to be
a female of the species. Her features were surprisingly

soft, even pleasing by human standards (although, by Calligar standards, she might have been ugly as sin; it wasn't possible to tell).

The older Calligarian next to Zyo was scowling fiercely, looking around the transporter room and shaking his head in disgust. "This serves no purpose," he snarled.

Zyo did not even afford him a glance. "Quiet, Alt. This discussion is ended."

"No, Zyo," said the one called Alt. "This is not ended." But he ceased speaking, apparently contenting himself with glowering at the *Enterprise* crew.

Pike stepped forward and, with a slight bow, said, "Master Builder Zyo, I am Captain Christopher Pike."

To Pike's surprise, Zyo thrust out his right hand. He noticed that the fingers of the Calligarian's hand were slightly longer and more slender than those of a human.

"You appear puzzled," said Zyo. "This is the correct earth greeting, is it not?"

"It is one of the better-known ones," said Pike, and he shook the extended hand firmly. "They taught us at the academy, however, not to be presumptuous. There are at least five known planets where a handshake is considered an obscene gesture, and one where it's a declaration of war."

"Oh, dear," said Zyo. "That sounds most unpleasant." He released Pike's hand, turned, and noticed Spock. Automatically he brought his right hand up and split his fingers into a $\vee$ shape. "Peace and long life."

Spock raised a surprised eyebrow but nevertheless lifted his own hand in the Vulcan salute and replied, "Live long and prosper."

Number One automatically followed suit, as did Barry. Boyce tried to make the gesture as well and found that he couldn't. He shrugged.

"You are well versed," said Pike.

"Your computer records were quite up-to-date. Oh, Captain," said Zyo, "I must apologize for the way in which I handled—or should I say, mishandled—that. Scanning your computer was the most efficient way we had of learning your idioms and dealing in a comfortable manner with you. And I was concerned that if we did so in a manner that alerted your alarms, you would be needlessly concerned."

"You could have asked permission," Pike pointed out.

"You might have said no," Zyo said reasonably.

Pike gave a very small smile. "Well . . . what's done is done. We won't let it get in the way of our future associations. May I present the rest of my command crew?" He gestured to each one as he spoke, and they bobbed their heads in turn. "My first officer, Number One. Science Officer Spock. Chief Engineer Barry. C.P.O. Garison. Chief Navigator Tyler . . ."

His voice trailed off a moment as he saw that Tyler was inexplicably staring at the Calligarians as if he'd seen a ghost. "Tyler?"

"Oh . . . sorry, sir," said Tyler, blinking, making a visible effort to bring his mind back on track. Now what in hell was wrong with him?

"This is Alt," said Zyo, gesturing to the frowning Calligarian next to him. "Whereas I am the Master Builder, Alt is Master of the Status."

"I must admit, the meanings of your titles are a bit obscure to me," said Pike.

"Ah. I shall explain it to you in short order. But let me introduce the two other young people accompanying us. This"—and he gestured to the youthful male—

"is my son, Macro. And this is my daughter, Ecma."

Macro's face was an unreadable mask, but Ecma smiled openly at them. "This is a great honor," she said, and her voice had an almost musical ring to it.

Pike, despite his distant cordiality, immediately found her to be a complete charmer. Inwardly he warned himself against having this sort of reaction to anyone; he did not want to lose his professional distance. After all, he'd almost done that with Vina, he thought, and look at the problems that had led to.

He heard Tyler gasp next to him and was faintly annoyed. He turned and saw that the navigator was indeed gaping at her openly, apparently unable to contain some sort of fixation he'd developed for her the moment she'd appeared in the transporter. Why in the world had he become so abruptly obsessed with Ecma . . .

Ec . . . ma . . .

Ma.

Oh, Lord. It hadn't been something as inane as Tyler calling for his mother. He'd been muttering the name of a female he had not yet met.

Tyler caught his glance and in a low voice affirmed what Pike had already figured out. "It's her!"

Oh, perfect, thought Pike. This just got trickier.

Chapter Five

A FINE ARRAY of foods from all over the Federation had been set out for the reception, and Zyo seemed to delight in sampling all that was being offered. The one known as Alt at first seemed intent on standing over in a corner and glowering, but the extremely personable Boyce appeared to assign himself the duty of drawing Alt out of his self-created shell. During the buffet Pike cast an occasional glance in Boyce's direction and couldn't help but smile as Boyce serenely plied Alt with some sort of booze, the nature and origin of which Pike felt a bit safer not knowing.

Pike also could not help but notice that Tyler was spending an inordinate amount of time in close conversation with the woman called Ecma. For her part, she seemed eminently entertained by him, and Pike couldn't help but feel a certain degree of discomfiture. So much so, in fact, that while Zyo was in what appeared to be a deep conference with Spock and Number One, Pike drifted over to Tyler and, with a loud clearing of his throat, asked Ecma if she might not excuse Tyler for a few moments so his captain could have a brief word with him.

"Is there a problem, Captain?" asked Tyler, perplexed.

Pike slightly swirled the liquid in his glass. "Why don't you tell me?"

"If you mean that I've been talking with Ecma—"

"Do not forget, Lieutenant," Pike said, "where your priorities are."

"They're right where they always are," Tyler deadpanned. Then, when he saw that his captain was not remotely amused, Tyler was all seriousness. "Sir, I find her a fascinating individual. She's bright, witty, and extremely interested in m—in us. But I have no intention of being remiss in my duties as a Starfleet officer."

"Good," said Pike. He took another sip, but his gaze never left Tyler. "See that you don't."

Tyler nodded and turned back to Ecma. Pike, for his part, still felt a degree of uncertainty. Tyler was an excellent navigator and a reliable officer, but he also tended to be hot-blooded and even excessively romantic—a combination that could be extremely dicey.

Zyo put his drink down and said in a voice that portended announcement, "Captain Pike . . . officers . . . you have been most patient, and extremely civilized. I believe that this would be the appropriate time to explain to you just who we are and what's going on."

Pike put down his drink and folded his arms. "I could not agree more."

Zyo nodded slightly and put down his own glass. "The Calligar," he said, "as you might have surmised, are an extremely advanced people."

"Far more advanced than you," added Alt, his speech slightly slurred. "No offense."

"None taken," said Pike. Inwardly he was amused. Advanced they may be, he thought, but if he could judge by Alt, they couldn't hold their liquor worth a damn.

Zyo was also aware of Alt's slightly inebriated state, but he seemed to be enjoying it as much as Pike. "Yes, we are advanced . . . but we are also something of an insular people. We have no planetary neighbors, which fact undoubtedly helped shape our development. We keep very much to ourselves. Our philosophy is one of total isolation."

"We have our own philosophy," said Pike. "One that stipulates that we do nothing to interfere in the affairs of other planets."

"A solid philosophy."

"But it has not made us isolationist," continued Pike. "Simply . . . cautious."

"Ah, now you see, in that respect you might be more advanced than ourselves." Zyo smiled. This prompted a snort from Alt, but then he started to teeter backwards, and it was only Macro's quick intervention that prevented him from tilting over completely. Ecma cut off a quick giggle and buried her face in Tyler's shoulder to smother it—a gesture that made Tyler immediately self-conscious—and he gently pushed her off himself.

"However," continued Zyo, "although we have never sought out contact, there have been arguments, long carried on purely in a hypothetical context, that if we were contacted by others, we could not simply turn away."

Now Ecma spoke up. "My father is one of the chief proponents of that philosophy. And Alt, for that matter, is one of his chief opponents."

"That is correct," said Alt firmly. Then he belched.

"Since I am the Master Builder," said Zyo, "I am the overseer of the advancements of the Calligar. Alt,

44

for his part, is responsible for watching over our philosophical and societal growth. Of course, since our society is dedicated to not growing—"

This actually seemed to stir Alt from his haze, and he stabbed a finger at Zyo. "That," he growled, "is a gross oversimplification. You know that, Zyo. But then again, maybe you're simplifying matters because you feel that these . . . persons . . . could not hope to grasp the subtleties of Calligarian philosophy. Of the Harmony, and the Worldmi—"

"Alt."

Zyo had snapped at his peer with a fierceness that was, curiously, without heat, but filled with unmistakable warning. Alt's eyes seemed to cloud over for a moment, as if he was mentally reviewing what had just been said, and then his eyes widened slightly. Apparently he was surprised at his own words. He looked down, chastened.

Zyo, utterly composed, turned back to Pike and said, "Curious that I would be more attendant to our philosophies than Alt. Then again, I would seem to be a bit more clearheaded," he added pointedly before continuing. "Because of our dislike of expansionism, we have no active program of space exploration— indeed, no vehicles beyond what is needed to service our Worldnet."

"That's what you call the cities that encircle that world?" asked Number One.

"Quite correct. That world was once our homeworld—still is, to some degree. Oddly enough," said Zyo, pacing in a small circle, his hands behind his back, "we almost destroyed it through pollution and misuse. Several of your centuries ago it became virtually unlivable, and what we had intended to do was move on to other planets, other worlds. But then we realized, as a people, that that was totally inappropriate. We were viewing space expansion as a means of

45

solving a pollution problem. As a means of a late repair to our own environmental and societal slovenliness. What we would have done, in all likelihood, was continue our irresponsible ways on other worlds.

"Instead, it was agreed—"

"Who agreed?" asked Pike. "You have some sort of governing board?"

"It was agreed," repeated Zyo with a tone of voice that indicated that Pike was stepping beyond the bounds of what Zyo wished to discuss, "that we had to solve our own problems without taking the chance of visiting them upon other worlds. That if we could not solve the difficulties within our own sphere, we did not deserve to continue as a race."

"Interesting decision," said Pike.

"It was the only one that seemed"—Ecma appeared to be searching for the right word—"humane," she said finally.

"What developed is the scientific breakthrough that I'm sure your sensors have already detected. The self-regenerating plasma that fuels our Worldnet."

"It would appear to be, on the surface," said Spock, "in violation of the laws of thermodynamics."

"We appealed the laws to a higher court," Zyo told him evenly. "From that discovery extended the creation of the Worldnet, and our many other advancements. And the philosophy of keeping to ourselves took hold as well, pervading much of our thinking. Here, in our relatively remote section of the galaxy, such an ideology seemed eminently workable. At the same time, isolationism can seem a very narrowminded way in which to go about living one's life.

"It would appear, however, that the fabric of the galaxy had its own answer to that."

"The rift?" asked Pike.

Zyo nodded. "The rift."

"So it's not a phenomenon that you created?" asked Spock. He actually sounded quite surprised.

"Not at all," Zyo said. "Utterly natural. Much of the time it is virtually and literally undetectable. However, every"—he seemed to be doing a quick calculation—"every 33.4 of your years, it opens."

"Brigadoon," said Tyler.

Everyone looked at him, and Tyler, momentarily embarrassed, said with a shrug, "It's an old story. A place where everyone sleeps the entire time except for one day every hundred years."

"Interesting," said Zyo. "Brigadoon, then, if you wish. The rift opens and stabilizes for approximately seventy-two of your hours."

"Approximately?" said Pike uneasily.

"Yes. So I would suggest you monitor the rift's activities quite closely. Unless you wish to be permanent guests," said Zyo. He continued to circle the briefing room as he said, "We became aware that, in other parts of the galaxy, life was developing and advancing. I admit to some curiosity on our part as to the nature and direction that it was taking. There were some, like myself, who wished to interact with those developing civilizations. Others"—he glanced very quickly at Alt—"did not. No matter. When you made your communication to us through the rift as it was just beginning to open, it caused quite a flurry of discussion, I can assure you. It's quite fortunate that your subspace radio transmissions move faster than the speed of light, or the temporal nature of the rift might have caused your transmission to reach us after you were long dead."

"Indeed," said Pike. "So . . . where do we go from here?"

Zyo spread his hands. "We wish to discuss philosophies with you. Subtleties that are difficult to discern from our scan of your computers. We wish to know you as potential . . . neighbors, if you will."

"Oh, nonsense," snapped Alt. "We want to study you to make sure that you're not warlike barbarians. Someday, this century or next, you will make incursions into our own space under your own power. We need to know what we'll be dealing with."

"Even should that time come," said Pike, "and I can assure you that it will be long after all of us are gone—but even if that time comes, the Federation will respect your desire for privacy. If you make it clear that you do not wish to be contacted, then we will honor that privacy."

"Now you say that," said Alt. Much to his credit, he seemed to have shrugged off some of the intoxicating effects of the liquor. But he still wavered as he walked slowly toward Pike and continued. "However, as you yourself just pointed out, contact with us can continue long after you are less than a memory. Who knows what the future of your Federation may hold. Therefore, it is in our best interests and out of concern for our personal privacy and safety that we be kept apprised of you."

"We have no secrets," said Pike, spreading his hands. "I am certain that we will be able to work together and allay your concerns."

"That is all we wished to know," said Zyo. "Tomorrow I will show you around one of our major cities, so you can get a feel for what the Calligar are like. In the meantime, to give you some indication as to our own sincerity"—he turned toward Spock and Number One—"while perusing your computers I noted very recent research that has been developed by a man called Richard Daystrom. Is that correct?"

"Dr. Daystrom designed the *Enterprise* computers," said Spock. "Since their original installation there has been further research developed."

48

"Improvement in data access capability," Number One told him. "In fact, next month we were scheduled . . ." Suddenly she stopped, uncertain if she should be discussing the upcoming schedule of the *Enterprise,* and she looked to Pike. Pike gave a small shrug and gestured, and Number One continued. "We were scheduled to lay in at a Starbase and have the new components and work installed in the ship's computer. Voice access and replies instead of only paper printouts and screen arrays. Daystrom has designed the new components, and they're in the process of being built."

"They're in your cabin," said Zyo.

They stared at him uncomprehendingly. "I beg your pardon?" said Number One.

"I arranged for the completed components to be in your cabin," Zyo said calmly.

"But . . . they won't *be* completed for another two weeks," Number One told him.

"Yes, but you see, your scientists had already done all the work." Zyo smiled. "We didn't use our advanced technology to do any of that work for you. We merely followed those plans to create the actual hardware for you. It does not detract from the accomplishments of your Dr. Daystrom at all; indeed, if you wish, once you get to your Starbase you can remove the components we have given you and install the Daystrom-issued ones. They will be indistinguishable, I can assure you."

"You're telling us," said Pike in astonishment, "that you studied the advancements in design made by Dr. Daystrom that were in our computer library base and were able to turn those designs into actual working models . . . in a day?"

"Certainly not, Captain Pike," said Zyo. "Not in a day."

"How long, then?"

49

Zyo couldn't help but smile, and he tried not to sound too smug.

"Five minutes," he said.

No one could recall a time that they had seen Number One actually dashing down the hallway. But this time she most definitely was, her legs pumping furiously. Crewmen were jumping to get the hell out of her way.

Right behind her came Spock, and the Vulcan was inwardly amazed at the woman's speed. Despite his superior Vulcan physiognomy, he was hard-pressed to keep up with her.

Moments later they were in her cabin, and there on a dresser was a large case. Number One flipped it open and gazed in astonishment at the contents.

There were all the components that she had only read about, nestled in some sort of cushioning that held them immobile. She pointed at one. "That's the A3 Interface Module."

Spock nodded and tapped a flat piece with a circle in the middle. "This is the Model 83 Logic Integrator."

She looked up at Spock. "This is incredible. It's all here. All of it. Everything I've read about."

It was the closest that Spock had ever—for that matter, that anyone had ever—heard Number One get to genuine excitement or enthusiasm. Within a moment she had managed to mask completely whatever exhilaration she might be feeling.

Number One's main interest, beyond her duties at helm, was computers. In that she overlapped, naturally, with Spock, and they had spent many hours discussing the limitations of their current systems and speculating about the possibilities for the future. Spock continually got the impression that Number One's abilities were beyond what she habitually let on, and he wondered at odd moments just how much she was capable of.

It seemed now he might have the chance to find out. She looked him in the eyes with an intense gaze and said, "Can we do this? Can we install this?"

Spock pursed his lips a moment in thought. "We shall have to run full diagnostics to make certain that these components are what they appear to be. Caution would dictate—"

She waved that off dismissively. "That will take an hour or so. After that . . . can we do it, Spock?"

Slowly he nodded. "I believe we can."

"Fantastic," she said. "Let's get to it."

"Now?" Spock was a bit surprised.

She looked at him evenly. "Do you have any better plans, Mr. Spock?"

He considered. "None at all."

"Then let's go."

Chapter Six

"THIS IS INCREDIBLE."

José Tyler was standing in the middle of a desert. He turned around slowly, feeling the intense heat of the sun beating down on him. "This . . . this is incredible," he said again.

From nearby Ecma was smiling, and she said, "Would you care to see something else?"

"Like what?"

"Like . . . anything." She shrugged, and the world blurred for an instant, replaced by a snow-covered mountainside. Tyler looked down to discover that he was up to his ankles in snow. His breath was coming out in little clouds. "Incredible," he said again, starting to feel a little repetitive.

The air was chilled and snapping around him, and he was glad that he was wearing the standard-issue gray jackets that landing parties usually sported when leaving the confines of the *Enterprise*. "There've been discussions, theories about holograph technology," said Tyler. "But this . . . this is beyond anything we can even begin to discuss. Holograph, but—"

"Substantial," affirmed Ecma. "Instantaneous creation of matter, and discreation as well."

"Discreation?"

"We can make it and unmake it," she said. She held out a hand. "Come."

He began to walk with her, utterly amazed at it all. It was difficult for him to comprehend that he was inside one of the satellite cities of the Calligarian Worldnet. The illusions—no, not illusions, the real holographs—that were created by the Calligarian technology were nothing short of astounding.

"I can't imagine the Federation ever having anything like this," said Tyler. He squatted, picked up a handful of snow, and began to shape it.

"Oh, you will," said Ecma. "We've studied the exponential growth rate of your scientific progress. We estimate that you will have developed similar technology within the next six of your decades."

"You mean in my lifetime?" Tyler shook his head. "Remarkable." Then he nodded in approval, feeling the heft of the snowball in his hand. "Good packing snow."

"Packing snow?" she asked.

He looked at her in surprise. "What, you never packed snow? Never made a snowball?"

She shook her head. "I've familiarized myself with it. I'm familiar with all of the environments that once existed on our planet. But"—she frowned—"why would you make a snowball? What purpose does it serve?"

He looked at her uncomprehending face, and then down at the snowball. Then he drew his arm back and hurled it.

His aim was just a bit off. It smacked satisfyingly against her upper right shoulder, and the impact caught her so totally off-guard that it knocked her right off her feet. She sat down hard in the snow with a surprised *"Whufff!"*

Tyler stood over her, laughing.

"Now what was the purpose in that?" she demanded.

"It was . . . well, it was supposed to be fun."

She pierced him with a steady stare. "Fun?" she said incredulously.

"Yeah. Fun." José was starting to feel a bit defensive.

"I don't understand. I'm standing here," she said, beginning to pull herself to her feet, "making no overt action against you. Being friendly. Obeying my father's instructions to give you a glimpse of our holotechnology. And what's the first thing you do? You use our technology to create a weapon—"

"Oh, for—"

"A primitive weapon, to be sure. But a weapon. And then you employ it against someone who is acting as your guide. Now I ask you, Lieutenant, are those the actions of an enlightened race? Of an intelligent and thoughtful civilization?"

He turned away from her, feeling embarrassed and ashamed. "Oh . . . look. I didn't mean anything by it. It's not like there was any hostility intended. It was just . . . just misplaced humor. That's all." He started to turn back to her. "You know, sometimes our sense of humor can be—"

The snowball hurtled through the air with pinpoint accuracy and hit him flush in the face. The snow went up his nose and made his eyes water for a moment, and he shoved the snow off his face with astonishment.

Ecma was laughing and pointing. "You were right, Lieutenant. That was very funny!"

"Ohhhh! Oh, you—" And he lunged playfully after her. She dodged away and rolled down a snowbank.

Tyler leapt after her, sliding down on his belly in pursuit.

The Calligarian architecture was some of the most impressive that Pike and Boyce had ever seen. A stroll down one of the main streets allowed them to admire the graceful, arched spires that were above, below, and around them. Pike couldn't detect any sudden increase in the angle of the street that they were on, but still they seemed to be ascending. Above them the stars were twinkling through the clear dome that covered the entire city, and Pike could make out the large connectors that led into another city nearby.

"What's the function of those huge cables?" Pike asked at length.

"Twofold," replied Zyo. "They link the various functioning systems of the Worldnet into one unifying whole. They are also the main means of transport between the different cities. If you wish to travel between the cities, your body is reduced to a particle stream and shot through the connector cables to your destination."

"You said they also linked the functioning systems," said Pike. "May I ask how?"

Zyo half smiled and said, "You may ask."

Boyce noticed that their presence was garnering a good number of looks from the passing Calligar people, but no one seemed to have anything to say to them one way or the other. They were objects of curiosity and cautious interest, much like a two-headed parakeet. But nothing more than that.

"Here is my home," said Zyo, and he passed through a solid door. The metal of the door seemed to ripple around him and then reseal itself.

Pike and Boyce looked at each other and then Pike gestured grandly. "After you, Doctor."

"You're too kind," said Boyce dryly. He looked at

the door, took a deep breath, and strode forward. He hit the door and kept on going, and then, a moment later, there was no hint that he had ever gone through.

Pike took a breath and realized that Boyce might, at this moment, be dead, and he could be following the doctor into oblivion. "In for a penny, in for a pound," he muttered, and he walked through.

He felt a bizarre tingling sensation, quite unlike anything he had ever experienced before. He stopped breathing because, just for a moment, he felt no need to breathe. It was as if the metal was supplying his body with whatever it needed to survive, and Pike realized that if he never took another step forward or backward he could probably survive indefinitely within the confines of the door. Not that that would be the most fulfilling of lives to live.

But he did indeed take another step and a moment later reemerged.

There was no room on the other side.

At least, nothing that Pike could readily discern. All around him was absolutely nothing, breathtaking in its nothingness. Just pure white, for as far as he could see. Nothing above him, and nothing . . .

Nothing below.

Pike grasped, fighting an immediate feeling of vertigo. His mind told him that at any moment he was going to start plummeting to some great unknown depth.

But no such plunge was forthcoming. Instead he simply stood there, the whiteness seeming to laugh at him.

Of Boyce and Zyo there was no sign at all.

The snow-covered hills had given way to a tranquil forest setting. Ecma wandered along the well-trod path with easy certainty, and Tyler followed behind her.

56

She moved with a grace Tyler found absolutely intriguing, and every so often she would cast a glance over her shoulder at him. He found her captivating.

All of his internal warning buzzers were going off. He had a nasty habit of developing immediate crushes on women and imagining all sorts of possibilities with them. And then the fantasies would invariably not pan out. Garison had once given him the tag "The Latin Lover," and although it had been done tongue-in-cheek, Tyler had felt constrained to turn the tables on Garison by living up to the title. The fact that, within a month of being so dubbed by Garison, Tyler had romanced away Garison's girlfriend had done nothing to endear Tyler to Garison.

So Tyler's problem was that he was never certain when he was attracted to a female—which was often —whether it was out of compulsion to maintain his image, or because he genuinely felt something.

"Tell me about yourself," he said as he stepped over a log. "All I know about you is that you're Zyo's daughter. Do you have a mother? Can I meet her?"

"No," said Ecma slowly. "She is gone."

"Oh. I'm sorry," said Tyler. "She died, huh?"

"It was her time," said Ecma with what sounded like a sort of forced detachment.

It was clear to Tyler that she had said all about that that she wished to say, so he changed subjects. "Do you have a job or something?"

She nodded as she pushed aside a branch. "Yes. My job is that I am Zyo's daughter."

"And what does that entail?"

She glanced back at him and smiled. "Are you trying to get information out of me, Lieutenant?"

"Well, now, I—"

She laughed that delightful laugh of hers. It had a bell-like quality that accentuated the alienness of her (as if red skin and two slits instead of a nose weren't

57

sufficient.) "It's quite all right. It's understandable that you're curious about us. We, after all, are openly curious about you." She paused. "My father is the Master Builder, as you know. I am his apprentice." She smiled thinly. "That does not sit well with my brother."

"Why not?"

"Because he is the elder. But my father believes that I am the more techno inclined."

"Are these kinds of things usually done on the basis of age?"

"That depends whom you talk to," said Ecma. "If you believe my brother, then yes. If you attend to my father, then no."

Tyler tripped slightly over a root but then righted himself. From up ahead he heard the sound of water running . . . a waterfall, he realized. It had been so long since he had heard one that it filled him with a dull ache. He hadn't seen a waterfall since he was eleven years old.

Ecma had said that this extraordinary holotechnology would exist within his lifetime. Imagine being able to, for example, be in a starship, but use holotechnology to create scenes from home, or wherever. Somehow his lifetime seemed . . . well . . . a lifetime away.

The path angled down, and Tyler saw the source of the waterfall. There was a gorgeous lake that spread out in front of them, and the waterfall was emptying into it. The surface was like glass, and the air was thick with the scent of pine.

He turned toward Ecma and started to speak, and to his shock, he saw Ecma was pulling her clothesoff. "Uhm . . . excuse me . . . what do you think . . ."

She had already removed her shirt, and Tyler was taking note of the fact that it appeared, biologically,

58

she was extremely similar to earth females. "Look, Ecma . . ."

"Is something wrong?" she asked. "Come swimming with me."

"I don't think that would be appropriate."

She removed the remainder of her garments, and the rest of her development was apparently parallel to humans as well.

God! He was doing biological comparisons! He really had been out in space too long.

"The water is wonderful," Ecma was saying. "This is one of my favorite places." She turned and leapt into the water, cleaving it cleanly.

Watching her swim through the water, he felt there was blood pounding through every cell in his body—not excluding his hair and fingernails. Ecma spun about in the water and, facing him, waved for him to jump in.

"Ooooohhh boy," he said.

"Doctor!" shouted Pike into the blankness. "Phil!"

"You don't have to shout, Captain," came Boyce's calm response.

A door seemed to open straight out of the nothingness, and Boyce stepped out, looking at Pike in concern. Zyo was next to him. "I'm right here," continued Boyce.

"Zyo, what"—Pike gestured helplessly—"what is all this?"

"Well, I was just explaining to the doctor," said Zyo patiently. "Our homes are very subjective."

"Subjective?" Pike clearly didn't understand.

"It's the ultimate in being made to feel at home, Captain," said Boyce expansively. "You're not seeing it yet because your mind isn't calm enough."

"Seeing what?" said Pike, trying to hide his exasperation.

"Our personal environments are subjected to individual whim and taste," said Zyo. "It's very subliminal."

"Subliminal?" said Pike, sinking down into a chair. "How can it be subliminal?"

"Decorations, fixtures, and so on all stem from your subconscious mind," said Zyo easily. "As a result, you are never subjected to the design whims of the homeowner. You always create your own personal environment."

"You mean each individual does?" asked Pike, drumming his fingers on the teak coffee table to his right.

"That's correct," said Boyce. "I, for example, am at this very moment seeing a room done up entirely in Louis XIV furniture. I have no idea what you're seeing."

"But I'm not seeing . . ." Then Pike's voice trailed off as he came to the slow realization that he was, in fact, sitting in a chair and rapping on a table. He glanced around. The entire room had taken on a very nautical flavor, with a barometer hanging on the wall opposite and a variety of heavy, polished furniture that looked as if it would have been at home in the cabin of a captain of a Spanish galleon. It seemed to have sneaked up on him: one moment the blankness, and now this.

"Very impressive," he said finally.

"Not to us," said Zyo graciously. "I'm pleased you find it so interesting. Do you paint, Captain?"

"You mean portraits and such?" He shrugged. "I dabbled with it in my youth. Never was very good."

"Over here, then." Zyo gestured for him to follow, and Pike got up from his extremely comfortable seat. He slowed when passing Boyce to ask, in a low voice, "Louis XIV?"

"Call me sentimental. What do you see, Chris?"

"Just the interior of my quarters, as usual," said Pike blandly. "You know me, Doctor. No imagination."

Tyler's imagination was running wild as he started to pull open his jacket.

He could see himself peeling down and leaping into the water with her, swimming toward her with sure, strong strokes. He saw himself pulling her to him, the two of them causing the water to bubble and come to a boil, her legs wrapped around him, the . . .

The captain. Showing up unexpectedly, standing on the shore, hands on his hips, scowling fiercely. The anger, the lecture, the snickering back on the ship when . . .

He cleared his throat, the vocal cords of which seemed to have become paralyzed, and he called to her. "Uhm . . . I think I'd better stay here."

"Oh, but the water is so splendid," she said.

"Not half as . . . uhm." He cut himself off again. He sat down on a rock and waved weakly to her. "I think . . . yeah, definitely, I'd better stay here. Tell me . . . tell me more about your people. What do you believe in?"

"Believe in?" She was doing the backstroke. She *had* to be doing the backstroke, now, didn't she? Damn. *Damn.*

"Uh . . . yeah. Like . . . do you believe in God? Or in some sort of maker of all things?"

She brought her legs down (mercifully, mercifully) and trod water, one of the least inflammatory things she could have done. "Of course," she said.

"Okay. Uh . . . what do you believe?"

"My father. He is the maker of all things. He is the Master Builder, as was his father before him, and his mother before him, and so on back." She grinned. "And someday I shall be the maker of all things . . .

and won't that infuriate my brother?" She suddenly spun in the water and dived under, her buttocks momentarily projecting cheerily in the air before disappearing under the surface.

"Yes, so you said," said Tyler, even though she couldn't hear him. For that matter she couldn't see him now, either, but nevertheless he crossed his legs and coughed once loudly.

She broke the surface a few feet away from him and continued to tread water. Trying to stick to business, Tyler said, "And, uh, what do you think happens to you after you die?"

At that a shadow crossed her face momentarily, and then she brightened, although it didn't seem to be without effort. "What does that matter?" she said.

"Well . . . I'm interested."

"I'm not," she said. "I'm interested in all manner of things. Bioengineering, holography . . . all sorts of things. But not in what happens to you after you die. I'm not going to die for a long, long time. I enjoy living much too much."

She paddled forward and emerged from the water, Venus on the shell, the water rolling off her. Her skin was curious, the water beading on it as if she had a water repellent on her body. She brushed the drops away and, still smiling, came toward him.

He took a step back and said, "You know, as a Starfleet officer—"

"You wanted to know more about our philosophies?" she asked. "We don't believe in prevaricating. We don't believe in tiptoeing around our feelings." She ran her fingers up his shirt, and the nearness of her was intoxicating.

"There are"—he cleared his throat loudly—"there are certain rules. . . ."

She nibbled at the base of his neck and then ran her

tongue up, tracing the line of his jaw. Then she buried her face in the nape of his neck.

"Well, it's . . . it's actually more guidelines than rules," he said. She was reaching up and massaging his temples in a manner he had never experienced. That, combined with the way her mouth was playing across his throat, made him dizzy.

Well . . . the captain had said to find out all there was to find out about these people . . . he was just following orders, after all.

Pike's communicator sounded, and he flipped it open. "Captain here."

"This is Barry, sir," came the engineer's voice. "This energy system they have here . . . it's amazing."

"They're giving you free access?" asked Pike, casting a glance at Zyo. To his surprise, Zyo shook his head.

Barry immediately confirmed Zyo's negative warning. "No, sir. There are certain sections where they're telling me I can't go. They say it's too advanced for me." The annoyance, even offense, in the engineer's tone was unmistakable. Barry had never been particularly good at concealing irritation.

"As you know, Captain," Zyo said, "we are cautious when discussing details of our technology. We do not want to do anything that will accelerate you beyond the level that you are ready to reach."

How condescending of you, Pike thought briefly, but he immediately quelled the judgment. Zyo was right, of course. It was merely a reflection of exactly how the Federation felt about their own technology. On a planet where the furthest someone had progressed was the invention of the revolver, the *Enterprise* would never show up and explain the detailed workings of a hand phaser.

"Be satisfied with what we are shown, Mr. Barry," said Pike. "Whatever you learn will be enough."

"Aye, sir," sighed the engineer.

Pike turned back to the canvas in front of which he was standing. An image was half completed on it, and Zyo was studying it in appreciation, as was Boyce. "Very impressive for a first-time artist," said Zyo approvingly.

"I didn't know you had it in you, Captain," said Boyce.

A "canvas" was only Pike's name for it, since it hardly had a scrap of canvas on it. It was a piece of solid, clear material, about two by three feet, or at least that's how it had started out. Pike had been placing his hands against it at Zyo's instruction and bringing an image to his mind with as much strength as he could. Slowly a picture had been forming out of whatever materials composed the "canvas," appearing as if by magic. It seemed, to Boyce's practiced eye, to be an Orion female in mid-dance step, but he couldn't be quite sure. The outlines had formed first, and now Pike was busy assembling the details.

Yes, it was an Orion female, all right. The green skin was unmistakable. She was nude, a bit more erotic than Boyce would have expected from Pike. The captain had been making murmurings about going off and being a trader of such women not too long ago, a notion that Boyce had made light of. Now he started to wonder if maybe he hadn't been just a bit hasty.

Her chin was tilted back, her eyes filled with fire and lust, her upper teeth just slightly chewing on her lower lip. Her arms were arched over her head, her hips thrust outward. Remarkably, Boyce could even tell that she was covered with a sheen of sweat from her dance.

He leaned forward and muttered to Pike, "Somebody you know?"

64

"No," said Pike.

"That wouldn't happen to be that girl you mentioned? Vi—"

"No," said Pike, even more firmly. The sort of voice that he used only when he was covering something, and Boyce wisely chose not to pursue it.

"So," said Zyo as Pike turned up the shade of green in the dancing girl just a notch, "tell me . . . about your enemies."

Tyler was drowning in her, and that was when a rough hand grabbed him by the scruff of the neck.

He heard Ecma gasp, and then he was swung around to find himself staring into the face of Macro, twisted in rage.

"Hi," said Tyler.

Macro hurled Tyler heels over head, sending him tumbling into the mud and dirt nearby. Tyler was immediately on his feet, just in time to see Macro charging at him. From behind him the naked Ecma was shouting something angrily, and Macro wasn't paying any attention to her.

Tyler knew from the very first contact that Macro was exceedingly strong. Macro had made no effort at all when he had used Tyler for a shotput. Nor did he seem to have an evenness of temper to augment it.

"Macro, *stop it!*" shouted Ecma, and she grabbed at his arm. Perhaps the lack of clothes on her part was damaging to her authority. She certainly didn't seem to have much impact on Macro, because he shoved her aside as if she weighed nothing and came once more at Tyler.

Tyler put his guard up, and Macro attacked with no particular artistry or even, apparently, a plan. Macro swung several quick rights, none of which managed to get through Tyler's guard. Tyler struck back with a quick flurry of rights and lefts, several of which landed, snapping Macro's head back. It was extremely satisfying, and Tyler danced around him, keeping his fists and feet in motion, stinging fiercely with his jabs and ducking or blocking each of Macro's vicious rights.

Satisfying until Macro suddenly landed a left with enough force to rattle Tyler's teeth. Tyler sat down hard, the world spinning around him. Sloppy. Damned sloppy. Macro had set him up and then switched hands. How could he have been so stupid?

"You keep away from my sister," snarled Macro.

"He didn't do anything," Ecma was saying angrily. "He was trying not to, at any rate. I wasn't giving him a lot of options."

"Cover yourself," said Macro angrily.

"No. I have nothing to be ashamed of. Lieutenant, do you think I have anything to be ashamed of?" She stood there defiantly, her hands on her hips.

"Not from where I'm sitting," said Tyler. He was trying with all his might to stop the world from spinning around.

And suddenly Macro reached down and lifted him completely off the ground. Tyler's feet were dangling high, and in a desperate maneuver he slammed a foot into Macro's stomach. Macro grunted but otherwise didn't seem to notice.

"You are so . . . so suffocating, Macro," Ecma was saying angrily. "You've always been like this, ever since I can remember."

"And ever since I can remember, you have done whatever you wanted in order to anger me!"

"The Worldnet does not revolve around you, Macro," snapped Ecma, "and you would do well to remember that!"

Tyler felt Macro's grip tightening in anger, cutting off his air. "For an advanced race," he gagged, "you have some . . . pretty petty squabbles."

Macro seemed to notice him for the first time. He glared into Tyler's eyes and snarled, "Oh, you think so?"

"It had . . . crossed my mind."

Macro turned quickly, stomped over to the lake, and—before Ecma or Tyler could react—shoved the navigator under the water. Tyler, caught off-guard, began to choke. Macro eased up on his grip ever so slightly; Tyler's lungs reflexively tried to draw in air . . . and only got water.

He heard Ecma yelling, but it was from a distance, and it seemed to be growing more distant with each passing moment.

Chapter Seven

NUMBER ONE WIPED THE SWEAT from her brow and drew herself up the computer core's Jeffries tube once more. She was in close quarters with Spock, who was checking over the data rerouting systems, and he tossed a glance at the first officer. Her concentration on her task was total; she had not said anything to him in the past five hours beyond crisp instructions or demands for information. She was not one for small talk.

She studied the calibrations once more and then wiped her hands. "All right," she said slowly. She actually sounded nervous for a moment. "All right, I think that's it."

Spock nodded, his back pressed up against hers. "I believe you are correct."

"So let's see what we've got. You installed that voice-integrating circuit up on the bridge?"

"As you instructed." He carefully modulated his response so as to disguise his irritation over the fact that this was the fifth time she had asked him about it.

"Good." She gave the systems one more check.

"I've done the primary setups at this end, plus imprinted a preliminary interface program. It should be ready."

With an inclination of her head she indicated that Spock should slide down out of the tube first. He did so and then helped her down. They looked at each other for a moment and couldn't help but notice how disheveled and even a bit tired both of them appeared.

"Let's go get cleaned up," said Number One, "and then get back up to the bridge to run a test. Sixteen hundred hours?"

"That seems a logical plan."

She nodded, and they started toward their respective cabins. Spock paused a moment at the door to his and said, "Number One, should the captain not be present for the preliminary test?"

She considered a moment and then said, "I'd rather not."

He raised an eyebrow. "If I may ask . . ."

"Because if it doesn't work, I don't want him to be there to see me fail." And with that she turned and walked away.

Spock watched her go and, arms folded, shook his head slowly. "Fascinating," he said.

"So the major enemy of the Federation is the Klingon Empire," said Zyo thoughtfully. He was studying the completed portrait of the green Orion dancing girl and nodding appreciatively. "Yes, that is what we garnered from your computer banks as well."

"I haven't had that much personal contact with them," Pike said. He was staring at the barometer and was surprised to see that, according to the dial, a storm was brewing. He wondered what that meant. "But they can be extremely deadly. And they are formidable enemies."

"But why? Your philosophies are so similar."

Pike looked at Zyo in astonishment. "Are you certain you read the correct files?"

"Oh, quite certain."

"But they believe that they have a right to conquer whatever they wish!" said Pike. "They believe that they are stronger than the Federation and can do what they want, where they want. They think they are destined to be the dominant race in the galaxy."

"They believe this because they feel they are the stronger."

"Yes."

"But your own theories of evolution and natural selection," said Zyo, "would seem to indicate that the—what's the phrase?—the survival of the fittest is, in fact, the natural and correct order of things. Do you believe that?"

"I believe that evolution is the true manner in which mankind rose to dominance on earth, yes," said Pike slowly. "But—"

"And the Klingons believe that through natural selection they are the dominant species, just as humans grew to be the dominant species on earth." Zyo seemed amused. "So how are you different from the Klingons in that respect?"

Pike looked at Boyce for help. The doctor shrugged. Pike looked back at Zyo and said, "The difference is that Klingons see only physical strength as the determinant of superiority. Their definition of strength is based entirely on the concept of being able to subjugate others. But man's dominion over the earth had nothing to do with physical strength or desire to subjugate. It had to do with survival, not conquest."

"Yet in striving for survival mankind wound up conquering much of their environment. Even nearly destroying it, much as we did ours." Zyo shook his head. "It's not the concept of conquest that is so disturbing to you, Captain. It's the concept that humankind would be on the receiving end of that conquest—just as your planet, and the life forms on that planet, were on the receiving end of your own continued existence, be it called conquest or survival or whatever you wish."

"The Klingons are different from us," said Pike firmly.

"Oh, I quite agree."

"Good," Pike said, looking to Boyce in satisfaction.

"I agree that they are different in that they are the stronger, and their claims," continued Zyo, "have a great deal of basis in your own philosophies. And it is the veracity of those claims that you find so annoying about the Klingons. It's not because you're so certain that they're wrong. It's because you're afraid they might be right."

Pike stared at him and then said, "what are you saying? That you're on their side?"

"Not at all."

"Because if they encountered you, they would try to conquer you," said Pike. "As would any number of warlike races that the Federation knows of. And if that happened, then you would have the chance to experience firsthand just how different the Klingons and the Federation are from each other."

Zyo nodded slightly. "You are no doubt correct."

"They would try to conquer you," Boyce put in to bolster what his captain was saying.

With an agreeable smile Zyo said, "They would try. But they would undoubtedly run into . . . trouble."

"We've got trouble."

Number One had just emerged onto the bridge, and Spock was right behind her. Viola, who had stepped in to monitor the science station while Spock was gone, moved aside as Spock came forward. "Specify," Spock said. Number One went to the command chair to take her place, but her full attention was on Viola.

"The rift is closing," said Viola.

"But it hasn't been seventy-two hours," said Number One. "It's been . . ."

"Forty-eight point nine," Spock told her. "It would appear that our passage through the temporal ripple, and the interaction with our own time warp field, accelerated the rift's instability."

"Time to full closure?"

Spock began to do mental calculations, and then to make sure he said, "Computer . . ."

"Working," said the computer.

Number One and Spock looked at each other, and Number One actually smiled before covering it quickly.

The computer's voice caught everyone on the bridge—with the exception of those who had installed it—completely off-guard. They looked in astonishment at one another and then at the air from which the voice had seemed to emerge. The crew knew that Spock and Number One had been hard at work at updating the computer, but the actuality was something else again.

"Time until closure of rift," said Spock.

"Thirty-two minutes," announced the computer, which jibed perfectly with what Spock had determined.

"Raise the landing party," said Number One quickly. "We've got to get out of here. Now."

"So tell me about your system of government," said Pike.

"There isn't all that much to tell," replied Zyo. "It's fairly simple. We have a advisory board, and we attend to what they tell us to do."

"But you must have some influence for the contact with us to have been made."

"Some influence, yes," said Zyo modestly.

"Can we meet this advisory board?"

"I'm afraid that's—"

Pike's communicator suddenly beeped, and he pulled it out. "Captain here."

"Captain," came Number One's voice, laced with urgency. "The rift is closing."

Pike looked in surprised betrayal at Zyo, but he could immediately see from the Calligarian's expression that it was just as much a surprise to him. "You must leave immediately," said Zyo. "Otherwise—"

"How long have we got?" Pike demanded.

"Thirty-one minutes, eleven seconds," came Spock's voice.

"Contact the rest of the landing party," said Pike immediately. "Beam everyone back aboard now."

"We've already brought back Chief Barry," said Number One. "But we have been unable to raise Mr. Tyler."

Pike looked at Zyo in alarm. "Where's my navigator?" he demanded.

Zyo frowned a moment, and then his face cleared. "Yes . . . of course. He's with my daughter, as I recall. But I see no cause for concern. He's in perfectly good hands."

Macro's hands were firmly on Tyler, shoving his entire body under the water. Tyler was pounding in futility on Macro's strong arms and was wondering obliquely just what he had to do to get the infuriated Calligarian to let go of him.

He thought he heard his communicator beeping at him, and then it was knocked free of his belt, sinking to the silty bottom of the lake.

Frantically, his lungs screaming for air and getting

73

only water in response, Tyler felt the side of Macro's hand brush against his mouth. He bared his teeth and clamped down with everything he had. To his satisfaction, he heard Macro yowl in pain, and he managed to kick free of the Calligarian's grip. He surfaced, sputtering and coughing up water. He was still standing knee-deep in water, though, and Macro was lurching toward him again.

Suddenly the world shifted once more, and they were standing on a desert plain. Ecma was in the process of pulling her clothes on, and she was saying angrily to Macro, "Try to drown him now, you idiot."

Tyler was on his hands and knees, still violently coughing up water. Nearby was his communicator, beeping insistently. Tyler started to roll over to get to it, and that was when Macro came toward him and stepped on the communicator. His large foot crushed the device into small pieces.

"Still no response from Tyler," Number One said as Pike walked onto the *Enterprise* bridge. "Everyone else is aboard." She rose from the command chair. "Nineteen minutes to rift closure."

Pike immediately took his place in the chair and said "Bridge to Engineering. Prepare hyperdrive, time warp factor two." He turned to Number One. "Lay in a course for the rift."

Viola, who had now stepped in at navigation, said what was on the mind of everyone on the bridge. "But sir . . . Mr. Tyler . . ."

"Give me an open channel to the Calligar," said Pike. The moment he was on he said, "Zyo. This is Captain Pike. We have still not ascertained the location of Lieutenant José Tyler. It is imperative that he be found within"—he paused—"fifteen minutes.

Otherwise there may be serious consequences that would be regrettable for all concerned."

Tyler got to his feet quickly and ducked under Macro's swing, which brought the Calligarian off balance. Tyler used the moment to his advantage and drove a furious mix of rights and lefts to Macro's gut. Fueled by anger and, to a certain degree, mortification, Tyler let himself be pumped up by it, let it drive him. He felt Macro stagger under the assault, and before the surprised Calligarian could retaliate, Tyler drove a left hook to Macro's chin that knocked him flat.

Macro seemed stunned by the sudden turnaround, and Ecma stood over him with satisfaction in her voice, saying, "I hope you feel like a complete fool, Macro. You certainly deserve to."

"I would tend to agree," Tyler said urgently, picking at the smashed bits of his communicator. "But right now I think I'd better find out what they wanted on the *Enterprise*. It could be important."

"Nine minutes, sir," said Spock.

Pike was a block of wood, staring at the Calligarian homeworld.

"Energize phasers," he said quietly.

Number One turned to him in surprise. "Sir?"

"Do it," he said.

She turned back and, a moment later, announced, "Energizing phasers."

"Give me an open channel," he said once more, and once he had it he said, "Attention, Calligar. You have one of my people. You will return him immediately, or I shall be forced to interpret this as a hostile action and open fire on one of your satellites."

Within seconds the image of a hurt-looking Zyo was

on the screen. "Captain," he said, sounding disappointed, "do you truly think threats are necessary?"

"They may be," said Pike. "One of my men is missing and you are endangering our ability to return to our sector of the galaxy."

Zyo shook his head. "It is very clear to me, Captain, that you and yours still have a way to go before we can be entirely comfortable with expanded contact. You automatically assume there is some sort of hostile intention. Such an attitude would indicate that, despite your protestations of peaceful and elevated intent, you are still fundamentally warlike enough to see attacks where none are planned."

"What I see," said Pike, "is time slipping away. And if you cause me to lose a crew member and make me leave someone behind, you are going to have a physical manifestation of my displeasure."

"I understand fully, Captain," said Zyo. "Perhaps . . . I understand more than you wish. Do not be concerned. I shall attend to this personally."

Ecma and Tyler emerged from the holography center in time to see an extremely annoyed Zyo standing just outside. His arms were folded across his chest, and he said, "Might I ask what you've been about?"

"I was just showing the lieutenant the center," she said ingenuously. Tyler smiled gamely.

"I can imagine. Ecma, we'll talk of this later. Lieutenant, you must depart immediately."

"What?" Ecma looked horrified. *"What?* But . . . but why?"

"There's no time to discuss this," said Zyo. "The transport center is nearby. We must go immediately. Your captain was quite emphatic."

"But—"

"Later, Ecma," said Zyo. "Lieutenant . . . *now.*"

Macro, looking sullen and angry, emerged from the

holocenter as well. His petulant gaze fell on Tyler, but he said nothing.

Ecma took his arm urgently. "Lieutenant, stay with me. There's so much we could—"

But he was pulled away from her as Zyo brought him forcefully to the building designated as the transport center. Ecma followed, Macro trailing behind.

They entered the smallish building, and Tyler saw almost nothing extraordinary about it. There seemed to be no controls, no pads, no nothing. Just the empty room that occupied the entirety of the building. Zyo quickly guided him to the middle of the room and then stepped back, saying, "My regards to your captain."

Tyler was looking at Ecma's saddened eyes. This was all so insane. He had just met her. He couldn't have such strong feelings for her . . . hell, who was he kidding? Of course he could. He was The Latin Lover, after all. But this felt . . . different. If . . .

"Come with me," he called to her.

Her eyes widened, but before she could say anything Zyo answered, "That is impossible."

"But—"

"Good-bye, Lieutenant," said Zyo.

Macro had entered and was standing just behind Ecma. The world of the Calligar began to fade out before Tyler's eyes, and he saw Ecma's stricken expression.

And he saw Macro reaching around from behind Ecma and beginning to fondle her. Her jaw moved tightly, but she did nothing to stop him. Zyo saw none of it.

José Tyler let out a shriek of fury and lunged toward them, and the next thing he knew he was hurtling across the *Enterprise* transporter room and smashing into the console of Chief Pitcairn, who let out a yelp of astonishment.

"Send me back!" he snarled.

"Like hell!" retorted Pitcairn as he punched his communications grid. "Bridge, this is the transporter room. Same thing as before—beams were activated by outside agencies. Lieutenant Tyler just materialized."

Tyler immediately bolted from the transporter room and made it up to the bridge just as the *Enterprise* was swinging around and aiming itself straight toward the rift.

"Captain, you've got to send me back!" said Tyler.

Pike stared at him as if he'd grown a third eye. "Get to your post."

"One minute, fifteen seconds," said Spock.

"Captain, it's an emergency. Ecma is—"

"Now." The air fairly crackled with Pike's cold fury at not getting instant obedience.

Tyler was seething as well, but there was no way he was going to stand up to his captain. His every move carefully controlled, he went to his navigation station, Viola getting out of the way as quickly as he could.

"One minute," Spock announced. "Fifty-nine, fifty-eight—"

"Hyperdrive on line," said Number One.

"Captain, the rift is closing at an accelerated rate," said Spock. "Revising countdown—twenty-nine, twenty-eight—"

The rift, its edges coruscating, became more narrow with each passing second.

"Engage!" shouted Pike.

The *Enterprise* surged forward and a split instant later had vaulted into the rift.

Time rippled and shifted about them once more, even more intense than before, and Pike felt as if his mind were being torn apart. His gaze was riveted to the viewscreen, the universe a shimmering haze of twisting and spiraling colors.

They seemed to snap together, take on a shape that was remarkably familiar. And he saw something . . . saw something impossible.

It was a starship rushing toward them in a dazzling burst of color that enveloped it, coming from within and without. Another starship, and they were on a direct collision course.

Pike tried to shout an order, but he couldn't hear anything over the roaring around him, the roaring of time, the roaring of the blood in his head. He didn't know if anyone else could see what was coming toward them, knew that it was too late even if they could because it was here, it was *here*. . . .

And then it was gone.

And he realized, in a moment of insane clarity, that it had been them . . . *them* . . . some sort of bizarre afterimage. Them on their way to where they had come from. An old song flitted through his mind— "Hello, I Must Be Going."

And then they were gone. Or rather, they were back. The world snapped into glorious normalcy, the stars acquiring their usual alignment.

"Hard about!" shouted Pike, and Number One, with a steady hand, brought the ship around. They were just in time to see the rift vanish.

Tyler's hands tightened on the controls at navigation. There was no sign of the temporal distortion ever having been there.

From behind him he heard Pike say, "Mr. Tyler."

Slowly, steeling himself, Tyler turned in his chair and said evenly, "Yes, sir."

Pike seemed to contemplate him for an eternity, although it was in fact only a few seconds. And then he said, quite simply, "Set course for Vega."

Tyler's jaw fell for just a moment, and then he quickly composed himself and said, "Yes, sir."

"And Mr. Tyler."

"Yes, sir."

"I expect a full report on my desk within three hours. A *full* report, Mr. Tyler."

Tyler nodded slowly. "Yes, sir."

"That goes for all of you," he said, turning to the rest of the bridge crew. "Starfleet is going to want points of view from all concerned here. This was a first contact, and we're going to play this by the book. Mr. Spock, Number One . . . how are those computer components going?"

Number One inclined her head slightly in Spock's direction, indicating that the junior officer was welcome to respond. For answer, Spock said, "Computer . . ."

"Working."

"Report status of computer and bridge."

"All systems are functioning normally. Course has presently been set for Vega IX. Awaiting order from captain."

Spock turned in his chair and looked patiently at Pike. Pike, too experienced to let his astonishment show, merely nodded. He seemed to be frowning, though, as he said "Hyperdrive, time warp factor one. Engage."

As the *Enterprise* catapulted into hyperdrive Spock could not help but ask, "Captain, is everything in order? You seem—"

"It's the computer voice," said Pike. "Somehow it seems famil—" Then his eyes widened, and he turned in his chair towards his first officer. "Number One . . . the computer. That was your voice."

"Yes, sir," said Number One.

"You programmed the computer with *your* voice?" he said incredulously.

"You may change it when we reach Starbase if you desire," she said flatly.

"No. No, not at all," he said. "I had no intention of

80

doing so. I was just curious as to why you used your voice as the pattern for the *Enterprise* computer. It would hardly have been an arbitrary selection, and I can't see you being vain enough to—"

"It had nothing to do with vanity, sir," said Number One crisply. "I wished to use a voice that commanded respect."

"I see," said Pike.

"In addition," continued Number One, "Studies have proven that female voices cut through noise with greater efficiency than male voices."

"So you're saying female voices get more attention."

"Correct, sir."

"That being the case," said Pike, "you'd think there'd be more female commanders."

Slowly Number One turned in her chair and said, "Yes, sir. I would."

"Should I be concerned about my command future, Number One, vis à vis your ambitions?"

"No, sir."

"Good."

"I'll be wanting a bigger ship, sir."

He watched her for a good long time after that to see if he could catch a hint of a smile.

But he never did.

SECOND CONTACT

Chapter Eight

"ALL SYSTEMS FUNCTIONING NORMALLY," said the voice of Number One.

Mr. Spock turned away from his science station and said, "Captain, computer diagnostic checks are completed. All systems functioning normally."

The captain turned in his command chair and smiled, his eyes twinkling with amusement. "Now that's a relief," he said with a sigh. "With all the problems we've been having recently, it's good to know that *something* is up to snuff around here."

Spock merely inclined his head slightly in deference and then added, "Certainly the arrival of Dr. Daystrom would have been diminished if the computer had been malfunctioning."

Captain James T. Kirk stood and stretched, once again regretting the loss of his old chair. It had had a far more cushiony feeling to it, and the squared-off armrests had been more comfortable than the narrow ones on this new chair. Why was it that people felt an overwhelming need to improve things that needed no improving? As much as was occasionally gained from such things, far more was lost.

"Considering Dr. Daystrom's last visit with us," observed Kirk, "I would hardly think that he'd care to experience computer malfunctions again." He took a step forward, flexing his arms back. "Mr. Sulu, time until we rendezvous with the transport?"

"Nineteen hours, sir," said Sulu briskly.

"Good. In that case, I'll attend to our other guests for a—"

The turbolift door hissed open. This drew immediate attention, since all authorized bridge personnel were already on duty.

The commodore stood there in the open doorway, youthful excitement in his face. He was grinning openly. His was the type of face that looked better when it was grinning; forced severity of manner did not suit him at all. Every time the commodore endeavored to be all business, it seemed to Kirk that he was, in fact, doing his best to pretend—that, indeed, he might even be trying to imitate someone.

Next to him was McCoy, who called out, "The commodore passed his physical with flying colors, Captain. Then he asked if he could see the bridge, and I thought—"

"By all means," said Kirk, and he waited for the elder officer to walk out of the turbolift.

But the commodore simply stood there, staring at the bridge as if in a trance.

"Commodore Tyler," said Kirk, catching the older man's glance.

Tyler turned to look at Kirk. He was a bit heavyset but still had the look of a man who worked out. His graying hair was quite thin on top. But he had a general air of youthfulness, accentuated by the fact that he seemed to enjoy flirting with the female officers whenever he had the chance. "Yes, Captain."

Kirk gestured in a "come on in" manner. "Don't just stand there, sir. Feel free."

Tyler took a tentative step in and then walked fully onto the bridge. The turbolift hissed shut behind him as McCoy also stepped out. He glanced to his left, looking at something that didn't appear to be there, and then said, "We always had a security man posted right there. Valdini, I think his name was. It was the damnedest thing—he always had this self-conscious smile on his face. I think he felt foolish, standing there for no damned good reason other than protocol." He turned toward Spock and said, "You remember him, Mr. Spock?"

"Yes, sir," said Spock.

"You know what ever happened to him?"

"He was killed in action on Argus X, on stardate 3619.2"

"Oh." That seemed to take the wind out of Tyler's sails for a moment, and then he gave a small sigh. "You try and make sense out of things, and all you encounter is more senselessness."

He walked down slowly across the bridge, looking around in wonderment. "You know . . . it's amazing how different it all looks . . . and yet how much the same. The two-tier setup, the positioning of the stations—that's all just as it was in my day. It seems so primitive now, the things that we considered to be so advanced. And who knows what there'll be in the future, when this ship is considered an antique."

"There are some"—Kirk cast a wry eye at Spock— "who consider her an antique right now. Along with her crew."

"Ohh," scoffed Tyler, "I hadn't heard anything like that. Have you, Spock?"

"Yes, sir," said Spock flatly.

Tyler studied Spock a moment, taking in the un-equivocal manner in which he spoke and even the

87

slightly imperious way in which he surveyed the others on the bridge. "You know, Spock . . . you used to smile a lot more."

McCoy looked astounded. "You're joking. Spock? What in the world would he have to smile about?"

"Undoubtedly, Doctor," said Spock dryly, "the fact that you had not yet been assigned to the *Enterprise* was something of a consideration."

Tyler looked surprised and said to Kirk with superb feigned indignation, "Captain, I'm surprised. Your officers squabbling with each other in front of other crew people—it's most undignified. Don't you think?"

Kirk smiled at that. "In my opinion, Commodore," he said in a stage whisper, "I think that the doctor and Mr. Spock have maintained their 'squabbling' more out of habit than anything else. Oh, long ago there may have been actual heat between the two of them, like two determined boxers going around and around, each refusing to fall. Nowadays, though, I think they keep at it because . . . well . . . it's expected. Rather than trying to convince each other of the respective superiority of their philosophical positions, they use each other as mental emery boards to keep their wits sharp."

McCoy and Spock stared at Kirk, who smiled innocently. Uhura, Chekhov, and Sulu stared determinedly at their stations, trying not to laugh out loud.

"Are you quite through?" asked McCoy.

"I think so."

"Then I will thank you," he said stiffly, "to play amateur psychologist on your own time."

"This is my bridge," replied Kirk, "on my ship. This *is* my own time. And that 'amateur psychologist' comment—you wound me, Bones. After all . . . dammit, Bones, I'm a captain, not a doctor."

"Then take care to remember that," said McCoy

stiffly, and he pivoted on his heel and walked off the bridge. But just as the turbolift door shut Kirk heard an unmistakable guffaw.

Kirk walked past the crew lounge and heard, to his surprise, the unique strumming of the Vulcan lyre. It had been ages since he'd heard that, it seemed, and he stepped in to discover Spock seated there, his long fingers moving smoothly over the strings and rendering delicate, haunting melodies. All around him were crew members, ensigns and junior-grade lieutenants. Kirk grinned at that. Most of these officers were learning how to walk and feed themselves, or hadn't even been born—hell, their parents might not have even met, Kirk realized, let's be honest—the first time that Spock picked up a Vulcan lyre and filled the rec room of a ship named *Enterprise* with the eerie strains of its music.

The young officers seemed entranced by it, and Kirk couldn't blame them. It was somewhat spellbinding. Oddly, Kirk was old-fashioned enough to prefer a tune that he could hum, and he had yet to be able to distinguish a particular song. It all seemed a rather eclectic agglomeration of notes—and yet, somehow, it always managed to work as a single melody.

Kirk had learned that the best way to appreciate the music of the Vulcan harp was on a subliminal level. Instead of concentrating on the music he allowed his mind to wander, letting it be carried wherever the notes might take it. It was (dare he say it?) fascinating that Vulcan music could stir so many emotions, especially since Vulcan philosophy was so tightly geared in the other direction.

He drifted along on the chords, let thoughts and images waft free-form through his mind. He never saw the same thing twice when he listened to Spock's music. Sometimes the faces of former lovers would float before him, and sometimes he found himself in a simpler time, home, in the fields of Iowa, gazing longingly at the skies and waiting for that far-off time when he could apply to the academy. How ironic . . . once again, just as it had been when he was a child, the notion of the academy was far off . . . but far off in the opposite direction—in the past.

This time, though, he pictured nothing from his past, or at least no single event. Instead he saw what his past had been for so long, and what his present was, and the future. Every one of the notes that drifted from Spock's harp was there in his mind as the twinkling of a single star.

Stars hadn't twinkled for him in quite some time. That was the first thing that he had noticed when he made it into space—the twinkling was the distortion through the earth's atmosphere, but out of the confines of that atmosphere the stars were individual, steady and unblinking beacons. And each beacon was calling to him individually, summoning him. That had been much of what had driven him through his existence. Every single star was an invitation, a personal invitation to him, James T. Kirk. And it would be the height of rudeness to refuse such an unselfish, unqualified invitation.

And so he had spent his life accepting those invitations, one after the other. And he would continue to accept them until his final day, when he would simply go to join them forever.

That was when the music ended.

For a moment Kirk felt a bit disoriented, which was par for the course when he was getting really involved with Vulcan music. He cleared his throat and joined in the applause that was already sounding throughout the rec room.

Then Kirk glanced over to one side and noticed

Commodore José Tyler, seated against a wall. His face was wet with tears, and at first he wasn't applauding, apparently caught up in whatever was on his mind. Then he seemed to pull himself together and, wiping the tears away, joined in the enthusiasm.

Spock acknowledged the applause with a slight nod of his head and then looked up. Uhura was hanging toward the back of the room, smiling and nodding in appreciation.

His fingers began to move across the strings again, and this time the opening notes of the tune seemed a bit more sprightly than the soulful tune that he'd played earlier. And then, to Kirk's surprise, he heard Uhura begin to sing along with it, her voice arcing in her lovely mezzosoprano. Kirk realized, from the confidence with which she sang, that she knew this tune, perhaps had sung it along with Spock sometime in the past.

The words, though, were clearly not part of any traditional Vulcan song. It might very well have been that Uhura was making it up on the spot. But if she was, she was doing a marvelous job.

She circled Spock in a playful, tigerish fashion, moving with lithe confidence, and she sang,

There was a man and ship of fame,
We lost them both, but back they came,
And women don't dare breathe their name,
They'll turn their charm on you. . . .
The man's still got those sexy ears,
In alien love, he has no peers,
He's not slowed down by extra years,
The ship brings him to you. . . .

Oh girls in space be wary, be wary, be wary
Girls in space be wary, You know not what he'll do.

Uhura laughed lightly, and another round of applause sounded in the rec room. Kirk watched, however, as Tyler got up and, smiling gamely, made his way out. After hesitating a moment Kirk got up and went after him.

He found Tyler walking down the hallway, lost in thought, and quickly matched his stride. "Very moving music, wouldn't you say, Commodore?" he asked.

"Oh," said Tyler, "unquestionably. In my case, it moved me right out of the rec room." He glanced sideways at Kirk. "It's fascinating to see how different captains of the *Enterprise* handle their crew. Pike was much more of a hardnose than you are, Kirk. You don't mind my comparing the two of you, do you?"

"I have nothing but admiration for Christopher Pike," said Kirk easily.

"You seem far more accessible than he. The crew clearly respects you, but you don't seem to feel the need to drill in the concept of spit and polish. It makes for a somewhat relaxed atmosphere, but there's no interference with professionalism and efficiency. Indeed, it probably helps. It's healthier. Now Pike, well"—he whistled—"he ran a tight ship, Pike did," said Tyler. "One of the tightest I've ever seen. He had a very military bearing, more so than anyone else in the fleet. On occasion he would try to be 'one of the crew.' Never worked. And he would always retreat to his more formal attitude. He was comfortable that way. His first officer was just like him—even worse, although I don't mean that in a negative sense. She and he, two of a kind. There were rumors about them, you know."

"Rumors?" asked Kirk with an amused grin.

"About how they were actually . . . well, never mind." Tyler gave a dismissive wave. "It's disrespectful, I suppose, even to talk about it."

"Indeed," Kirk said gravely. Then he thought about it and said, "Actually, as much as I admire Chris Pike, I have a hard time picturing him trying to let down his hair. What type of things did he do?"

"Well . . . once he boxed with me."

"Really? How'd you do?"

"Oh . . . it was just a sparring match. I think it ended in a tie, actually. Yes, I remember," said Tyler. "Never really got a clean shot in. He was just too good."

"I can imagine."

They got to Tyler's quarters, and Kirk paused outside. "Commodore . . . is everything all right?"

Tyler fixed him with a level gaze, his hands draped behind his back. "How do you mean, Captain?"

"You seemed . . . upset before."

"Oh. That. The . . ." He cleared his throat loudly and said, "Just remembering a young woman that I left behind. You ever get misty-eyed for the women that you couldn't make a part of your life?"

"Oh, yes, sir," said Kirk.

"There you are, then."

"If I may ask . . . when was the last time you saw her? Do you remember?"

"I most certainly do. It was 33.4 years ago."

"Thirty-three point . . ." Kirk frowned. "Commodore, that's the last time the rift opened. The rift that's our destination . . ."

"I'm quite aware of that, Captain."

"And you," Kirk said slowly, beginning to understand, "requested that you be assigned to attend the re-opening of the rift, based on your previous experience the last time the rift opened."

"Keep going, Captain," said Tyler. "You've almost got it."

"The woman you left behind . . . Commodore, is she—"

"One of the Calligar, yes." He stepped into his cabin. He smiled and said as the door closed, "Stimulating, isn't it?"

Chapter Nine

THE TRANSPORT SHIP *Secord* pulled within range of the *Enterprise* right on schedule, prompting Kirk and his senior officers to head down to the transporter room to greet them. To Kirk it was something of an oddity —in a couple of respects, almost old home week.

Stepping into the turbolift with Spock and McCoy, Kirk said briskly, "Transporter room." Then he continued, to neither of them in particular, "You know, I find much of this situation to be extremely ironic."

"First psychiatrist, now philosopher," said McCoy dourly. "The skills you're picking up in your old age are absolutely amazing."

"Don't you want to hear why it's ironic?" asked Kirk. He almost sounded hurt.

"Not especially," McCoy informed him.

He turned to Spock. Spock merely looked at him impassively.

"All right, I'll tell you," said Kirk.

McCoy sighed.

"It's ironic," Kirk said, "that here we are, going to explore a rift in space. A division, a separation. And we are doing so with the aid of several people with whom we've had our own personal rifts: Ambassador Robert Fox, with whom we had sharp disagreements that almost resulted in all of us getting killed; Dr. Richard Daystrom, whose drive for success caused him to suffer a separation, not only from himself, but from reality, for a time; and Commodore José Tyler, officer from an *Enterprise* almost from another time, who has been separated from a particularly interesting female he left behind on the other side of the rift. Mr. Spock, wouldn't you consider that ironic?"

"No, sir."

"Well, then, how would you characterize it?"

The turbolift doors opened, and Spock faced his captain. "Contrived," replied the Vulcan. Then he and McCoy walked on ahead.

Kirk followed, shaking his head slowly in disappointed disgust. "Absolutely no sense of drama," he murmured.

Scotty was waiting for them in the transporter room, handling the transporter himself, as was his habit when VIPs were being brought aboard. He glanced at the young woman who normally operated the transporter and said briskly, "Now ye be sure to watch an expert at work, Tooch."

"Yes, sir," said Tooch. Her long brown hair swung around her shoulders, and the young engineer whose heart still beat in Scotty's chest felt a moment's stirring. Then, inwardly, he sighed.

"Problem, Mr. Scott?" asked Kirk.

Tooch was busying herself checking the programmed transporter patterns of the individuals coming aboard, and Scotty took a moment to say softly to the captain, "All the distances we travel, and there's no greater distance than age. Isn't that ironic?"

Kirk looked triumphantly at Spock and McCoy, but

they hadn't heard. He reminded himself to mention it to them later.

"The *Secord* is signaling readiness," said Tooch.

"Bring them aboard, Mr. Scott."

"Aye, sir," said Scotty, and he manipulated the controls with practiced ease.

The transporter platform began to shimmer, and moments later several familiar—and a couple of unfamiliar—forms appeared on the transporter platform.

The men who were familiar looked somewhat older, somewhat more tired, reflected Kirk; but then again, that description could certainly be applied to anyone else in the room, with the exception of Tooch. Distance indeed.

Kirk stepped forward and extended a hand. "Ambassador Fox," he said.

Fox stepped down from the platform and shook Kirk's hand firmly. When Fox had been a younger man the gray in his hair looked distinguished. Now it just looked old. But he still carried himself well, and the additional years in the diplomatic corps had only added to his general air of self-confidence.

"Captain Kirk," he replied formally. "It has been a long time."

"It certainly has."

Fox quickly surveyed McCoy, Spock, and Scotty. "And the same command crew, I see."

"Why fiddle with perfection?" asked Kirk.

"Indeed. A few more gray hairs all around, but none of us is spared that. It is good to see you again, Captain. I look forward to working with you and your extremely capable people."

"Thank you." Considering the disdain and arrogance with which Fox had treated them last time out in the business with Eminiar VII, this was something of a turnaround.

97

Fox gestured toward a tall, slightly frail-looking Andorian. "This is Thak, Andorian chargé d'affaires, and also one of their top scientists."

Thak bowed slightly at the waist and spoke in the softly modulated, faintly lisping voice that effectively covered the fact that Andorians were among the most deadly warriors in the Federation. "It is most satisfying to meet you, Captain Kirk. And your officers."

"And this," continued Fox, "is Shondar Dorkin, a top Tellarite expert on societal development."

Shondar Dorkin did not even bother to say anything but merely grunted as introductions were made. Dorkin and Thak had their respective assistants with them, and both of them seemed to ignore their assistants entirely.

One individual remained on the transporter platform. He stood tall and impassive, staring fixedly ahead. He was dressed much the same as Kirk remembered him from those many years ago, but somehow he seemed . . . shorter. Yes, that was it. His shoulders were stooped with age, and perhaps something more. When Kirk had last seen him he had carried himself with overwhelming dignity. That seemed to have been leached out of him.

"And," said Ambassador Fox, "I'm sure you remember Dr. Richard Daystrom."

"Of course. Doctor Daystrom." Kirk proffered his hand once more.

Daystrom stared at it as if Kirk had tossed him an obscene gesture. Then, very slowly, he reached up and shook Kirk's hand. There was no firmness to the grip, and Daystrom's palm felt clammy.

"Captain," began Daystrom, his voice still a strong, basso tone. But then he faltered, as if he'd wanted to say something but couldn't recall what it was.

Kirk immediately said, "You remember Mr. Spock

and Dr. McCoy," and he put just enough emphasis on the latter name to subtly cue the *Enterprise* chief medical officer that he wanted his immediate attention to this. McCoy was extremely prompt on the uptake and said, "Dr. Daystrom, it's good to see you again."

Daystrom smiled gamely, and there was so much pain in that smile that it made Kirk ache. But he responded immediately to McCoy's practiced bedside manner and visibly relaxed.

"You look tired, Doctor Daystrom," McCoy continued.

"Yes . . . yes," rumbled Daystrom, rubbing his forehead. "It has been a very long trip, and I am . . . fatigued."

"We have personnel just outside to show all of you to your quarters," said Kirk. He raised his voice slightly, addressing everyone in the transporter room. "As soon as the *Secord* is out of range we will get underway to our destination. We estimate arrival in—"

"Twenty-six point three hours," said Spock briskly.

"So we will have a briefing at fourteen hundred hours," Kirk continued, "to make sure that everyone is up-to-date and we all know our respective jobs."

"Are you implying that I cannot do my assigned duties?" demanded Shondar Dorkin gruffly.

Kirk kept his face impassive, long practice in dealing with Tellarites serving him well. "No, Shondar," he said, addressing the Tellarite by his title. "I am concerned that we all know one another's parameters, so that none of us interferes with you in your most important activities."

His voice was carefully neutral, and the Tellarite did not notice the faint sarcasm at all, because one man's sarcasm was a Tellarite's mark of respect.

"Good," said Shondar. "That is an excellent way to proceed."

"I'm glad you approve," replied Kirk.

Moments later the exploratory team assigned by the Federation to make contact with the Calligarians was being escorted to quarters while Kirk, Spock, McCoy, and Scotty hung back and watched them go.

"Bones," said Kirk softly, "I want you to keep a close eye on Dr. Daystrom. His nervous breakdown was years ago, and Starfleet swore to me that he was fully recovered, but—"

"I studied his medical file before he came aboard," said McCoy. "He's still as brilliant a computer genius as ever. And he's recovered from his breakdown, thanks to years of therapy. But Jim, the human mind is a delicate instrument. Once broken, it can be repaired, but the cracks don't completely heal. Especially, in my opinion, in someone with such an unrelenting intellect as Dr. Daystrom."

"You'll talk with him," said Kirk.

"I'll talk with him," affirmed McCoy.

Kirk nodded approvingly, and then after a moment he said, "Considering all the difficulties we had with Ambassador Fox the last time we worked with him, he seemed extraordinarily sincere in his praise for us."

"There is an old saying in the field of diplomacy," said Spock.

"And that is?"

"The entire key to diplomacy is sincerity. Once that can be faked, the rest is simple."

Kirk stared at Spock for a minute and then looked at McCoy. He gestured with a nod of his head in the direction of the Vulcan and said to the doctor, "He's been hanging around you too long. Mr. Spock"—he turned back to his first officer—"I do believe you're developing into a cynic."

"First a master of logic, and now a master of cynicism," said McCoy.

Spock nodded his head slightly in acknowledgment. "I have had excellent models to study, Doctor. In that I have been most fortunate."

Chapter Ten

RICHARD DAYSTROM sat in his quarters, staring at the computer screen. He ran his fingers across it gently, like a father caressing a child.

"Computer," he said softly.

"Working."

"Identify me."

"Dr. Richard Daystrom," said the computer. "Inventor of the duotonic systems serving as the basis for computer systems in use by Starfleet. Winner of the Nobel and Z-Magnees prizes."

He nodded. A perfectly decent short ID. "And what have I done lately?" he asked.

"Suffered mental collapse."

He grimaced. "And since then?"

"Recovered from mental collapse."

"And since then?"

"Specify."

"Have I done anything . . ." He searched for the word. "Have I done anything noteworthy?"

The computer did not hesitate. "Negative."

He sat there for a moment and then lowered his head, tapping his temple against the edge of the computer screen. He only registered in the back of his mind that the door to his quarters had just opened.

"Hello, Doctor."

"Hello, Doctor," Daystrom replied to McCoy. The edges of his mouth were tight. "Checking up on me already?"

"I'm not checking up on you," said McCoy, sitting opposite Daystrom.

Daystrom swung his chair around to face him. "Not only are you checking up on me," he said patiently, "but you're doing an extraordinarily bad job of lying about it."

Rather than pursue it, McCoy took note of the fact that the computer was on and asked, "What are you doing?"

"I am running a diagnostic."

"On the computer?"

He smiled a smile of gentle self-mockery. "No, Dr. McCoy. On myself."

McCoy nodded at that. "And what is your diagnosis?"

"Not a very flattering one."

It was curious, McCoy noted. When Daystrom spoke it was in a low, flat monotone. Moreover, he had developed the nasty habit of not blinking for extraordinary lengths of time. It was extremely disconcerting.

"Doctor," said McCoy softly, "I'm not going to mince words with you. I've studied your medical file. You must have known I was going to do that."

"You are the chief medical officer," rumbled Daystrom. "I would have been shocked if you had not."

Daystrom didn't sound to McCoy like someone

who was capable of being shocked right now. In fact, he didn't sound like someone who was capable of feeling anything at all. "Doctor—"

"Please," said Daystrom, raising a slender hand. "We are both men of titles. Please call me Richard. And I shall call you—"

"Dr. McCoy."

Daystrom blinked impassively, and McCoy put a hand on Daystrom's forearm. "It was just a joke," he said. But he felt the tension beneath Daystrom's skin. The man was like a wound-up spring. "Please . . . call me Leonard. Or Bones."

"Bones?"

He shrugged. "Nickname I picked up. Depending who you talk to, it's short for either 'Sawbones' or 'Skin and Bones.'"

"I had a nickname in my younger days," said Daystrom. Again he was speaking in that flat monotone rather than sounding wistful over a memory from his youth.

"Really? What?"

Daystrom looked at him with those dead eyes. "The Freak."

"I see." McCoy looked down and then up. "Richard, what in hell are you doing here?"

"Starfleet is interested in the Calligar computer technology, which is presently utterly unexplored. In the first contact between the *Enterprise* and the Calligar, they were not willing to discuss their computer developments at all. It is hoped in certain circles that their attitude will have changed in the intervening decades. I am still an expert, despite all my widely discussed mental difficulties—I was written up, you know, in a very esteemed medical journal."

"I know. I read it," said McCoy.

Daystrom raised a sardonic eyebrow. "What did you think?"

104

"I thought the author was more interested in showing how clever he was than in exploring the difficulties that you suffered."

"I am a genius," said Daystrom. "That is not a boast, that is a quantitatively determined fact. The concept is that an advanced thinker should be advanced enough so as not to have to worry about such petty things as mental instability."

"Historically that concept has not been consistently true," said McCoy.

"No, Leonard," said Daystrom gravely. "It has not."

Daystrom rose and walked slowly across the cabin as if pacing it out, and then back across to his chair. He leaned against the back of it, the knuckles of his hand working beneath the skin. His eyes, if focused anywhere, were focused inward.

"You have no idea," he said softly, "how many people were thrilled that I collapsed. How many people rejoiced in seeing it. When you are a genius you give little care or thought to the people whom you surpass in your drive to succeed. You see them as stumbling blocks or obstacles to your goal. Nothing more than that. And every time a genius surpasses one of the lesser people he takes pride in the divine rightness of that act. The strong survive by stepping on the weak. You understand that, don't you, Leonard? Genius is a great, crunching, giant maw, chewing up sparks of humanity and spitting out the fat, the dross, the gristle, and keeping for its own meal the protein. The quality. The meat of humanity."

"Richard—"

He turned that unblinking gaze on McCoy. "I assure you, Leonard, there is nothing wrong with me. I am merely waxing philosophical. I am not a danger to this ship, this crew, or this mission. My intellect is still intact . . . a most fortunate state of affairs, considering that my family, personal fortune, and personal pride are not." He seemed to give the matter some more thought, and then he said, "Leonard, are you concerned about me?"

McCoy pondered that and then said, "I'm concerned for you. I'm trusting that you'll be able to do your job. Your confidence may have deserted you—you may be able to look at a half-full glass and only see it as half empty—but I believe that you can handle whatever we come up against."

"That's good to know," said Daystrom. "That's very good to know. Now . . . if you wouldn't mind, I'd like some time alone."

"All right." McCoy stood. "I want you to know, though, that my door is always open."

"That sounds rather drafty," said Daystrom evenly.

"Just so you know," said McCoy, and he walked out of Daystrom's quarters. Daystrom waited until McCoy's footfall faded.

Then he leaned forward and said, "Computer."

"Working," said the computer.

He interlaced his fingers and said, "Identify me."

"Dr. Richard Daystrom," began the computer.

And Daystrom listened, his interwoven fingers drawing tighter and tighter until he thought that his knuckles were going to snap. And his chest began to shake. . . .

"He's going to be fine," McCoy said to Kirk.

Kirk looked up from his desk. "Good," he said. "That's good to know. The last thing we need on something as delicate as this is for something to go wrong with the mental balance of one of our key personnel. I'd like you there for the briefing."

"I wouldn't miss it for the world," said McCoy.

Chapter Eleven

"THIS IS ANOMALY T-128—the rift," said Kirk, "as it was nearly four decades ago—and as it will soon be again."

On the viewscreen of the conference room the rift was undulating in all its trans-spatial glory. Kirk looked around the room at all his senior officers, as well as the team of diplomats and scientists that had been assembled by the Federation.

All of them were studying the file footage with extreme interest and fascination. Shondar Dorkin leaned over and muttered something in gruff Tellarian to his aide, who in turn laughed in a grunting, piggish manner. It was probably some off-color remark about the rift, and Kirk was extremely pleased that he hadn't understood what had just been said.

Kirk could not help but notice, however, that Commodore José Tyler was watching it more closely than anyone. Indeed, he seemed almost spellbound by it. Kirk knew what was going through his mind and prayed to whatever gods might be listening that the commodore wasn't setting himself up for some major disappointment.

"You have already been briefed as to the specifics of the rift's makeup," said Kirk. "In less than nine hours we will be at the site when the rift opens sufficiently to allow access to the Calligar."

"How do we know they'll be expecting us, or will even want to see us?" said Sulu. He had read up on the Calligar and knew how isolationist they were capable of being.

"That has been prearranged," Spock said. "When the rift is preparing to open it does not do so immediately. There are certain 'birthing pains,' if you will. A series of small, almost undetectable fissures that are created as the rift prepares to open fully. Virtually pinpoints by our standards—however, more than sufficient for communication via subspace radio to be achieved."

"Starfleet has been communicating with the Calligar!" said Shondar Dorkin, suddenly becoming excessively bombastic. "My government was not informed of this! With beings of the Calligarians' power there can be no exclusive communication without threatening the very treaty and power structure that—"

"The Tellarite government was informed, Shondar," said Spock with infinite patience.

"Nonsense! You're lying!"

"Vulcans do not lie." Thak now spoke up in his slightly creepy whisper. "For whatever reason, it would seem they neglected to tell you."

"*Neglected!*" blustered Dorkin. "That's the most—"

"Shondar," said Kirk, making sure to put the accent on the second syllable, since to do otherwise would have been seen as a lack of respect. "Either your government was not informed due to some oversight on the Federation's part, or else you were not informed through some oversight on your government's part. Either way, it would seem to indicate that someone slipped up somewhere. Can we all acknowledge that what we have here is a snafu and move on?"

"A *snahphu!*" roared Shondar Dorkin. To Kirk's astonishment Dorkin leapt to his feet, knocking back his chair. "You dare! You *dare* call me a *snahphu!* You realize, Kirk, that with those words you have brought about war?"

"What?!" Kirk was dumbfounded. He looked around. "Will someone please—"

Ambassador Fox put up a hand and said, "Captain, it's the word."

"What word? What—" And then Kirk's eyes widened, and he realized. It was an effort not to laugh, but it became a bit easier when he reminded himself of just how serious the situation could become. "Of course. Shondar—"

Dorkin was already heading toward the door when he spun on his large heel and said, "What do you want, earther?"

"The word spelled S-N-A-F-U—pronounced in a manner similar to the Tellarite insult and obscenity that you think I said—is an acronym for 'situation normal, all . . . fouled up.'"

"What?" said the confused Tellarite. "What?"

Spock stepped in and said, "An old earth term referring to the idea that constant chaos and misunderstanding was a routine state of affairs."

"Having nothing to do with the word you think I said, which was not even on my mind," said Kirk.

"Captain Kirk humbly, grovelingly apologizes and requests forgiveness," Fox said.

Kirk glanced at him in annoyance. "Well, now, I didn't exactly—"

"Groveling apology accepted," grunted Dorkin.

He gestured for his aide to return to his seat as well and sat down once more.

"I'm glad that's settled," said Kirk, forcing a smile. "Even in this day and age we can have an occasional muck-up when—".

"A *mukkup!*" howled the Tellarite, leaping to his feet. "How *dare* you—"

Mercifully, it was the Andorian who put a hand on Dorkin's shoulder and, with surprisingly steely strength, shoved him back down. "Listen, if you please," he said firmly to the Shondar.

Kirk rolled his eyes. "I think the briefing might go a bit more efficiently if *everyone* just listened. Can we all do that?"

There were nods of assent around the table. Kirk rubbed his forehead, trying to ease the pain he was feeling, and he said, "I've totally lost track. Where were we?"

"Subspace radio," said Chekov helpfully.

"Ah, yes. Thank you. Via subspace radio we were able to communicate with the Calligar and affirm that they were indeed interested in maintaining contact with us. Their stated reason and interest was the same: to keep apprised of our progress and, in turn, give us some idea of what their technology and society are like."

"Do you have any idea who it was that you communicated with?" asked Tyler. "Was it Zyo? The Master Builder?"

"My understanding is that no names were given," said Kirk. "I have no idea who spoke on behalf of the Calligar."

Tyler settled back in his chair, looking thoughtful.

"When we arrive at the rift," Kirk continued, "we will wait for it to open to sufficient width and reach stability. We will not send anyone through if I am not

110

convinced that it will be safe for all concerned." Again there was nodding of heads, and Kirk turned to Spock to indicate that the science officer should continue.

Spock picked up smoothly. "The *Enterprise* will not pass through. It would appear that the size of the vessel the last time was a major factor in disrupting the rift and causing it to close prematurely. Instead we will be sending in a shuttlecraft mounted on a warp sled."

"Warp sled?" asked Fox. "Pardon my ignorance, but . . . being a diplomat, I'm not up on all the latest developments."

"A warp sled," said Spock, "is a small, self-contained warp propulsion unit that can be attached to a non-warp vehicle. It is capable of attaining warp three. However, the fuel consumption is very rapid, and a warp sled–mounted vehicle can only use that propulsion system for a maximum of one half hour. After that the shuttle would be entirely dependent on impulse."

"Which means it would be torn to shreds under the temporal stress, of the rift," Scotty added.

"The last time we went through," Tyler said, "we experienced all sorts of time fluctuations. It was almost a living hell."

"Ah," Scotty said, "but that was the old hyperdrive, sir. When the time warp and hyperdrive systems were consolidated and refined into the more modern warp drive, we also strengthened the warp field that protects the *Enterprise* from even the standard stress of faster-than-light travel."

"And the warp drive units on the warp sled?"

"Same thing, sir," said Scotty. "So it should be more than enough to protect the passengers from temporal strain."

"Good," said Tyler, looking extremely relieved. "I

111

can't say I'd be particularly eager to go through that again. Four decades later, and it was still one of the most grueling things I've ever experienced."

"How do we know this isn't some sort of trick?" demanded Shondar Dorkin. "We're sending our own people through and getting nothing in return. You could sit here like dunces for seventy-two hours, and then the rift could close while you foolishly allowed it."

"Other members of the Federation Council said much the same thing," admitted Kirk. "It would seem we live in suspicious times."

"Not like the old days, eh, Captain?" said Tyler, smiling.

Kirk nodded and then continued. "However, communications with the Calligar already attended to that. As part of their continued interest in us, and in keeping with the spirit of interstellar harmony, the Calligar have agreed to send through a representative as part of an exchange program for the duration of the rift's accessibility."

"*A* representative? As in one?" growled Dorkin.

"Yes, sir," said Spock. "One."

"We send in a group of top individuals, and they send one?" Dorkin snorted. "What are they saying? That one of them is worth the lot of us?"

"In some instances," murmured Thak, "I would be hard pressed to debate that notion."

Shondar Dorkin cast a suspicious glance at him with his piglike eyes.

"We are, to all intents and purposes, the guests of the Calligar," said Kirk. "They have done nothing to give us the impression that they are remotely duplicitous or planning any sort of double cross."

"I do not like it," grumbled Dorkin.

"Tellarites like nothing in this galaxy, which certainly fits in with how the galaxy views Tellarites," said Thak.

Dorkin turned toward him, growling. "Did you attempt to insult me, Andorian?"

Clearly exasperated, Thak said, "I did not attempt to. I succeeded. Your incessant belligerence is enough to drive a more sane being to distraction."

"Thak," said Kirk warningly.

"And what would Andorians know of sanity?" snapped Dorkin. "With your effete, lisping mannerisms. You call yourselves a warrior race! You wouldn't last five minutes in a young Tellarite's manning ritual!"

"Shondar Dorkin." Kirk turned toward the Tellarite. As captain it was his job to be as diplomatic as possible, but this was reaching the breaking point.

"Would you mind speaking in the other direction?" said Thak pleasantly. "Your breath is wilting my antennae."

Shondar Dorkin was immediately on his feet, as was Thak, who moved with deceptive speed. Ambassador Fox was sputtering in surprise. Tyler was grinning widely, as if enjoying the first good brouhaha he'd seen in some time. And Kirk was about to dress both of them down when the *Enterprise* captain was saved the trouble.

A stentorian voice boomed through the briefing room. Commanding. Angry. Full of authority and so deep that it almost made the furniture vibrate.

"Sit down and shut up."

Heads snapped around to look upon Richard Daystrom. He had not moved an inch from his seat. His fingers were steepled, his eyes were coldly burning, and he added, *"Now."*

There was quiet for a moment, and then the Andorian tilted his head slightly in that amazingly polite manner that he had. He sat. Shondar Dorkin remained standing for a moment, but the silence had come over them like a shroud, and a moment later he had settled into his seat as well.

As if there had been no disturbance at all, Kirk continued. "Since the Calligar have always dealt with us in a straightforward manner, we have no reason to believe they are not doing so now. In fact, the sending of a representative could easily be viewed as a gesture of confidence to us, to let us know that they are intending to continue that tradition of honest dealings."

"Fine," grunted Dorkin. "Whatever you say."

"The Calligar have even agreed to send their representative through first," said Kirk. "As soon as they have, we will send through our team, which will consist of Mr. Spock, Commander Scott, Dr. Daystrom, Commodore Tyler, Ambassador Thak . . ."

"Simply 'Thak' will do," said Thak. "I dislike titles."

"Thak," continued Kirk, "and Shondar Dorkin. We will remain in constant subspace communication, checking in at hourly intervals. Mr. Spock will be in charge. I assume you all understand that. I don't care how highly placed in your respective governments you are. His word is final."

Tyler cleared his throat loudly, and Kirk slowly turned to him. "Commodore, I am aware that you are the ranking officer, but—"

Shaking his head, Tyler put up a hand and smiled. "I was just kidding, Captain. This is an *Enterprise*-coordinated mission. Since Mr. Spock will be the ranking *Enterprise* officer on the scene, I'm more than happy to acknowledge his authority in this matter."

"Thank you, Commodore," said Kirk, not ungratefully.

The exchange had had the appearance of spontaneity, but actually it had been worked out ahead of time between Kirk and Tyler. Kirk had wanted the science officer to be the officer in charge on site, especially considering the makeup of the rest of the contact team. Tellarites and Andorians tended to regard humans with a mixture of amusement and contempt, but they had nothing but respect—however grudging at times—for the remote and coldly logical Vulcans. It was Kirk's gut instinct that things would go more smoothly with Spock running the show, and to his relief, Tyler had agreed.

"Ambassador Fox will be remaining here to act as official Federation intermediary with the Calligarian exchange representative. Now, are there any other questions?" asked Kirk.

There was a quick glance around the table. No one seemed to have anything to say.

"Yes. I have a question," Dorkin said. "I wish to know how long you think you can continue to treat Tellarites with such a lack of respect."

"You will generally find, Shondar," said Kirk icily, "that when it comes to matters of respect, one gets only as good as he gives."

Dorkin glowered at him for that, and suddenly his head snapped around. "What was that?" he demanded.

His gaze was focused on Tyler, who had murmured something to Scotty that had gotten a wide grin from the engineer. But the Tellarites, despite their apparently lack of auditory apparatus, had rather sharp hearing. "What did you say about me?" demanded Dorkin.

Scotty fired a warning glance at Tyler, but Tyler didn't particularly seem to care. Instead the commodore smiled a toothy grin and said, "I said you were a jerk."

115

There was dead silence, and then, to the shock of all concerned, the Tellarite actually seemed to smile. He rose from his seat, pointed a furry paw at Tyler, and said gravely, "Thank you."

Tyler looked at Scotty, and then back at the Tellarite. "Don't mention it."

Shondar Dorkin turned and headed out of the room, his aide at his side. He paused at the door, gestured toward Tyler, and said to the room at large, "Now there is a human who knows how to address a Tellarite with respect."

He strode out into the corridor and away from the briefing room, proud of his parting shot. And even his sharp Tellarite hearing did not pick up the gales of laughter that issued from behind the closed conference room doors as he sauntered back to his quarters.

Chapter Twelve

MONTGOMERY SCOTT strode through the engine room like a king surveying his kingdom. As he walked past, each of the young engineering officers would snap to slightly or suddenly cast a nervous glance at the station monitors they were supposed to be watching. It was widely acknowledged throughout Engineering that Mr. Scott saw everything—absolutely everything —that went on.

This was eminently true, and the ability was not limited to machines. Scott walked past the warp engine inductor monitor and suddenly took a step back. Ensign Hicks was on duty, and he looked a bit off. His eyes seemed bleary, his concentration not what it should be—and even when he was trying to concentrate for the benefit of Mr. Scott, his focus seemed weak.

"Mr. Hicks," said Scotty sternly, "turn around."

Hicks did so, his back ramrod-straight. "Yes, sir," he said.

Scotty eyed him carefully for a moment and then

leaned forward so that he was almost nose to nose with him. Hicks was wavering ever so slightly, as if he were a bush and a gentle breeze was causing him to sway in the wind. Then Scotty remembered—Hicks was to be the best man at the upcoming marriage of Crewman Flaherty to Ensign McGee, and last night had been the bachelor party.

"Breathe at me, Mr. Hicks," he ordered.

Hicks flinched and stammered, "Uh . . . uh . . . Mr. Scott, I don't see that—"

"Breathe. That's an order, lad," said Scott in no uncertain terms.

With a grimace Hicks opened his mouth and puffed tentatively in Scott's direction.

He wasn't drunk. Not by any means. Not remotely. Not even close. But the trained nostrils of Montgomery Scott could scent alcohol on a man's breath anytime up to a week or more after the beverage was consumed—at least, that's what he told people.

But not just that alcohol had been consumed; oh, no. Scotty's olfactory senses were even more refined than that.

"Again," said Scotty. Hicks, clearly unhappy, obeyed. Scotty looked him dead in the eye. "So Mr. Chekov was there, eh?"

Hicks's eyes opened wide in complete shock. Totally forgetting protocol, he stammered, "How . . . how did . . ."

"Ach. Lad, I can catch a whiff of vodka from twenty paces with the wind blowing against it. Mr. Chekov was invited." He shook his head in mock horror. The unspoken follow-up was clear: And I wasn't.

"Mr.—Mr. Chekov is Flaherty's direct superior," Hicks said.

"And what am I to you?" demanded Scott. "A pot roast?"

"Well, I—"

"I think that you're not entirely attending to your duties with maximum efficiency," said Scotty. "Would you say that working an extra shift would be sufficient to bring you up to maximum potential, Mr. Hicks?"

Hicks gulped. "Yes, sir."

"There's a lad."

Scotty turned and, to his surprise, saw Commodore Tyler standing right behind him. "Ah. Commodore. You've been through once on an inspection. Can't get enough of where the real work in the ship is done, eh?"

Hicks, grateful for the interruption, returned to his duties as Scotty and Tyler began to walk. "Far more impressive than in the old days, isn't it?" said Scotty proudly. "The more sophisticated the engines, the more room we need to make 'em work properly. They've certainly grown up, my bairns have."

"Remarkably complex apparatus."

"Complex, yes, but marvelously self-sufficient. The equipment has so many redundant check systems and self-maintenance programs, why . . . a blind man could be chief engineer and not lose a whit of efficiency."

"I tend to think you're undercutting your own influence and importance, Mr. Scott. According to the captain, you do everything but tuck the engines in at night."

"Well . . . I have been known to read them a story every now and then. If they've behaved themselves, of course, and eaten all their vegetables."

But Tyler was looking at Scotty thoughtfully, and now he was saying, "You know . . . you seemed familiar at the briefing yesterday, and now . . . I remember you now."

"Remember me, sir?" said Scotty.

"We didn't really interact all that much," said Tyler.

119

"I was on the bridge, you were down in Engineering. But you . . . ohhhh, yes. How could I forget? Lieutenant J.G. Montgomery Scott. From back on the original *Enterprise*. My God, have you ever left the engine room?"

"Not of my own volition, sir," said Scott with a smile.

Tyler nodded at that. "Was I to understand that that crewman was at his post and intoxicated?"

"No, sir," said Scotty firmly. "My boys know better than that. He was a bit . . . off his feed, however. I rode him about that. It won't happen again. There's no need for any formal—"

"Oh, of course not." Tyler waved off the very notion. "Actually, if anything, I was going to observe that you were riding him pretty hard."

"There's no such thing as too much discipline when it comes to the engine room, sir."

"What was the cause of the . . . offness? Some sort of event?"

"Bachelor party, sir."

"You present when the imbibing took place?"

"No, sir," said Scotty stiffly. "As a ranking officer, I dinna think it appropriate to be fraternizing with subordinates in that manner."

"I see. Meaning you weren't invited."

"No, sir," said Scotty with a small sigh. "Between two old war-horses, Commodore, I can't help but wonder . . . when did we become them?"

" 'Them,' Mr. Scott?"

"Them. The enemy, sir. The other people. The older generation. The opposition. Them. When did it occur? I was watching for it so I could avoid it happening, but it seems to have sneaked up on me—perhaps when I was taking one of those naps I seem to need more frequently these days. And I was wondering when I crossed that line."

"When?" Tyler was smiling. "You want an exact time?"

"I'm not certain when it was," Scotty said thoughtfully. "I didn't plan it that way. Just somewhere, it happened. One day I was one of us, and now I'm one of them. Do ye understand, sir?"

"Oh, all too well," said Tyler. "We all want to capture little pieces of our past, Mr. Scott. For some of us, it's something as simple as being thought of as 'one of the boys.' For others, it's . . . a bit more complex."

"Complexity is my area of expertise," Scotty said.

"Oh, I remember that all too well."

"Sir?" Clearly the engineer didn't understand.

"You think I forgot about it, don't you?"

Scotty's eyes narrowed. "Forgot about what, Commodore?"

"The still. The hooch that was made right in the engine room—"

"Sir!" said Scotty with great indignation. "Such an endeavor would be completely contrary to Starfleet regulations. I would never undertake such an—"

"Enterprise?"

Scotty blinked. "Yes, sir."

"Then perhaps I'm not remembering quite correctly," deadpanned the commodore. "When you get older the memory can play nasty tricks on you."

"I would think so, sir," said Scotty. "Might be a result of drinking all that illegal hooch in your youth. Rots your brain cells."

"No. Alcohol rots your brain cells. The booze that I remember simply ate the brain away. However, I bow to your expertise in the matter, Mr. Scott."

There was a beep on the wall comm unit, and Scotty stepped over and punched it. "Engine Room. Scott here."

"This is the captain," came Kirk's voice. "Commodore Tyler is down there with you?"

"Right here, Captain," Tyler replied.

"Commodore, we estimate ten minutes until we reach the site of the rift."

"I'll be right up. Tyler out."

He turned to Scotty and stuck out a hand. Scotty shook it firmly.

"It was a pleasure recalling old times, Mr. Scott."

"The same here, Commodore."

Tyler turned and left the engine room, and slowly Mr. Scott began his rounds again. Within minutes he was back at the station where the hapless Mr. Hicks was diligently going on about his business.

"Mr. Hicks," said Scotty, all sternness.

Hicks's back was to him, but Scotty could see him sag slightly, looking exasperated that he was still on the chief engineer's hit list. He turned slowly and, to his credit, drew himself to attention, shoulders squared. "Yes, sir."

Scotty inclined his head ever so slightly and said, "Go sleep it off."

"Sir?"

"You have the mother of all headaches, don't you, lad?"

"Not exactly, sir," admitted Hicks. "More of a close aunt."

"Fine. So go sleep it off. That's an order, lad."

Unable to believe the sudden turnaround, Hicks nevertheless nodded and walked quickly out of the engine room before (he figured) Mr. Scott could change his mind. Scotty watched him go and smiled inwardly before turning to another crewman some feet away and said, "And what do you think you're staring at? Do I look like a dilithium variance monitor to you?"

"Now that's a remarkable sight," said Kirk.

He had studied the file record of the original

122

encounter between the *Enterprise* and that freakish temporal phenomenon that had become informally known as "Pike's Rift," a name that Chris Pike had reportedly hated and discouraged whenever possible. As a result, most people in the field continued to refer to it by its scientific designation of Anomaly T-128. However, studying the records was nothing compared to standing on the bridge of the ship that was, in name if not fact, the first one to encounter the structural rip in the universe those many years ago, and staring at its image on the viewscreen.

Space was swirling around it in what seemed to be almost a bubbling miasma, evocative of what it might have been like at the very dawn of creation. In a way, Kirk felt that he was staring at a small leftover bit of cosmic history.

"The seams in the universe," he said to no one in particular on the bridge, "appear to be showing."

McCoy, standing to his left, responded, "Looks to me like the universe is coming apart at those seams."

Kirk glanced up at him. "Age is telling on all of us, Doctor. Maybe the universe needs to cut down on its fats and exercise more."

"That would certainly be my prescription," confirmed McCoy.

"Holding steady at five thousand kilometers," said Chekov.

"What's the rift doing?"

"Nothing, sir," Sulu said, glancing at his instruments. "At the moment it seems to be stab—" Then he stopped and looked again. "Energy flux, sir. Wave reading alpha niner and rising."

"Confirmed," said Spock from his science station. "The rift appears to be opening more fully. Its cycle has begun."

The turbolift hissed open, and Tyler stepped out onto the bridge. This time there was no tentativeness in his step, nor anything in his gaze aside from excitement.

Kirk glanced at him and then looked back at the screen. "Commodore," he said, "I thought you were going to be down in the reception bay with the other representatives."

"I was," said Tyler. "But now it would appear that I'm not. Strange how the universe works, isn't it, Captain?" He took a step down and stood just to McCoy's left. "I would not miss this for all the world."

The rift took swirling shape and slowly, slowly, began to separate. The crew watched with fascination bordering on astonishment. In a steady, calm monotone Spock gave out readings as the rift became more and more accessible. Within minutes it became wide enough to accommodate a shuttle, and then a starship, and then several. From within were hints of the whirling temporal vortex that constituted its interior.

Every scrap of information, every possible reading by the sensors that had been upgraded by years of improved technology was taken down and fed into the *Enterprise* computers. That information, in turn, was disseminated with lightning speed to the mainframe data base of the Federation, and from there to all the races that were participating in this grand and exciting adventure.

And yet, with all the remarkable alacrity at the command of the machines, it was a human eye that spotted something at the precise moment the instruments read it.

"Captain," began Spock, "sensors are indicating—"

"I see it," said Kirk. And next to him Tyler was pointing and saying, "There. At four o'clock."

Sulu glanced at Tyler and said briskly, "Two-twenty mark eighteen."

Tyler smiled. "Same thing."

"Magnification two, Mr. Sulu," said Kirk.

Immediately the screen shifted to focus on what had caught the attention of, by this point, everyone on the bridge.

A small vessel had emerged from the rift. Roughly the size of a shuttlecraft, but the design was amazingly simple—it wasn't much more than a cylinder. But it was moving with incredible speed.

"Sensors indicate that the vessel was proceeding through the rift at warp four," said Spock, "but reduced to half impulse the moment it emerged from the rift."

"Faster than our shuttlecraft," said Kirk in quiet amazement, "and it stops on a dime. Commodore, didn't they state in your first contact with them that they were not actively pursuing space travel?"

"So we were told," replied Tyler. "On the other hand, the Calligar have demonstrated that they are fully capable of rising to whatever occasion presents itself. After all, they were able to produce computer components at virtually a moment's notice. Having any kind of lead time at all to create a conveyance doesn't even seem a challenge."

The craft drifted closer and then came to a rest. It simply hovered there, as if staring at the *Enterprise* contemplatively.

"It's come to a dead stop, Captain," said Sulu. "They are just inside transporter range."

"Not a coincidence, I would presume," said Kirk. He glanced at Tyler, who merely nodded confirmation. "Life readings?"

"Sensors detect one life form," said Spock. "Calligarian, based on records from the original transporter matrix when they first beamed aboard the *Enterprise.*"

"Saving bodily compositions for four decades," commented Tyler. "Talk about being thorough."

"You never know," said Kirk sagely. "Open a hailing frequency, Uhura."

"You're on, Captain."

"This is Captain James Kirk of the starship *Enterprise*," he said. "If you are the Calligarian representative, then I welcome you on behalf of the United Federation of Planets. Please identify yourself."

The vehicle did not respond. Instead it simply sat there.

Suddenly lights began to flash on the computer consoles. Kirk looked around, his concentration momentarily thrown, and Spock said, "Captain, we are being scanned."

"Ah-haaah," said Tyler slowly. "Doing it differently this time." When Kirk looked at him questioningly Tyler continued. "Captain Pike made his displeasure known when they originally scanned our computer banks in a clandestine manner. Obviously they recall that and decided to be more open about it."

"Shall I engage scanning safeguards?" asked Spock.

"No," said Kirk. He leaned forward, resting on one elbow. "We have nothing to hide. Let them scan to their heart's content."

The boards flickered for some moments more and then ceased. Then Kirk said, "Uhura, patch me in." When she nodded in confirmation he said, "Calligarian vessel . . . we have cooperated with you thus far. It's your move."

The move wasn't long in coming. Less than thirty seconds later there suddenly came a call from the transporter room. "Captain!" came the surprised voice of Tooch. "Transporter beams have been activated!"

"By whom?" demanded Kirk.

"Not by me, sir. Should I try to abort?"

"No. We'll be right down. Bridge to Security," he continued without missing a beat. "Security team to transporter room." He stood quickly and said, "Commodore Tyler, Mr. Spock, Dr. McCoy, would you join me, please? Uhura, summon the rest of the contact team to the transporter room. Mr. Sulu, you have the conn."

"Aye, sir," said Sulu, crossing to the captain's chair as Kirk vacated it.

No one spoke during the turbolift trip to the transporter room, but Kirk could almost feel the waves of excitement radiating from Commodore Tyler. This was a nostalgia trip for Tyler, Kirk realized—a return to one of the grand adventures of his youth, whereas for Kirk it was just another contact with an alien race.

Just another contact. My God, he realized, did I actually think that just now? When he had been a youngster on earth, dreams of alien races, of visiting places that were light-years away, occupied his every waking and sleeping moment. Had he now grown so blasé that the notion of meeting a new race—new for him, at least—had been reduced to "just another contact"?

Perhaps it was incumbent upon him, he realized, to do everything he could to maintain his youthful enthusiasm. Because the moment that meeting and interacting with new races became simply a part of the job—nothing to get excited about—then something very important and very primal in the makeup of James T. Kirk would have died, and the stars he loved so much would no longer belong to him.

The turbolift deposited them less than two hundred feet from the main transporter room, and Kirk could hear the babble of voices and the discussion that was going on just outside. There seemed to be some sort of disagreement. Now why was Kirk not surprised about that?

He was even less surprised to find that the source of the disturbance was Ambassador Fox.

Fox was blocking the doorway of the transporter room, informing the two security guards, Meyer and Boyajian, that had been summoned to the scene that they were not to take another step. Meyer looked irritated enough at this point to pick Ambassador Fox up and stuff him up a Jeffries tube, but he was clearly trying to employ restraint. Kirk's arrival prompted a sigh of relief from the security guard as he said, "Captain, Ambassador Fox is obstructing security procedures."

Fox turned to face Kirk. "Captain," he said with patience that sounded so extreme as to be condescending, "I think it would be extremely poor form for the representative of the Calligar to see, as his first exposure to us, a crewman pointing a phaser at him. It isn't exactly in keeping with the image that we're seeking to project."

"What I am trying to project, Ambassador," said Kirk, "is a ship with maximum consideration of crew safety. We're in the process of an unauthorized transportation, and although I tend to think it will be harmless, there are nevertheless certain procedures to be followed." He glanced at the guards, who did indeed have their weapons out. "Holster them," he said. "But be prepared to draw if threatened." As Meyer and Boyajian put their weapons away Kirk continued, letting a bit of the annoyance he felt slip through. "Be aware, Ambassador, that procedures also dictate that anyone interfering with a security officer attempting to carry out orders can, at the captain's discretion, be thrown into a holding facility. How closely do you want me to stick to regulations, Ambassador?"

Fox grunted his acknowledgment and stepped aside. Kirk was already concerned—whoever was beaming over had already arrived and was in there with Ensign Tooch. If there was any danger, Tooch was suffering it while Kirk was outside waltzing around with a bureaucrat.

Thak and Daystrom had watched the proceedings without comment. Dorkin, for his part, was chuckling softly to himself in a voice that sounded like sandpaper on metal.

Kirk turned away from Fox as if he were incidental —which, to Kirk, was the case—and walked into the transporter room.

There he saw his first Calligarian.

She had her back to the door, engrossed as she was in discussion with Tooch. Clearly the transporter operator was in no danger whatsoever; as a matter of fact, she was laughing lightly at something that the Calligarian had just said. Upon the doors opening, however, the Calligarian pivoted on her heel and faced Kirk and the others.

There was a gasp from just behind Kirk, and he glanced over his shoulder. It was Commodore Tyler. His eyes were wide with—what? Amazement? Joy? Shock? His mouth looked as though it didn't even dare to smile, for fear of breaking whatever spell had caught him up.

"My God," he whispered, "she hasn't aged a day."

The Calligarian smiled a lovely smile. "Hello. It's a pleasure to meet you all, and I come to you on behalf of the Calligar, who, once again, tentatively extend a hand of greeting. I am Ecma, the Master Builder."

"James Kirk. Captain of the *Enterprise.*"

One by one Kirk introduced the others to her. He noticed that Tyler was hanging back. Whether Tyler simply wanted his presence to be a surprise to her, or whether he was suddenly self-conscious, Kirk couldn't be sure. But finally there was no one else left, and Kirk said, "And this is—"

129

"I think I can handle this myself, Captain," said Tyler. He strode forward, stopped in front of Ecma, and smiled broadly. He took a deep breath and then said, "Hello, Ecma."

"Hello." She returned the smile, and he felt something. It was his heart, jump-starting. "And you are—"

The words didn't register at first. "Uh . . . Commodore Tyler," he said in confusion. "José Tyler."

"Hello, Commodore." She took his hand and shook it briskly.

His expression of shock was clear for all to see. And Ecma stared at him long and hard and said, "Is something wrong, Commodore?"

"Wrong? Ecma . . . don't you remember me?"

She stared at him in confusion, this woman from his past, this woman who was a direct link to his youth. The woman whom he had thought of more often than he cared to admit.

"Have we met?" she asked.

Chapter Thirteen

AND THEN SHE reached up and kissed him.

The taste of her, the smell of her was just as it had been those long years ago. And when she smiled up at him there was still that same impishness . . . although now there was something more in those eyes of hers. Years. That was it. Years, experience, and sadness.

"How, my dear lieutenant," she said, in a voice that was low and throaty, "how could you think that I had forgotten you? Hmmm? Even for a moment." She stroked his face briefly and smiled. "Your lack of confidence—"

"Lack of confidence?" said Tyler, and he harrumphed loudly. "Nonsense. Nor for a moment—not one moment—did I consider it a possibility that you'd forgotten."

And then he became aware of the others who were standing nearby, several of them smiling like damned fools. He turned to them and said, as if it needed any sort of elaboration, "The Master Builder and I have . . . met."

"Obviously," said Ambassador Fox.

"Gentlemen," Kirk now said, turning to them, "since we're not dealing with an indefinite period of time here, I suggest you get down to the shuttle bay."

"Captain," Tyler said abruptly, "would you be terribly averse to the idea of my switching places with Ambassador Fox?"

The Tellarite looked to Thak in confusion. "What is the purpose of his standing in a different place?"

"Better view," Thak informed him straight-facedly.

"Oh." Dorkin frowned. Actually, he was always frowning, but in this instance his frown deepened. "Why was I not invited to stand there, then?"

Kirk, wisely ignoring the exchange, looked from Tyler to Fox. Fox gave a small shrug. "I have no objection, Captain. I must admit that, while I took on my assignment without complaint, I was a bit disappointed over missing the opportunity to visit the Calligar homeworld. And it would seem clear that Commodore Tyler has certain . . . interests in staying aboard."

"It's of no relevance to me," said Dorkin.

Thak pointed out succinctly, "Actually, no one asked you." To that Shondar Dorkin merely grunted.

"Very well, Commodore. If you wish to serve as Ecma's official liaison during her stay with us, there seem to be no objections." Kirk tried to avoid smiling like an idiot, even though he found the entire thing to be utterly charming. "Everyone else, please retrieve whatever gear you wish to take and report to the shuttle bay. Launch in five minutes, Mr. Scott?"

"Aye, sir," said the engineer readily. He held up his hands. "It's been a while since I've done any shuttle piloting, but I know I haven't lost m'touch."

"I have every confidence in you, Mr. Scott," said Kirk. "Master Builder Ecma, I'm sure that the Commodore would not mind showing you to the quarters assigned to you for the duration of your stay . . . and then, if you don't mind, others of my crew would appreciate the opportunity to talk with you."

"I'm here to be of service to you, Captain," said Ecma with a slight bow.

Everyone emptied out of the transporter room, and Fox hung back a moment to speak to Kirk. "Could we make departure in ten minutes, Captain?" he asked. "Now that I know I'm going, I have a number of things I'd like to get together to bring with me. Research material that I was going to discuss with whoever came over here, and I would—"

"Ten minutes, Ambassador, but no more," said Kirk, sounding stern. "You'd better hurry."

"I will, Captain." And Fox, true to his word, set off down the hallway at something quite close to a run. Kirk nodded in approval as he watched him go. "It's nice to see a man of his advanced years still able to get so excited about something."

"Is he that much older than you, Captain?" asked Ecma.

Kirk thought about that a moment. "You know . . . when I was younger, he seemed much older than me. Now, somehow, he seems less older. Does that make any sense to you?"

"As much as anything about humans does," said Ecma. She smiled at Tyler, who actually grinned sheepishly. "You were going to show me to my quarters, Lieutenant?"

"Commodore, actually," he said. "But you should really call me José. Or Joe."

"All right, Joe," she said graciously. He extended an elbow to her, and she took it smoothly. Together they walked off down the hallway, Kirk and McCoy watching them go.

"They make a handsome couple, don't you think, Captain?" asked McCoy.

"They do indeed, Doctor."

"For people of 'advanced years,' of course," amended the doctor.

At that, Kirk grinned. "You're never too old to be young, Doctor."

Crewman Hicks woke up and forgot where he was.

Obeying the orders of the chief engineer, the slightly foggy Hicks had returned to his quarters to sleep it off. But not too long after he had drifted off . . . just as he was starting to slip into REM sleep . . . something startled him awake. A random, distant engine noise, perhaps, or an unexpectedly loud laugh as someone walked past his cabin. Whatever it was, it jolted him to wakefulness, and he sat up in the dark, confused and thrown off through a combination of his fatigue from the late-night partying the night before and the mild hangover he was still suffering.

He glanced at his chronometer and gasped. "Oh, my God! I'm supposed to be on duty!"

Still in a haze, he lunged to his feet and ran out the door. Even as he emerged at high speed, however, he suddenly remembered that he was supposed to be in his cabin resting, at the orders of Mr. Scott. He tried to put on the brakes. Under ordinary circumstances it would have been a momentary and unimportant lapse.

However, the particular moment that Hicks had chosen to bolt from his cabin happened to coincide with the moment that Ambassador Fox, already feeling winded but no less determined, was loping around the corner from the other direction.

The result was that the two men smashed into each other. Hicks was not injured in the least, but even as he crashed into Fox he heard what sounded like bones snapping, and it wasn't from him. Fox went down hard on his right hip, and there was another nauseating cracking noise.

Hicks had merely staggered and was now leaning against the wall, rubbing his chest. But Fox was lying on the floor, moaning, and grimacing in pain.

"Ohhhh, my God," said Hicks.

"Broken femur," McCoy was saying. "Broken hip. Two cracked ribs; one of them came close to puncturing his lung."

They were down in sick bay, McCoy, Kirk, and the stricken Hicks. Hicks was making vague gestures with his hands, saying, "It was an accident! I barely bumped into him. All that happened was that I knocked him down. I didn't mean to—"

"We know you didn't mean to, Ensign," said Kirk. He was trying to act consoling, but at the same time he couldn't mask his annoyance. "However, that doesn't excuse the fact that if you'd watched where you were going—"

"I know, sir," said Hicks, looking downcast. "I'm really sorry. I just bumped him—"

"Old bones can be extremely brittle," said Kirk.

Hicks looked at McCoy in momentary confusion, and McCoy said in irritation, "Not *me*. Bones in the body."

"Oh," said Hicks.

From over on the medibed Fox called, "I'm feeling fine! Really! Just let me get up—"

McCoy turned and said sharply, "You stay right where you are, or I'll break your other hip by sneezing on it." Whether that threat worked to intimidate him or not, the result was that Fox settled his head back down on the pillow, his face a portrait in misery. McCoy looked back at Kirk and pointed at Fox. "Next time you're thinking about climbing up one of those damned mountains of yours," he snapped, "think about fragility, why don't you?"

Kirk was about to reply when there came a sum-

135

mons from the wall comm. Kirk went to it and tapped it. "Kirk here."

"Captain, this is Spock in the shuttle bay," came the Vulcan's voice. "I understand there has been a mishap with the Ambassador."

"High-speed collision with Ensign Hicks," said Kirk. He glanced in the direction of Fox's bed, where Hicks was now standing and apologizing profusely. "Ambassador Fox definitely took the worst of it."

"Shall we hold the shuttle for him?"

Kirk looked to McCoy, who had overheard. The doctor shook his head emphatically. "He's going to be here a while, Mr. Spock," replied the captain. "Best get going."

"Yes, sir."

"Remember, hourly communication. Good luck."

"You'll need it," muttered McCoy.

"Thank you, Captain. And please thank the doctor for me for his kind sentiments as well."

Kirk tossed an amused glance at McCoy, who merely scowled. "Better watch those facial expressions, Doctor. You're starting to look like a Tellarite."

"Why is that one piloting the shuttle?" groused Shondar Dorkin.

Scotty turned in the helm chair and speared the Tellarite with a look. "Because I'm capable of taking this craft apart with m'bare hands and reassembling it if need be. That's why." The engineer then turned back to his last-minute preflight checks and thought, Wouldn't mind taking apart something else in this shuttle. . . .

Spock entered the shuttle and looked at Thak, Daystrom, and the scowling Shondar. "Ambassador Fox will not be joining us, it seems. There was a mishap, and he is in sick bay."

"Hah!" said Dorkin. "I knew he appeared too frail

136

for the rigors of space travel. It's a shame you're not all built like Tellarites. You know what you would all be then?"

"Suicidal?" inquired Thak.

"Stronger!"

"Oh, dear. That would make it harder to die, wouldn't it?"

Dorkin aimed his gaze at Thak. "Tellarites are among the sturdiest races in the galaxy. Do you know what it would take to kill us?"

"A long, hard, look in the mirror?"

"No. It would take," said Dorkin dangerously, "more than you've got."

"Don't worry," said Thak guilelessly. "I can get more."

And now Daystrom, who was in a seat directly in front of them, slowly turned with gradual, dignified movement. "Are you aware," he said slowly, ponderously, "that with the amount of energy the two of you are expending in this nonsensical fighting you could power a ship halfway to Rimbor?"

Dorkin stared at him. "Halfway, you say?"

Daystrom's gaze flicked to Thak. "Sarcasm seems to elude him, doesn't it?"

"Most things do," agreed Thak.

Spock, in the meantime, took his seat next to Scotty.

Scotty grinned and called, "Hold on, lads. We're going to see what this baby can do."

"What?" roared Dorkin. "There's an infant on board? Why wasn't my government notified of this?"

The rest of the Shondar's protests were drowned out by the shuttlecraft engine as the small vessel leapt into space and toward the huge gap in reality.

The rift grew larger as the shuttle approached, propelled by impulse power. Spock kept a wary eye on the readings that were being produced by the on-board instrumentation, to make sure that the rift was staying steady. At the first sign of instability Spock would immediately abort the flight, because the last thing he had any intention of doing was jeopardizing the contact team. He glanced sideways at Scotty, and as if by some silent telepathy, Scotty returned the look. After all these years there were certain things that simply didn't need to be said.

One of those was the result of the significant look that Scotty gave to one particular activation square, because pressing that would bring the warp engines on line. Up until the firing of the warp engines on the sled, the shuttle could still veer off.

By the same token, they didn't dare enter the rift with only the impulse engines. If they did, they wouldn't last more than a few minutes . . . in subjective time, that is. So at some point, upon reaching the crest of the rift, a decision would have to be made. And it would have to be predicated on the idea that the rift was not going to change suddenly and strand them or, even more cheerfully, crush them.

"Approaching point of no return, from my mark," said Scott tonelessly. If there was any concern over the do-or-die aspect of the moment, he gave no indication of it. "Fifteen . . . fourteen . . . thirteen . . . twelve . . ."

Closer and closer still came the rift, shimmering and undulating in the depths of space. It seemed to be filled with colors, dancing mockingly and hauntingly in the blackness.

"Eleven . . . ten . . ."

"What in blazes is he waiting for?" demanded Shondar Dorkin.

"For the precise moment to push the ejector-seat button that will hurl you into space," Thak informed him.

138

Spock immediately became aware that Dorkin was now watching him with suspicion. There may be a more gullible race than Tellarites, he thought, but none came immediately to mind.

"Six . . . five . . . four," said Scott. For all that one could discern from his voice, he might have been counting down to the beginning of a sporting event. "Three . . ."

The rift called to them.

And with one final glance at their instruments Spock said, "Activating warp drive."

The shuttlecraft seemed to distend, its front leaping into the rift, less than an instant later followed by its back end.

On the bridge of the *Enterprise* Kirk watched the shuttle disappear into the darkness. He sat in his command chair, his face immobile, his thoughts private, and his prayers extremely personal.

Ecma stood in the center of her quarters, stark still, looking around. Tyler, near the door, watched her with interest and even puzzlement. Something about her seemed to have changed all of a sudden. In the transporter room, even on the way to her quarters, she had been pleasant, polite, even flirtatious. Much as she had been those many years ago, in fact, except tempered with maturity and even a mild, self-mocking wit.

Now, however, she seemed to radiate tension and apprehension. He couldn't help but notice the difference, but he was reluctant to say anything about it. So instead, aiming for something neutral, he asked, "Are these quarters okay?"

She didn't answer but instead faced him and said, "Do you think I could speak to your Captain Kirk? He is in charge of this ship, is he not?"

She sounded so formal, even distant. "Certainly," he said evenly, and he reached over and tapped the wall comm. "Tyler to bridge. Captain?"

"Kirk here."

"Would you be able to come down to Ecma's quarters for a moment?"

"Is there something wrong?"

"I don't think so. She just asked to speak with you. Of course, if you want to wait until the shuttle's underway . . ."

"They just entered the rift, Commodore, so now there's nothing to do but wait. I'll be down in a few moments."

"Thank you." He turned to Ecma and spread his hands slightly. "There. Okay?"

"Thank you."

She sat down on the edge of the bed very carefully, placing her hands just so on her knees. He looked at her with open curiosity. "Ecma," he said, "is your father—"

"Zyo has passed on to be with his predecessors," she said quietly.

"Oh. I'm sorry. He was a real forward-thinking individual. It's a damn shame."

"He had no choice."

He shrugged and walked slowly along the perimeter of the room. "I suppose none of us does."

She didn't respond but continued to stare off into space. That left Tyler with the next question, the one that had been weighing on him for years. The question of that last, awful image that he had beheld just before being beamed back to the *Enterprise*.

"And Macro?" he asked. "Your brother?"

That seemed to cause a flicker of response. "Yes. He is well."

"Ecma"—he dropped all pretense of trying to sound dispassionate—"when I beamed out, years

140

ago, the last thing I saw was him . . . and his hand on . . ."

She slowly looked up at Tyler, her eyes resembling glass. "What you saw . . . was not unusual among my people."

He stared at her. "What?"

"Your taboos are not ours," she said simply. "The jealousy my brother felt for you—his attempts to injure you—were not simply the actions of fraternal concern."

He was staggered by the concept. "So you mean you and he . . . you . . ."

She sighed, her hands fidgeting. "I am not what I was when we first met, Joe. In those days I was very . . . free. I reveled in that. I rejoiced in life because it seemed as if it would go on forever. And it helped me forget aspects of life that I would rather . . . have forgotten." She looked up at him, and her next words were like a hammer blow to him. "I have a son."

Tyler felt all the blood drain from his face. "A . . . a son," he whispered. "*His* son?"

She nodded. "You must understand, our genetic makeup is not like yours. We needn't worry about recessive genes being brought to dominance. Among our people brother-and-sister unions result in some of the best and brightest of our race."

"Well, I don't believe it's healthy," said Tyler, revulsion shaking him. "I think it's wrong, I . . ." He stabbed a finger at her. "It happened after your father died, didn't it?"

"As a matter of fact, it did. As the new Master Builder, it was incumbent upon me to—"

"I don't care what it was!" said Tyler with more fierceness than he thought he was capable of feeling. He took her by the wrists, squeezing them so hard that a human woman would have cried out in pain. "It's

141

wrong, and if your father had been around, he would have seen that. He would have said so."

She smiled mirthlessly. "Where do you think my father came from, Joe? Such a forward-thinking individual—you said so yourself. Who do you think his parents were?"

He shook his head, feeling a pounding in his temples. "I don't believe it."

She reached out to touch his face, and he reflexively pulled back. Seeing the gesture, she said sadly, "What a pity. You think of yourself as a citizen of the galaxy, Joe, and yet you are so provincial. So unwilling to accept viewpoints that are at variance with those that you grew up with."

He was silent, and then there was a chime at the door.

"Come in," called Ecma.

The door slid open, and Kirk walked in. Immediately he sensed the anxiety in the air, but instead of commenting he managed a small smile and said, "You wished to see me?"

"Yes, Captain. Thank you for making the time."

He made a "think nothing of it" gesture. "I always have time for guests—particularly such important ones such as yourself. So . . . what can I do for the Master Builder of the Calligar?"

"Nothing."

The flat response caught him off guard for a moment. He looked at Tyler, but Tyler was of no help, so he forced a game grin and said, "Well, if I may ask . . . since I can do nothing for you, then why—"

"You can do nothing for the Master Builder of the Calligar," she said, "because I am resigning that exalted title."

"Resigning?" The word came from both Kirk and Tyler, and it was Kirk who continued, "I don't understand."

142

"Then I will explain. No one in our history has ever resigned as Master Builder. It is not allowed. It is unthinkable. But that is what I'm doing. I am officially seeking asylum aboard the *Enterprise*. I do not wish to go back to the Calligar"—she looked up defiantly at Kirk—"and nothing in this galaxy can make me."

Chapter Fourteen

"FASCINATING."

The shuttlecraft circled one of the larger cities that comprised the Calligarian Worldnet. The city issued an unmistakable homing beacon, guiding the shuttle to that particular city platform. Scotty steered with sure hands, trying not to let himself be distracted by the awesome sight of the perpetually burning Calligarian homeworld.

An aperture opened in the top of the domed city, and Scotty looked to Spock the moment that it appeared. Spock gave a small nod, which was all the instruction that Scott needed to angle the shuttlecraft down toward the opening that had been provided.

Once through, the dome shut behind them, and Scotty followed the continuing summons of the homing beacon until it brought them to a landing area that had apparently been set up specifically for them.

"Bring us in, Mr. Scott," said Spock.

"Aye, sir," replied Scotty.

On the landing area below they saw a number of

individuals waiting for them. Even from a distance Spock recognized one of them immediately as the Calligarian who had been introduced as Alt, the Master of the Status. And standing next to him appeared to be the one called Macro. He did not recognize any of the others.

Scotty landed the shuttle smoothly, except of course the landing was not smooth enough for Shondar Dorkin, who complained loudly and made sure to let Mr. Scott know that a cross-eyed Tellarite child could have done a better job bringing the vehicle down. Scotty did not reply but instead contented himself with imagining the shuttle being brought down on top of the Tellarite's head.

Once Scotty had shut down the engines he opened up the door, and the contact crew emerged from the shuttle. What struck Scotty immediately was the almost overwhelming silence that seemed to pervade the entire city. It was as if everyone and everything in the area was listening, hushed with anticipation.

Alt stepped forward and inclined his head slightly. "Mr. Spock, I believe it was?"

"I am honored that you remember me," said Spock.

"And your Captain Pike?"

"He has retired," Spock said diplomatically. Now was hardly the time to cite chapter and verse of the final fate of Christopher Pike.

"And you are in command now?"

"I am in command of this contact team," Spock said. "May I introduce—"

And now it was Macro who spoke. He seemed surlier than when Spock had first met him. More irritated. The good doctor would have said that Macro looked like he had a burr up his butt. "Are you in command of the *Enterprise?* Or is perhaps that one— what was his name?" He seemed to be making a great effort to remember something, but Spock immediately perceived that Macro knew perfectly well whom he was thinking of. "Oh, yes. Tyler."

"Commodore Tyler has remained aboard the *Enterprise*," said Spock quietly, sensing the waves of hostility that seemed to be undulating from Macro. "The arrival of your Master Builder prompted him to remain behind to serve as her liaison."

"Yes," said Macro softly. "Yes, I would think that he did. And he is the commander of your ship?"

"No. The commander is Captain James T. Kirk."

Macro tilted his chin defiantly. "And why is he not here? Are we not worth his time?"

"The current directive from Starfleet," Spock said patiently, "is for ship commanders to remain aboard their ship whenever possible."

"We prefer to deal with leaders of men," Macro told him.

And Mr. Scott, with quiet confidence, said, "If Mr. Spock led us into the gates of hell, I'd follow him whistling. Is that sufficient leadership for ye?"

Alt watched all of this in silence, but he was unable to keep the look of distaste off his face. "Macro is correct in our belief that leaders should be the preeminent contact points. However, for the time being we will not stand on ceremony. Macro," he said, and it was clear that this was part of some ongoing and rather acrimonious discussion, "we shall talk of this —yet again—later. In the meantime, I will thank you to display at least a modicum of tact."

Macro bowed slightly and said, "As you wish, sir."

"Good." He turned back to Spock. "You do not inquire as to the absence of Zyo."

"The fact that Ecma introduced herself as the Master Builder—a term that Zyo described as a lifetime appointment—would indicate that he is deceased."

146

"Yes," said Alt slowly. "Yes, that is quite correct. He was the greatest supporter of this sort of contact. I must admit that, at the time the first contact was made, I thought it the worst possible decision. I have, however, had a great many years to ponder the matter. Furthermore, despite my initial fears, it is clear that contact with you did not bring the end of our civilization as we know it. Perhaps the time has come for cautious experimentation and contact. That is not, of course, something I would have admitted to Zyo while he was alive—the notion that he was right about something."

"That, sir," said Spock, "is a sentiment that I can easily comprehend."

Scott stifled a smile. He knew exactly what was crossing Spock's mind. McCoy would certainly have had something pithy to add had he been present.

"These," said Alt, "are members of our ruling council," and he gestured to the half-dozen Calligarians who were standing nearby.

"A ruling council?" It was Shondar Dorkin who had spoken now in that gruff voice of his. "There was no indication in any previous reports of any ruling council. What's the reason for the change?"

"None of your business," snapped Macro.

Slowly Shondar turned his piglike gaze on the Calligarian. "I'm making it my business," he said.

"Gentlemen," said Spock with quiet authority, "the purpose of this encounter is the peaceful exchange of ideas. I hardly think that hostility will go very far in supporting that intention."

"Quite correct, Mr. Spock," said Alt quietly. "Quite correct." He made a sweeping gesture. "If you'll follow me, you'll find that we have developed quite a thorough itinerary for you. Do you have any objections to being split up in order to provide maximum efficiency?"

"Not at all," said Spock. He tapped the wrist comm units that had been distributed to all members of the group before leaving the *Enterprise.* "We will be able to stay in communication with one another, of course."

"Oh, of course," said Alt. "Now . . . introductions?"

Briskly Spock introduced each of the members of the contact team to Alt, Macro, and the council, who were introduced to them in turn. Alt then gestured for them to follow, which they did as they walked slowly across the city.

The Calligarians they passed seemed to give him barely passing interest, as if they had adjusted to the presence of the outsiders that had decided to live with it. As they walked through the city Alt said, "Did you have any difficulties passing through the rift?"

"The improved warp field was more than sufficient to shield us from the mental strains of the temporal passage. However, the fuel consumption was greater than we anticipated," said Spock.

"You won't run into difficulties returning, will you?" It was Macro who had spoken, and his voice was perfectly emotionless, making it impossible to determine whether or not he would be sorry to see such an event occur.

And Scotty spoke up. "Ach, no. We'll only have a wee margin for error, but we've come out of tighter difficulties than that. Although—I'm curious. Do you have the technology that would enable us to repower our warp sled attachment?"

"Oh, certainly," said Alt. He didn't even bother to look at Scott. "We couldn't give it to you, though. We're fairly firm about that. For that matter"—and now he glanced at Scott—"we have the capability of re-forming the dilithium crystals that power your main vessel. We could create self-regenerating crystals, in fact."

Clearly, Scotty was unsure whether Alt was kidding him or not. "Honestly?"

Macro snorted loudly. "Of course."

"That's amazing."

"What's amazing is that you haven't done it yet," Macro told him.

Scotty frowned at that, but Macro now lapsed into merciful silence. For that Scotty was extremely grateful. Then he said, "If ye don't mind my asking, I'd be interested to know about the composition of that dome. The opening seemed to appear out of nowhere. Is it some sort of force field, or a material similar to transparent aluminum?"

Alt glanced at Macro, and this time Macro seemed to be making an effort to answer without hostility. "Actually, it's bonded artificial atmosphere molecules."

"Bonded . . . you mean," said Scott, trying to grasp it, "you've essentially created a shield out of thin air?"

"That's certainly one way to put it," agreed Macro. "When the aperture was opened for you, it was actually a force bubble that was being created from the molecules themselves. It stayed with you upon your entrance while maintaining the seal of the dome. Once you were safely inside, it released you to go on about your business while snapping back to its original form and protective shape."

"You make it sound almost alive."

Macro stopped to face Scott, halting him in his place. And when he spoke, it was with passionate intensity as he said, "Of course it's alive. All of it is alive."

Scotty frowned at him. "What's that ye say?"

"Ah," said Alt. "Mr. Scott, here we are."

They had stopped in front of a gleaming silver disk that was about six feet across. Alt gestured to it. "You, Mr. Scott, are the chief engineer, according to the ship's records that we scanned. I see no reason not to fill you in on our latest advances, although we don't promise to give you the specifics on how things work."

"That's quite all right," said Scotty. Inwardly, he was confident that all he had to do was glance at something, and he would be able to replicate it from memory.

"Good. Step on this platform, and you'll be shunted to the engineering center. One of our top people will be there to greet you."

"Yes," said Macro. "His name is Regger, and he is my son."

"Your son?" Scotty said.

"Yes, but don't worry. He's nothing like me."

Everyone looked at Macro in surprise, and the look of utter innocence on his face drew involuntary laughter from several of the council members. This, in turn, engendered chuckles from Thak, Scotty, and even Shondar Dorkin, whose large belly jiggled in a manner somewhat akin to Santa Claus.

Spock, for his part, looked at the perpetually un-smiling Richard Daystrom, who merely shrugged.

Alt, shaking his head, said, "I admit, Macro, there are times you surprise me tremendously."

"It is a foolish individual who does not know his own shortcomings," said Macro, "and I am far from that. Might I suggest that the scientist Thak accompany Mr. Scott? Shondar Dorkin and Mr. Spock can accompany Master of the Status Alt and the rest of the council to discuss philosophies and political situations while I bring Dr. Daystrom to the computer communion center. That should satisfy the individual areas of expertise."

The contact team members looked at one another,

exchanging silent opinions, and Spock finally said, "That would seem a satisfactory agenda, Macro."

Thak walked over next to Scotty, and the two of them stepped onto the gleaming platform. In a low voice Thak said, "Anything that means I don't have to stay close to the Tellarite is devoutly to be wished."

"I hear ye," replied Scotty, also quietly. Then, in a raised voice, he said, "What do we have to do to activate—"

"Just think of where you wish to go," Macro told him.

"Ye mean all I have to do is think about visiting the engineering section, and—"

Mr. Scott and Thak vanished as if they had never been there.

"Where the devil—" exclaimed Shondar Dorkin. Not that he was particularly concerned with the welfare of the two of them. If he never saw them again, he would not have cared. But it was the abruptness of their disappearance that had startled him.

"Do not be concerned," Alt told them. "They are merely on line."

Chapter Fifteen

"OUT OF THE QUESTION."

The gathering in the conference room was small, consisting of Kirk, McCoy, Fox—held immobile in a floatational chair—Ecma, Tyler, and Uhura, who was acting as recorder. In point of fact she was redundant, since the computer was keeping automatic records of everything that was transpiring. But in situations such as this one, certain protocol was required.

It was Fox who had spoken, and he was shaking his head vehemently. "It is absolutely out of the question."

"Ambassador," said Kirk quietly, "it is not up to you."

"Captain"—Fox turned the chair to face him—"I'm afraid it is."

There was an uneasy silence for a moment, and then Tyler spoke up with quiet authority. "I can personally assure you, Captain, that you will have the full support of Starfleet in this matter."

"I wouldn't extend such assurances, Commodore," said Fox offhandedly. "With all due respect, it is quite evident that you are not thinking clearly. Your judgment has been impaired by your involvement with this"—he gestured towards Ecma—"individual, who is clearly exerting some sort of undue influence. Now, I would not be presumptuous enough to imagine—"

Tyler started to rise. Keeping his temper in line had never been one of his strong suits. "You bureaucratic, hidebound son of a—"

"Commodore!" said Kirk with a sharpness that would have been more appropriate for addressing a subordinate. Tyler, however, said nothing but simply settled back in his chair.

McCoy, for his part, was watching Ecma carefully. There was something about, something about her body language that didn't seem quite right. He had spent years developing the knack of telling at a glance if someone was in good health, and his sixth sense was warning him now. "Master Builder," he said softly, "are you all right?"

She looked at him with eyes that seemed momentarily glazed, and then she smiled gamely. "I'm fine, Doctor. Just a bit . . . overstressed from recent events."

"I'm not surprised," said McCoy cautiously.

"Well, I am surprised," said Fox. "I am surprised at you, Master Builder, that you would jeopardize developing relations with your people by suddenly announcing that you don't wish to return to them."

"She has her reasons," said Tyler, "and I repeat, Starfleet will support her."

"And Starfleet is answerable to the United Federation of Planets," shot back Fox, "and I am the official representative of that august body. Captain"—he turned to Kirk—"do you have any idea of the immense delicacy of the situation?"

"I think so, Ambassador," said Kirk quietly. "It is your concern that the Calligar will be distressed over the defection of their Master Builder, not to mention the fact that her leaving their confines would probably be in violation of their philosophy of isolationism. Am I right?"

The question was addressed to Ecma, and slowly she nodded. "The contacts made with your UFP are ground-breaking for my people," she told him. "That contact would not be possible without my father's influence."

Uhura looked up from monitoring the computer record. "I beg your pardon . . . I thought you said your father was dead."

"That sounded very much like present tense," Kirk affirmed. "I am a bit confused myself on that."

Ecma coughed slightly and said, "My father and his philosophies live on in spirit among my people, just as philosophers and wise men long dead among your people influence you. I tend to speak of him as if he were still alive."

"Very understandable," said Tyler.

Kirk wasn't sure he completely understood it, but he let it pass. "Let's deal with the issue at hand."

"The issue is how we're going to convince the Master Builder here that the course she intends to take could be suicidal for continued relations with her people," Fox said. "Whatever reasons she has for doing this, I can't believe that she would want to jeopardize the work that her father began and that we are endeavoring to continue."

Kirk turned and fixed him with a gaze. "Ambassador," he said, lowering the temperature in the room several degree with his voice alone, "I understand you feel strongly about this, but if you interrupt me one more time, I'll return you to sick bay, and you will participate in this conversation over the conference-room viewscreen. Am I making myself clear?"

Fox glowered at him but said nothing.

154

Kirk looked back at Ecma for a minute. "Now then, Master Builder—"

"Ecma, please," she said.

"Ecma, then . . . you've told Commodore Tyler, and now myself, that you wish to stay with the Federation. I assume that you have given the commodore some sort of reason for this desire." From the corner of his eye he noticed Tyler nodding. "But you have not shared them with me. I am asking you to do so now."

"It's personal, Captain," said Tyler before Ecma could say anything.

"I'm afraid that's not good enough, Commodore."

"I'm afraid it will have to be, Captain."

"No, sir," said Kirk. "Perhaps Ambassador Fox has a point when he says matters of diplomacy, such as defections, are up to the diplomatic office—and since he's on site, he has that authority. And perhaps you can argue, as the highest-ranking Starfleet officer present, that you have authority. But gentlemen"— Kirk smiled unpleasantly—"the bottom line is, this is my ship. My crew. When I say jump, they say how high, and if I order my security team to clap the lot of you in the brig, they'll do so without hesitation. Are we clear on this point as well?"

"You're threatening to strong-arm us," said Fox.

"That's correct. I have a history of strong-arming to get my way, and one consequence of that history is that you survived Eminiar VII. I'm too old to start being delicate, Ambassador, and if you don't like it, you are cordially invited to walk home. And with all due respect, Commodore, you can join him."

Kirk rose from his chair and started to circle the briefing room, hands behind his back. "Commodore, you're asking me to put my head on the block while Ambassador Fox there would be more than happy to drop the axe on it. Now, I'm willing to stick my neck

155

out—God knows I've done it often enough before—but I have to have some idea of what's at stake here. I will not go into this blindly." He stared at Ecma. "It's up to you, ma'am. Tell me why you wish to defect. Is it because of Commodore Tyler? Is there something else?"

Ecma was silent, seemingly turned to stone. The only sign that she had even heard Kirk—that there was anything going through her mind—was that she was chewing on her lower lip.

"She wants to stay with me," said Tyler.

"That's not the reason," said Ecma. She seemed very distant. McCoy noticed that her breathing seemed irregular. "Oh, I feel very strongly toward you, Joe—I think perhaps I even love you—but that alone would not be enough."

Tyler seemed nonplussed by this but then recovered. "All right, then," he said. "You'll have to tell the captain about your brother."

"It's not my brother either," she said.

"Her brother?" asked Kirk.

Ecma forced a ragged smile. McCoy, for his part, had brought along a medical tricorder in his bag to keep an eye on Fox's vitals. However, he now subtly recalibrated it to monitor Ecma instead.

"Joe Tyler is morally outraged," she said, "because of my intimate relationship with my brother Macro."

"A relationship that produced a son," said Tyler darkly.

Kirk blinked in surprise, and Uhura barely managed to cover her reaction. McCoy was too busy eyeing her vital signs. Her pulse was racing, as was her heartbeat.

"It is not the happiest of relations for me," she continued, "but as I said to Joe, it is not unheard of among my people, nor is it taboo, as it is in your society. We have our own . . ." She coughed for a moment, seeming weak, but then she pushed on. "We have our own taboos. For that matter, as difficult as it is to believe, I love my son. But I love life more, and I—"

"Captain," McCoy said. "I think you should—"

But Kirk hadn't heard him. "Love life? Is someone threatening your life?"

Her breath was coming in gasps now, and McCoy was immediately on his feet, the tricorder clearly in evidence.

"I don't want to be Thinned," she gasped, and her body seemed to be turning to rubber. "I . . . I don't . . ."

"Thinned? What the hell is 'Thinned'?" demanded Kirk. "Commodore—"

"News to me," said Tyler in confusion. "I never—"

"Captain, the woman is erratic!" Fox snapped.

"Jim!" McCoy said. "Her heartbeat is arrhythmic, respiration up."

"It's not time yet! It's not right!" She was on her feet, her body quivering, and then she started to keel over. Tyler caught her, lowering her back to the chair, and McCoy was immediately on the intercom summoning a team from sick bay.

And she screamed, mustering the air to cry out, *"I don't want to die!"*

"Die?" said Fox. "What in hell is she—"

"Shut up!" snapped Tyler. "Just shut up!"

Her bones might as well have dissolved for all the strength her body seemed to display. She started to slide off the chair, and Tyler lifted her up into his arms. She seemed weightless.

"Do something for her!" Tyler shouted at McCoy. "That's an order!"

"I don't know her full biological makeup," said

157

McCoy. "Drugs that help us might kill her. I have to get her down to sick bay."

As if on cue the medical team from sick bay burst in with an antigrav table and crash cart. Tyler immediately put Ecma's quivering body on the table, and Kirk was right next to her. "You're in the best of hands," he said.

Her eyes were half closed, but suddenly they snapped open, and strength seemed to surge into her right arm. She reached up and grabbed Kirk by the forearm in a viselike grip. "Don't send me back!" she hissed. "Please . . . I'll die . . . please . . ."

"I won't," said Kirk. "I promise. I'll grant you asylum. You have my word."

Her mouth moved, but she was unable to get a word out, and then her head slumped back. Her hand released its hold on Kirk, and McCoy snapped, "Get her to sick bay. Now!"

The medicart rolled out, and Tyler started to follow, but McCoy froze him with a look. "I don't need a goddamned audience," he said sharply. He turned and then glanced back over his shoulder and added, *"Sir."*

There was silence in the briefing room for a time after Ecma had departed in such haste. And then, very softly, Ambassador Fox said, "Captain . . . you were not serious, of course."

Kirk seemed to answer from a great distance. "Serious?"

"About not sending her back. Our interaction with the Calligar is very delicate. Something like this—one of their highest officials—"

"Ambassador," said Kirk slowly.

"Now hear me out!" Fox said. "My God, Kirk, I'm not inhuman. I saw how upset she was—the woman is clearly terrified. Nor am I foolish enough or insensi-

158

tive enough to ignore Commodore Tyler's obvious affection for her.''

"What the hell do you know about it, Fox?" said Tyler with obvious disdain.

Fox shook his head ruefully. "I know that look you gave her, Commodore, and the way she looked at you. There's a connection between the two of you. It's unpredictable, and you never know when and where in this vast galaxy you're going to find it. But you two have found it, and under ordinary circumstances I'd be happy to shake your hand. But these are far from ordinary circumstances. Our relations with the Calligar are still extremely tentative. We have no idea how they're going to react when they find out about this, but I think the chances are pretty damned good that they're not going to be thrilled about it. You're going to put this entire affiliation into jeopardy over the desires of one person."

"Two persons," said Tyler quietly.

"It is not fair," Fox went on as if Tyler hadn't spoken, "to jeopardize all the good and hard work that has been done to bring matters to this moment in time. Your obligation, Captain, is to your mission. And that mission is to firm up relations with the Calligar. Not to risk antagonizing them."

"I will thank you, Ambassador," said Kirk, "not to remind me of what my mission is." He paused. "You do, I admit, have a couple of valid points about priorities and where they should be placed. The fact of the matter is that you are quite possibly right."

Tyler looked at Kirk with open hurt in his face. "Captain, I cannot believe—"

Kirk put up a hand to indicate he wasn't finished yet. "Now, the fact is that we don't know for sure how the Calligar are going to react until we tell them. So I think we'd better tell them and see what happens from there."

"The bottom line, Kirk," said Fox. "You're forgetting that. I know this is your ship. I know all that. But I believe that due to my rank and position, I'm entitled to know. If the Calligar want their Master Builder back, are we going to give her to them?"

"I've given my word," said Kirk firmly. "I'm not going to take someone who says her life is at stake and ship her back to die. I simply will not."

"Even if it means losing an alliance that could be of tremendous benefit to the future of the Federation?"

Kirk stood, towering over the immobile Fox. "What good is our future, Ambassador, if our morals and sensitivity to human need becomes a thing of the past?"

"Very high-sounding, Captain," replied Fox. "Just one problem: Ecma isn't human. The Calligar aren't human. You're superimposing human attitudes on other beings, trying to cross that gulf between humanity and the rest of the galaxy by fashioning a net of morality with Terran philosophies as the anchor points. I'm surprised at you, Captain. It doesn't work that way. You know it, and I know it, and moreover, the Prime Directive knows it."

"This is not a Prime Directive issue."

"It damn well is. We're not to interfere in their society. We're not to do anything such as—"

"Such as blowing up computers that maintained a centuries-long war?" Kirk asked evenly.

Fox's face became hard. "Will you stop tossing that up at me?"

"For some reason," said Kirk with false heartiness, "it seems to keep cropping up."

"The actions you took were entirely out of self-defense."

"And that made them all right?" said Kirk challengingly.

"That made them at least understandable."

"And what made it understandable was that we were acting in defense of ourselves and you. So understand this: We are now acting in defense of Ecma. And her life is worth defending as much as anyone else's."

"And more so than a few that come to mind," growled Tyler.

"Therefore," said Kirk, "the bottom line that you're so fond of is that we have a situation here that's going to have to be worked out. Shipping her back in a box is not one of the options. This will, however, require the skills of an Ambassador. So you're going to have to . . ." He paused, trying to come up with a word, and none seemed appropriate. "Ambass," he said with a shrug.

"Let me get this straight," said Fox. "Tyler wants her to stay because he loves her. You're going to support that view because of some misbegotten—I don't know—Lancelot complex you have. And you're expecting *me* to try and smooth all this over?"

"That's exactly right."

"Why?"

"Because it's your damned job," Kirk said. "Because I'm telling you to. And because, Ambassador, whether you like it or not, you owe me."

Fox scowled, shook his head, and swung the chair around. As he exited the briefing room he was muttering to himself in a rapid string of unintelligible sentences.

Tyler turned to Kirk and said, "Thank you, Captain. If you don't mind, I'll go down to sick bay to await word."

"If Doctor McCoy will allow you in, then by all means."

As soon as Tyler left Kirk turned to Uhura with a

questioning glance. "Well? Don't you have anything to say on the matter?"

Uhura shrugged. "Only that if I were in trouble, I can't think of anyone I'd rather have on my side."

He smiled wanly. "Thank you, Commander."

"That, and also that you're in deep trouble."

"You're telling me."

Chapter Sixteen

MONTGOMERY SCOTT was screaming inside his own head.

He could not hear anything otherwise. There was nothing surrounding him, nothing interacting with him . . . there was no *him*.

He was suspended in time for eternity, and even though he had ceased to exist, he couldn't help but have a sensation of forward movement. All of existence was roaring past him, a headlong rush that streaked by him, surrounded by a hum and torrent of air that seemed to be crackling around him.

And suddenly, just like that, it was over.

Scotty staggered slightly, and the voice that had escaped him now seemed to catch up with him. *"Aaaaahhhh,"* he managed to get out, taking a quivering step forward.

Next to him was Thak, similarly disoriented. The Andorian was slightly faster to recover, though, and he put a hand on Scotty's shoulder to steady him.

Scotty nodded once in appreciation and then, taking a deep breath, looked around.

Lining the walls were a series of narrow tubes with what appeared to be pulsing blue plasma, similar to what covered the surface of the planet below. Long tubes stretched up and out the ceiling of the cavernous room, going off to who knew where.

In the center of the room was some sort of unit that was unlike anything Scotty had seen before. It stood in its own independent canister, and visible through the clear top of the canister was a device big as Scotty's fist. Small spokes protruded from it, and it flashed alternately in black and red.

Scotty and Thak stepped tentatively off the flat silver disk that was identical to what they had been standing on moments earlier. The room was filled with a slow, steady hum.

"What in the world," asked Thak. He and Scotty walked toward the canister in the middle and then circled it slowly, not getting closer than a couple of feet.

"Looks a bit like a dilithium chamber," Scotty said, "but that's certainly not a crystal in there. Hmmm." He rubbed his chin. "Some sort of energy redistribution device, do ye think?"

"A trafficking device? But wouldn't something like that have to be considerably larger?"

"Aye. We have similar nodules on the *Enterprise*, and they're much larger—and that's just for powering a starship. Can ye imagine how large such a unit would have to be to deal with the power redistribution needs of an entire world?"

"About as large as that device right there," came the softly amused voice.

They turned and saw the speaker. It was another Calligarian who seemed to bear a general resemblance to Macro, although his face seemed a bit softer and his neck somewhat longer. He also had slightly stooped shoulders, giving him the appearance of perpetually straining to hear what was being said to him. "You must be Regger," Scotty said.

"Yes, sir," said Regger. He nodded to Scott and Thak. "And you are the gentlemen from the Federation."

"Aye, that we are."

"I hope our shunt transport wasn't too disconcerting for you."

"Is that what that was?"

"Yes. Basically your particle stream was inserted into a free-flow accessor and shot through to here via a preprogrammed route derived from your neurons."

"How long did it take?" Thak asked. "It seemed positively endless."

"Actually, it was instantaneous. Far faster than your transporters."

Scotty whistled and took a long, inspecting look around, his hands on his hips. "This is quite a setup you have here. And that device there—you say it is for channeling energy?"

Regger nodded and walked to the canister in the middle, placing his hands on it. "The Illidium Pew-36 Explosive Space Modulator," he said with satisfaction. "I designed it myself. Improved energy efficiency throughout the Worldnet by seventeen percent."

"'Explosive'?" said Thak nervously.

"Oh, don't worry. That refers to the data processing aspects. Not to actual explosions."

"Well, that's a relief," Thak said gamely.

Scotty was studying the device, his eyes narrowing. "Amazing," he said. "Simply amazing. If there was a way to apply this to our engines—"

"You had a start on it," Regger said casually. "Your data base described something referred to as a 'transwarp' drive. Correct?"

"Ach," Scotty snorted disdainfully. "That boondoggle. It never worked right."

165

"No," Regger corrected. "It was never designed right. But the basics were quite sound, and if Starfleet researchers pursued it, they would find the design flaw and fix it."

"What are you saying?" asked Thak. "Are you claiming that you could fix—"

"No," said Regger. "I'm afraid that I can't hold your hand and lead you through, much as I'd like to. You seem decent fellows. But it has to do with politics, disputes between philosophies and such. I've never involved myself with any of that. I just enjoy the pure research. What I'm saying is this: If the transwarp system were made to work, you would not believe the possibilities. It would totally restructure your concept of what's possible in terms of speed. You'd have to recalibrate your entire definition of warp."

Already possibilities were dancing through Scott's head. "I never thought that—"

"No," said Regger. "I didn't imagine that you would have."

For just a moment he had sounded extremely arrogant, and Scotty looked at him suspiciously. But then Regger smiled a relaxed smile and said, "Come. Let me show you some of the energy readings generated by our plasma burn. I think you'll find them most impressive."

"I find your concept of IDIC most fascinating," Alt said. "Infinite Diversity in Infinite Combination."

They were in a central Calligarian meeting hall, simply but comfortably filled with furniture that twisted in shapes that didn't seem as if they could be remotely comfortable. They were, however—so much so that the perpetually dissatisfied Shondar Dorkin was moved to comment on it positively.

"That is the Earth definition for it," said Spock. "IDIC is derived from a Vulcan term. The acronym is

166

a convenient method for Terrans to sum up in English what is, in fact, a concept that Vulcan philosophers have been debating for centuries."

"Typical. Earthers prefer nice, quick, easy solutions," snorted Dorkin disdainfully.

Spock looked at him with open curiosity. "If that were true, Shondar, the Prime Directive of the Federation would never have been developed. What easier solution is there to any problem than simply to employ superior technology or firepower—something forbidden by the noninterference directive?"

"What simpler solution?" laughed Dorkin. "I'll tell you what simpler solution there is: Ignore the problem. Turn away. Say 'It's not my predicament, so I will simply not interfere.' That, my Vulcan associate, is the easiest way to handle something. Just walk away."

And Alt leaned forward and said, "No. No, Shondar Dorkin. Actually, that's the most difficult thing to do."

"There is another Terran philosophy called Quakerism," Spock said, "or the Society of Friends. One of the foundations of their beliefs is that to bear witness to an act means that action must be taken to resolve it. All philosophies—intervention and nonintervention —have their individual demands."

Shondar Dorkin nodded slightly. "You have a point."

Spock found Dorkin's attitude fascinating. Although perpetually blustering to the point of insufferability, Dorkin actually seemed a most intriguing individual when discussing matters that were part of his expertise, such as different societies and their developments. It was something of a relief to Spock—up until that point it had seemed as if Dorkin would be nothing but a hindrance to the mission.

Indeed, it was Dorkin who was continuing the conversation as he said to Alt, "We have discussed various Federation philosophies, but we still know nothing of the day-to-day beliefs of the Calligar, beyond your desire for isolation. What drives you, I wonder?"

Alt pursed his lips for a moment and then glanced at the members of the council. They glanced at one another and then nodded.

"Our concept of day-to-day beliefs, as you put it, is predicated on the concept of the Harmony," said Alt, "which is why we find the concept of IDIC so interesting. We believe in being in Harmony with one another—and, most especially, with our surroundings."

"But when we first encountered you," said Spock, "you were in discord over how to deal with us."

"That is true," said Alt. "My view of your Federation and Zyo's were opposed. As Master of the Status, it is my job to keep the Harmony for all concerned. You see how responsive our surroundings are to our very thought. That stems from the Harmony. Zyo, however, as Master Builder, was responsible for the actual working mechanics of our world and our progress. In other words, I am responsible for the mind, while he was in charge of the body."

"And the mind and the body were divided."

"Yes. It was Zyo's contention that your incursion into our environment—even in so relatively minor a manner as subspace transmission—was going to impact on the Harmony. That the only way to maintain the Harmony was to incorporate your existence into ours."

"To absorb us?" said Spock cautiously.

But Alt shook his head. "To acknowledge you. This was opposed to my feeling, which was to ignore you utterly. But it was Zyo's feelings that prevailed, and Zyo's plan that we followed."

"How did this plan prevail?" asked Dorkin, narrowly beating Spock to the question. "How was it decided?"

"It was decided."

"How?" repeated Dorkin more insistently.

But Alt's face hardened. "It simply was. It was decided through the Harmony. The idea was made a part of us, and eventually we opted to accept it. You see, gentlemen, we must live in the Harmony. For there is nowhere to go."

"What do you mean, 'Nowhere to go'?" Dorkin asked. "There's all of space to go to. Certainly now that you've seen that contact with other life forms is hardly the end of life as you know it, you're not going to hide in these sky cities."

"That," said Alt firmly, "is precisely what we intend to do. We have lived in this manner for hundreds of your years. We have no intention of changing it now."

"But certainly you must," said Spock. "Necessity would seem to demand it. For example, I do not comprehend how you deal with population expansion. If you are confined to these satellite cities, and they are immutable in terms of size or expansion, certainly, at some point, your people will outgrow it. How do you intend to make allowances for that?"

"We have," said Alt simply. "That is all you need to know."

Now Dorkin was starting to get his hackles up. "We did not come all this way for you to be obstructionist with us."

"Obstructionist?" Alt actually seemed amused by the notion. "We have permitted you into our lives. We did not have to do that. We do not have to do that in the future. We are trying to be attentive to our place in the galactic scheme of things. But we are, at our heart, a reclusive people. We prefer our privacy when it comes to matters of a more personal nature. Just as we have our tightly drawn limits, so must you learn and understand the limits of what we will and will not share. We have spoken of the Harmony with you. Do not ask us to volunteer more than we feel comfortable doing."

"Then, sir, if we may, I would like to discuss further something you already brought up," said Spock. "The notion that your 'Harmony' interacts with your environment. How does it do that, sir? Purely from a mechanical point of view."

"Your Dr. Daystrom will be able to answer that for you," said Alt. "We have a computer system. It's main terminus is in the Southern Pole satellite."

"May we inspect it?"

"No, Mr. Spock, you may not," said Alt firmly. "However, Dr. Daystrom is being guided by Macro to one of our computer access facilities where the Harmony is maintained."

Spock began to have uneasy feelings and recollections of such ominous entities as Landru and the Oracle. "Is this computer facility . . . something you worship?"

Alt's eyes opened wide, and he started to laugh. The other council members joined in, although it was difficult for Spock to tell if it was because they thought it was funny or because they felt it was appropriate to laugh when Alt laughed. "My dear Mr. Spock," he said, "do you worship the computers aboard your ship?"

"No, sir."

"Nor do we make ours the object of any devotion. Our computers are tools, nothing more. We interact with them to facilitate our ability to control our environment. They are machines. Useful machines. That is all. Do not ascribe to us the primitive delusions of more simpleminded races."

"No offense was intended, sir."

"Nor is any taken. Now, then . . . there is something else that we discerned from your computer banks as being remarkably influential on your culture. Something that your ancestors apparently worshipped, but it was not a religion, not a school of thought, not even a deity. We are a bit confused as to its nature and are most curious about its origin and impact."

"If I can be of help, I will," said Spock.

"Good. So please tell us, then"—and he leaned forward, his fingers steepled—"what exactly was this mighty entity known as 'television'?"

As with all the buildings that Daystrom had observed, this one seemed unassuming. The Calligar were clearly far more interested in function than form. He stood outside a moment next to Macro, his arms folded, surveying it. "So what is this place? Your computer center?"

"A means of accessing the computer," said Macro, "not the center itself."

"And what do you access it for?"

"All manner of things. It's . . . meditative," Macro said uneasily. Suddenly he turned to Daystrom and said, "Be aware that I am still not pleased about this situation. I am cooperating because it is the desire to maintain the Harmony. But that is the only reason. So it would be in your best interest not to ask a large number of questions, because I'm not going to answer them, and you'll just annoy me further. If there's something that I think you should know, I will tell you. Other than that, kindly be quiet."

Daystrom opened his mouth to speak but then closed it again. Squaring his shoulders, he followed Macro into the computer communication center.

He hadn't been sure exactly what to expect. A series of computer stations, perhaps. Or maybe rows of chairs with helmets for participants to fasten on that would tap them in neurally.

Instead they walked into an atmosphere of such suffocating silence that Daystrom felt as if he could barely breathe.

The only noise at all was the sound of Daystrom's boots on the polished floor. He immediately became conscious of his tread, and a moment later, of his breathing. Even his own heartbeat sounded like thunder.

Macro, who was larger than Daystrom, didn't appear to make any sound at all. Evidently he was wearing some sort of cushioned soles. Or maybe he just absorbed sound the way a black hole sucked in light.

The lights in the large chamber were dim, punctuated by cones of pure white light piercing down from overhead. It was impossible for Daystrom to make out just how many people were in there, or how many individual beams of light were being generated. Three, four, five dozen. Maybe more.

Under each of the lights stood a Calligarian. Young and old, male and female, all were there. They stood absolutely immobile in the stark light. They looked neither right nor left; they seemed not to be breathing until Daystrom looked very closely to see a very slow, very shallow rising and falling of their chests.

He stepped very close to a random male, staring straight into the male's eyes. That was when Daystrom found they weren't even really looking straight out. Instead their gazes seemed to be internally directed, as if they were staring into their own souls.

Daystrom looked them over with a mixture of amazement and something akin to horror. "What are they doing?"

"Communing."

"Communing with—"

172

"Themselves. They exchange and study philosophical thoughts with one another, with the computer . . . it's a kind of free-form association with everyone and everything that makes up their environment. Abuse of their surroundings by the Calligar is what led to our initial difficulties so long ago. Only by constant awareness of ourselves and the Worldnet can we avoid such an onerous fate."

"That's a very interesting ideology," said Daystrom. "How does this work specifically?"

Macro actually smiled at him, a toothy and unpleasant smile. "Magic," he said.

Daystrom looked at him uncomprehendingly. "Magic?"

"The system of neural interaction would be beyond your ability to replicate or even fully grasp," Macro informed him airily. "I can just as well tell you that small elves are responsible for it, or a race of giant cyclops with beams emerging from their great eyeballs. Those, at least, you could understand."

"Your confidence in my comprehension is most flattering," said Daystrom dryly. "I am the preeminent mind in computer development in the Federation. I would like to think that means something."

"To those in the Federation, I'm sure it does. But does the preeminent rat in the maze have the power to understand the tools used to construct the maze?"

And then he laughed, loudly and nastily.

Daystrom glanced around and said, "I'd like to try the communing, if you don't mind."

The laughter immediately stopped. "I do mind," said Macro with quiet menace. But that menace was tinged with uneasiness.

"Why, may I ask?"

"The brain of a human being would not be sufficiently strong to cope with it."

Daystrom took a step back and studied Macro

173

thoughtfully. "Are you saying that," he asked, "because you have a great deal of disdain for human beings? Or because it's neurologically true?"

Macro smiled thinly. "You will never know."

And suddenly a shaft of light lanced down from overhead, encompassing Macro. The momentary surprise on his face was immediately noted by Daystrom, who took it to mean that Macro was not expecting this sudden appearance of light. Which meant that the computer was communing with him of its own accord —something that Daystrom found to be personally extremely intriguing. Just how far did this computer's "own accord" go?

Macro stood frozen that way for only a few moments, and then the light vanished. For some moments afterward, however, he said nothing. Daystrom looked at him curiously and then said, "Macro? Is everything all right?"

"No," Macro said, lowering his gaze to Daystrom, and there was undiluted menace in it. "No, everything is not all right. My sister is trying to leave us. And if she does . . . then it will go very badly for you. Very badly."

The last time Daystrom had felt a chill like that pounding through his veins he had been leaning over the M-5, trying to convince the computer of its sanity while feeling his own slip away. It was not a feeling that one ever forgot. It was a feeling of menace to body and soul.

He felt that now, and he shivered under the scrutiny of Macro.

Chapter Seventeen

"ASIDE FROM THE FACT that she's unconscious and her vital signs are all over the place, there's nothing wrong with her."

Lying nearby in the medibed, Ecma didn't move, was barely breathing. The life-sign monitors were fluctuating and seemed to be descending, but then every so often they would jump upward slightly and hold steady.

Standing some feet away was McCoy, his arms folded and his face concerned. Kirk and Tyler were there as well, and McCoy—to Kirk's relief—had made no blustering, annoyed comments about spectators in the sick bay. Usually this meant either that he was confident the patient was going to recover with no problem, or else that there was little chance of anyone else's presence making any difference. Kirk had the uneasy feeling that in this case the latter was true.

"She can't have collapsed for no reason," said Tyler, his voice hitting slightly on the high end of the scale.

"Steady, Commodore," said Kirk firmly. He looked to McCoy. "There's no physiological reason? None?"

"Would you care to double-check her, Doctor?" asked McCoy dryly. "I'm telling you I can't find anything wrong with her. I've studied her physiognomy as much as I could, short of dissecting her—which would probably decrease her chances of survival substantially. I believe I have a handle on what makes her tick. The question is, how do I get her wound up again?"

Kirk thought a moment and then crossed to the computer station. He leaned forward, his knuckles on the counter, and said, "Computer, call up the visual record of the conference-room briefing of an hour ago."

The scene sprang to life on the computer screen. There were Ecma, Fox, and the others, all frozen in place. Kirk became aware that McCoy had joined him, and the doctor said, "What are you hoping to find?"

"Something. Anything. Some clue. Computer—run it forward."

"Speed?" asked the computer.

"Normal time, one-to-one," Kirk said. "However, focus on the individual identified as Ecma."

And the sequence began, except the screen was entirely occupied by Ecma's image.

They watched the whole thing through, up until Ecma's collapse with her shrieks of being afraid to die. "Freeze it," said Kirk. Then slowly he looked at McCoy. "Does that remind you of anything?"

"Should it?" asked McCoy.

"She seemed to be trying to tell us something," said Kirk. "Remember, she stressed that our taboos were not hers. But the implication is that she and the Calligar have their own taboos."

"We know they tend to play close to the vest," said McCoy. "Beyond that—"

"Beyond that we don't know a hell of a lot," Kirk

176

replied. "I think that she was trying to break one of those taboos just then. She was trying to tell us something, something that's part of their society, that they don't wish to share with outsiders. And something—some sort of imperative—prevented her from doing so."

McCoy frowned and started snapping his fingers as if that could jog his memory. "You know, that does sound familiar, that . . . " Then his eyes widened, and he stared at Kirk. "Yonada."

"That's what I was thinking," Kirk replied. "When the old man collapsed—"

"The instrument of obedience."

"Yes," said Kirk.

"The device that was surgically inserted that tied people in to the Oracle."

"Right."

"You think she may be tied in with some sort of supercomputer or something, and it's shutting her down via an implant!" McCoy sounded excited.

"That's it exactly," said Kirk.

"Perfect! My God, Jim, that's brilliant!"

"Thank you, Doctor."

"Really! That's a terrific answer."

"Good. So you—"

"Just one problem."

"What's that?"

"I already thought of it."

Kirk's face fell. "What? You already—"

"Yeah. I didn't just fall off the turnip truck, you know. I checked her over thoroughly for any sort of mechanical implant. There's nothing there."

Kirk was considerably crestfallen. "So just now you were—"

"Stringing you along, yes. Just to remind you which one of us is the doctor."

With an annoyed glare Kirk said, "You're becoming nasty in your old age, Bones."

And then they heard something strange.

Humming.

Quietly, singsong, almost as if a child were being eased to sleep.

They turned to discover Commodore José Tyler standing next to the medibed. He was holding Ecma's hand, slowly drawing his fingers across the top in a slow, soothing fashion. And he was humming to her. Nothing readily identifiable, or even especially coherent. Just slow, steady comforting.

Kirk and McCoy went over to them to watch in silent puzzlement, and then McCoy glanced up at the bioreadings. "Son of a gun. She's stabilizing. Lower than I'd want, but at least she's not deteriorating. I'm not sure why, but what you're doing is definitely helping, Commodore. Keep it up."

"Ecma is someone who likes to be in tune with her surroundings," Tyler said in between soft, gentle hums. "From what I saw, and from what Captain Pike reported about Zyo's home, her world is very thought-responsive. I just wanted to bring her in tune with me . . . and us. And I thought filling the environment with something soothing, like music, would get to her inside and out and might make things easier for her."

"I can order music piped in to sick bay," said Kirk.

And now Tyler was tenderly singing, "'Juuust me and my shaaadow . . .'"

"I know that song," said Kirk.

"Good. Sing it with me."

"But Commodore—"

"I'm pulling rank, Captain."

Kirk shrugged and joined in with "'Strolling down the aaavenue,'" and together he and Tyler continued, "'Me and my shaaaadow . . .'"

They went through the entire song twice, and

Ecma's breathing—which had been erratic—was slow and regular. And then at Tyler's urging they continued, launching into "Rockabye Baby," "Twinkle, Twinkle, Little Star," "Fly Me to the Moon," and the slightly off-color drinking song popular at the academy, "Down from Saturn and up Uranus." This was followed by McCoy leading Tyler in a rendition of "Dixie" while Kirk went to the intercom.

"Kirk to bridge. Uhura."

"Yes, Captain," she replied, and then she said, "Captain, I seem to have something else on the channel. It sounds like singing."

"That's correct. Uhura, I want you to program a selection of songs and have them fed into sick bay."

"Songs?"

"Yes, Uhura, songs."

"Any particular preferences?"

"No, none. Just something soothing."

He heard Sulu, who was in command, come in on the band. "Captain, this is Sulu. Is there a difficulty?"

"No, Mr. Sulu, just trying to arrange for some music to be piped into sick bay."

Sulu seemed to give it some thought. "May I recommend show tunes, sir? I've always been partial to show tunes."

"Opera." Chekov's voice could be heard. "If you vant true passion, it has to be opera."

"Three hours of corpulent divas braying in Italian. No, thank you," said Uhura disdainfully. "Actually, for pure beauty, nothing can top a madrigal."

"This isn't for recreation!" said Kirk in exasperation. "We have a patient down here who responds well to a musical environment. I don't care if you send us pop, waltz, or a Rigelian candigal, but get some music down here, dammit!"

"Yes, sir," said Uhura, who clearly hadn't realized that there was medical need. "Give me ten seconds."

Precisely ten seconds later a gentle, sweet, and haunting tone filled the air, and Kirk recognized it immediately. It was a recording of Spock playing his Vulcan lyre.

"I'm going to bring the lights down to fifty-percent illumination," said McCoy. "If what she needs is a peaceful environment, then that will certainly help."

"Good idea, Doctor," said Kirk.

Moments later the lights did indeed come down, and Kirk even found himself becoming almost hypnotically relaxed by the peaceful environment that had been created in the sick bay. Tyler was humming along with the Vulcan music and continuing to stroke her hand.

"It would seem, Captain," said McCoy in a low voice, "that a fair guess is that she's going through some sort of withdrawal."

"The question is, what is she withdrawing from?"

"I don't know," said McCoy. "The problem is that withdrawal generally gets worse before it gets better. In other words—"

"She may continue to deteriorate, and we've just bought her some time, is all," Kirk said slowly. "All right. But at least we've got her that." He grimaced. "Thinned, she said. What in hell was she talking about?"

"I don't know, but whatever it was," observed McCoy, "it certainly seems that it has fatal consequences."

"Bridge to the captain."

Kirk went to the wall comm and tapped it. "Kirk here. The music is fine, Commander."

"That's not it, Captain," said Uhura. "We're receiving a communication from the Calligar. They insist on talking to the leader of the starship, and they sound extremely unhappy."

Kirk exchanged glances with McCoy, and the doctor mouthed the words *They know.* Kirk nodded grimly. "I'll be right up, Uhura." Then he turned to Tyler. "Commodore, I think you might want to hear this as well."

"I should really stay here with Ecma," began Tyler.

But Kirk would have none of it. "Commodore, as ranking officer I think you should be present when this communiqué comes through. And for God's sake, stop acting like a lovesick schoolboy."

Tyler's face hardened. "You're out of line, Captain."

"No, I'm out of patience, Commodore."

The commodore's mouth twitched a moment, and then he nodded. "Very well. You're correct, of course. Doctor, please call me if there's any change in her condition."

"Of course," said McCoy.

Tyler placed Ecma's hand gently on her belly, took one more glance at the life signs that had stabilized, and then nodded to Kirk. "All right. Let's go."

Kirk tapped the wall comm once more. "Kirk to Ambassador Fox."

"Fox here," came the immediate reply.

"Where are you, Ambassador?"

"In my quarters, resting."

"Stay there, but tie in with shipboard communications through your computer. We're getting a message from the Calligar, and you might want to contribute."

Fox's voice was laced with sarcasm. "Is this where I'm supposed to defend a position that I don't agree with?"

"That's right, Ambassador. This is it."

"Splendid."

Kirk spun and headed quickly out of sick bay, followed by Tyler, leaving the eerie strains of the Vulcan harp behind him.

McCoy sighed and said to himself, "God, I hate

that creepy Vulcan music. They should have stuck with show tunes."

Kirk walked out onto the bridge, followed by Tyler, and said briskly, "Put them on visual, Uhura."

"Yes, sir."

The rift that had seemed to become a permanent fixture on the screen now vanished, to be replaced by images of several Calligarians and Mr. Spock, looking calm as always.

"Captain," said Spock as casually as if he were announcing the weather, "there appears to be a difficulty that has the Calligarians quite distressed."

"I think I'm aware of what that might be, Mr. Spock," said Kirk, emulating the Vulcan's stoicism.

"These gentlemen," said Spock, inclining his head slightly in their direction, "are Alt, the Master of the Status, and Macro and Regger, the brother and son, respectively, of the individual in question."

"The individual in question," Alt said, clearly trying not to lose his patience, "is our Master Builder. Ecma has apparently taken it upon herself to turn her back on her people. That cannot be allowed. She must be returned to us."

"May I ask how you became aware of the situation?" asked Kirk.

"I was informed by Macro," said Alt. "And Macro—"

"Has nothing to say to you beyond that I think you are deceiving, conniving cretins," Macro said fiercely. Then he pointed in the direction of Tyler. "I blame you for this, Tyler! You talked her into this. She was happy and content until she met you."

"I only knew her for a short time, and many years ago, Macro," Tyler replied. "I doubt I could have had that much influence on her beyond whatever discontent with your society she may already have had within her."

"The Master Builder's discontent is not at issue here," Alt now said. "What is at issue is the concept of continued trust and cooperation between my people and yours. That is impossible if we cannot trust you to return one of our most valued commodities."

"She's not just some commodity," Regger said. His annoyance seemed more focused on Alt than it did on the *Enterprise* crew. "She's my mother. She's our Master Builder. We depend on her. We need her. She's been training me all my life to take over after her, but I would never have the temerity to claim that I'm ready to do so." Now he turned toward Kirk. "Captain, I implore you . . . make her see reason."

"Right now I can't make her see anything," said Kirk. "She has passed out and is currently in our sick bay."

"Of course she is," said Macro. "She can't survive away from us. It's against the way in which she was brought up. It's against everything that we are. Her life cycle begins and ends with the Calligar, and if you think to interfere with that, then you have no one to blame but yourself for the consequences."

"For someone who has nothing to say," observed Tyler, "you certainly have trouble shutting up."

"Don't start with me, Federation man," Macro said fiercely, stabbing a finger at Tyler.

"Captain," came Fox's voice, "if I may . . ."

Kirk took a breath. This had been a calculated risk on Kirk's part. He had dealt before with Fox, and others like him. But he had anticipated that the Calligar were not going to be ecstatic about the situation, and he believed that one of the things that could get him through this extremely delicate situation was presenting a united front. The last thing he

183

needed was internal bickering. Which meant that he had moved hard and fast to get Fox on his side, appealing to everything from his diplomacy to his humanity.

"Go ahead, Ambassador," he said.

"This is Ambassador Fox," he said, and the viewscreen, at the silent command of Sulu, cut away in the lower right-hand corner to display an image of Fox from down in his quarters. "Obviously you feel strongly about this situation. Just as obviously, so does Captain Kirk."

"Ecma is subject to Calligarian law," Alt said.

"I would tend to agree," said Fox, "and were we, in fact, on Calligar, there would be no question. However, gentlemen, we are in Federation space. That makes Ecma's request for sanctuary subject to our laws, and granting of such request is left to the captain's discretion on a case-by-case basis."

"And in this case," Kirk said quickly, while heaving an internal sigh of relief, "I am using that discretion to give the Master Builder, however temporarily, sanctuary. You should be aware, by the way, that she has stated she abrogates all rights to her title."

Alt looked dumbfounded, as if this had never occurred to him. He looked at Roger questioningly, and even Regger seemed amazed. "That would mean, Captain," said Regger slowly, "that I would now be the Master Builder. A most exalted title. But one that I would gladly relinquish to she who has done far more than I to deserve it."

And now Macro, to the surprise of all, turned on Regger and said, "You insufferable little snot. The way you talk, you act as if you never wanted it. I know what you're all about, Regger, and don't think I'm unaware. It's what you've always wanted, isn't it? It's a foolish father who doesn't know his son."

Kirk was extremely pleased at that moment that he

had managed to present a united front, because watching the internal bickering among the Calligar emphasized what an unseemly sight that could be.

Regger looked hurt and betrayed, and he ignored his father as he said straight into the monitor, "Please . . . excuse my father. He is extremely upset, as are we all, and he is saying things that are inappropriate and untrue."

"And Ecma has been saying things as well," Tyler added. "Things like—"

"Things like . . ." Kirk said, motioning for Tyler to be silent for a moment. Slowly he sat in his command chair, looking extremely casual, as if he had all the time in the world. He even smiled slightly.

"Like what?" said Macro impatiently.

"She told us about thinning. And about how thinning would mean her certain death if she returned to you."

Tyler looked at Kirk questioningly, but Kirk didn't return the stare. Of course, Kirk had no idea what specifically Ecma had been talking about, but there was no reason to tip the Calligar off to that.

Indeed, the expressions of the Calligar were a sight to behold—utter astonishment, to put it mildly. Then Alt seemed to pull himself together, and he said firmly, "She would not have. You are lying, Captain. But that doesn't matter."

"People of Calligar," Fox now said, "the last thing the Federation wishes to do is cause a difficulty. However, our commitment to the right of free will makes it—"

"If I may," Spock now managed to get into the conversation, "I am certain that some sort of equitable compromise could be reached if we merely keep the lines of communication open."

"We will be more than happy to keep those lines open," Alt said tersely, "but our communication

185

consists of this: Gentlebeings. You will return the Master Builder to us, and you will do so quickly. As much respect as we have for your good intentions, and for you, Kirk, as the leader, we cannot see any other way."

"It's his fault!" Macro said again, pointing at Tyler. "Things would have gone perfectly well—"

Tyler felt his temper flaring. "And have you considered that maybe you're at fault, you repulsive pig?"

"Commodore," said Kirk dangerously.

But Tyler wasn't paying attention. Instead his gaze was locked with Macro's, and he said, "And that maybe it's not so much that she's running to me as that she's running from you? Maybe she's tired of your insular, nonexpanding world. Or maybe she's just tired of you."

"Uhura, cut the audio," ordered Kirk. She did so, and he immediately spun his chair to face Tyler. "Commodore, you're not helping."

"My apologies, Captain." There was no edge to his voice. He spoke flatly and evenly.

"Uhura." He nodded to have the audio brought back on line. "Alt, Mr. Spock is correct. We are both intelligent, reasonable peoples. I'm certain that we can work matters out to the satisfaction of all concerned."

"Are you willing to bet your crew on that, Captain?" asked Alt.

"What do you mean?"

"He means," Macro now said, "that until such time that you return Ecma to us, we will hold on to your contact team."

"You can't do that!" shouted Tyler.

Ambassador Fox was *hmphing* as well. "I would like to think," he said tautly, "that the Calligar can deal with us in a more equitable manner than extortion!"

186

"If it's good enough for you, it's good enough for us," said Macro.

Regger looked uncomfortable. "Father, this—this isn't right. . . ."

"Shut up. If it's good enough for them, it's good enough for us."

"Sir," Spock said patiently, "you cannot reasonably equate the two. In the case of Ecma, she is asking to remain with the Federation. In our situation, you are holding us against our will."

"Semantics," said Macro dismissively.

"No, sir. Facts."

"That really doesn't matter now, does it?" said Alt. "Here is the reality of the situation. We are not barbarians, Captain, nor are we kidnappers. However, we know what we want, and we know what we're entitled to. Send the Master Builder back to us. Until that time, the Federation contingent will stay with us. And I remind you, Captain, that the rift will close roughly sixty hours from now. That does not leave you a great deal of time. I suggest you use it wisely."

And with that, the transmission from the Calligar blinked off.

Kirk sagged back in his chair and rubbed his forehead. "Perfect," he said. "Just perfect."

Chapter Eighteen

ALL THE MATERIALS from the shuttlecraft were brought into the large common room that had been arranged for the convening of the contact team. Extending from the common room were a series of bedchambers for Spock, Scott, Daystrom, Thak, and Dorkin. It took the team only a few minutes to discover the subjective nature of the room's interior furnishings, and for the first time that anyone could remember, Shondar Dorkin had absolutely no complaints with anything—particularly the decor.

What spoiled the charm of the setup for the group was the knowledge, passed on to them by Mr. Spock, that matters had gone seriously awry back on the *Enterprise.* This drew, expectedly, the loudest bellow from Dorkin.

"That idiot captain of yours is going to get us all marooned here!" he yowled.

"I am quite certain," said Spock confidently, "that is not the captain's intent."

"Aye. If there's a way out of this, Captain Kirk is the

man to find it," Scotty affirmed. He smiled at Spock, who, unsurprisingly, did not smile back.

"Well, I'm certain that's an unbiased couple of commentaries from people who have served with Kirk since before the dawn of time," said Dorkin sarcastically. "You're staking your personal freedom on his ability to work us out of this."

"Captain Kirk seems quite capable," Daystrom said. "And he is also quite resourceful. If anyone can get us out of this, he can."

"Well, that's fine for all of you. If you're content to sit around waiting for Kirk to save us, then that is perfectly fine for you," said Dorkin. "But as for me, I prefer to be in command of my own destiny, thank you." And now he was on his feet and heading for the door.

It came as a surprise to no one except the Shondar when the door refused to open.

"Hey!" he snarled, and he hit it once. When it ignored him he snarled again and hit it again. He had no more luck the second time. He whirled. "We're being made prisoners!"

"That was the logical next step," said Spock.

"This is infuriating!" said Dorkin. "We do not have to stand for this! They won't leave us in here forever. As soon as we see one of them, I say we attack. Vulcans are formidable fighters, as are Andorians—although neither of you, of course, can come close to the pure brawling power of a Tellarite."

"Why in the name of Ghu should we want to?" asked Thak in amazement.

"Physical force would accomplish nothing," Spock said. "It would not garner us knowledge that we need. Injuring or killing Calligarians can only exacerbate the situation. And even if we were able to get to the shuttlecraft, we would not be able to get outside the dome unless the aperture were opened for us. We do not need a show of strength. We need information."

"So what do we do?" asked Thak.

"We wait," said Spock.

In the sick bay of the *Enterprise* Kirk and Tyler were once again observing the unmoving form of Ecma. Kirk was leaning over her and, in a soft but insistent voice, saying, "Ecma. Speak to us. We need to talk with you, Ecma."

She did not reply, and furthermore her breath seemed a bit labored. McCoy glanced warily up at the medical readings, endeavoring to ignore the Vulcan harp music that had been playing in his sick bay for what seemed like an eternity. If Spock hadn't been completely off the ship and uninvolved in the decision, McCoy would have sworn it was part of some Vulcan master plan to drive him insane.

"The withdrawal is becoming more pronounced," he said at length.

"But withdrawal from what?" said Kirk in frustration. "What's the exact nature?"

"I'm not sure," said McCoy, his professional detachment a marked contrast to Kirk's own attitude. "If I were sure, we could come up with some sort of substitute. The music definitely seems to have helped, but—"

And suddenly the vital signs started to drop precipitously. The scanning board began blinking faster, and an alarm signal sounded.

"Damn," said McCoy, grabbing up his instruments. "Medics!"

As if they had materialized from thin air, two medics showed up with stabilizer units. McCoy hurriedly set the calibration.

Ecma's body was covered with sweat and trembling

horribly. She was moaning softly, and from her mouth emerged faint whistling noises, as if she had a sucking chest wound.

"Do something!" said Tyler.

"Shut up!" snapped McCoy. He was rapidly preparing a hypo.

"Pulse and respiration dropping, Doctor," said one of the medtechs. "Bottoming out."

"We're losing her," said the other medtech. "Vital signs at less than minimal."

"Brain-wave activity is discordant."

It had happened so fast, and Tyler was shouting to her, "Come on! *Come on!* Whatever's happening to you, make it stop! Make it stop! You can *beat* it! *Make it stop!*"

"Hold her down," said McCoy. He placed the hypo against her forearm. "I'm giving her five ccs of cordrazine."

"Five?" said Kirk in shock, remembering what the drug could do in even the smallest of doses.

"My studies show her body should be able to handle it," said McCoy, and then in a softer voice he added, "I hope."

He injected the stimulant, and the result was, as always, instantaneous.

Ecma's eyes snapped open, her mouth forming a perfect ○ shape, and she shrieked. Her hands swung up, snapping the restraints and knocking aside the two medtechs. The medisensor lock around her middle, however, was significantly tougher. She tried to sit up, but it held her in place. If she'd tried to slide out, she would have succeeded, but her mind was too chaotic at the moment for any such lucid plan. All she was trying to do was sit up, and that she could not accomplish.

There was enough time for Kirk and Tyler to get on

191

either side of her, grab her by the shoulders and force her back down. Kirk glanced up at the monitor board and saw all the gauges at the top of the scale. Though McCoy had certainly kicked her back up into high gear, the problem was that, as high as she was, she wasn't going to stay there, and they had to make sure she didn't come crashing back down in flames.

"Ecma!" Tyler was shouting. He leaned against her, grabbed her face with both hands, and forced her to look straight at him. Her eyes weren't focusing on him, weren't focusing on anything. "Ecma! Listen to me! Remember—'Just me and my shaaaadow—'"

With superior strength her arm coiled up, and she shoved him fiercely away. He stumbled back and knocked over a medical cart.

Ecma was trying to shove Kirk away as well, and he twisted about and got her left arm immobilized. The right one was pushing at him with everything she had. "Ecma! Stop! Whatever is happening to you, it's in your mind! Your mind is trying to shut down your body, for some reason none of us knows! You can stop it! You can! There's nothing biologically wrong with you. You have to have the force of will to overcome it. We can't do it for you! No one can. This is your fight! Yours! Now start fighting it! Come on! Fight your fight! *Fight your fight!*"

It was some hours before Spock, Scotty, and the others received their first visitor: Alt showed up, inquiring after their health.

This drew a coarse and sarcastic laugh from Dorkin. "Why should you care? You're the ones who are keeping us prisoners."

"We are all prisoners, in a way," said Alt. "Prisoners of circumstance." He sat down on a chair that appeared seven different ways to the seven individuals in the room. "We do not wish to keep you here until the next cycle of the rift. The chances are that most of you will be deceased by the time that happens."

"I would, in all likelihood, still be alive," said Spock. "Vulcans are notoriously long-lived."

"It's because they never shut up long enough to stop living," sniffed Dorkin.

"That is one theory," said Spock graciously. And then, totally unexpectedly, Spock turned to Scotty and said, "Mr. Scott, perhaps now would be the time to . . . I believe the phrase is 'crack out' . . . the provisions you brought with you."

Scott looked at him in total befuddlement. "Provisions, Mr. Spock?"

"Yes." He indicated the supplies Scotty had brought that had been unloaded from the vanished shuttlecraft. "Particularly the bottle."

The chief engineer's jaw dropped. "Now how did ye—"

"Mr. Scott," Spock said, sounding as close to surprised as he ever came. "I have known you for far too long to be unaware of your usual definition of supplies."

Scotty shook his head in amazement as he went to the supplies chest. Daystrom, Thak, and Dorkin were looking at one another in confusion. "Will someone kindly tell me what the blazes you're talking about?" demanded Dorkin.

For reply, Scotty pulled out a bottle of Scotch and held it up for all to see. "Muh hat's off to ye, Mr. Spock. After all these years, I guess there's just not very many surprises left."

"The price we all must pay, Mr. Scott." And then Spock turned to Alt and, much to Scotty's surprise, said, "Would you care to sample Mr. Scott's provisions, Master of the Status?"

Alt raised an eyebrow. "If it is Mr. Scott's wish. I do not wish to impose."

"Certainly not, don't think of imposing," said Thak with soft sarcasm. "Keep us against our will, that you have no trouble doing."

"I have already said that is not our desire," said Alt, taking the proffered open bottle from Spock. "It is due simply to the demands and the unfortunate necessities of the situation. Ecma is a very valuable individual."

"And if she were less valuable?" asked Spock.

"It would make no difference. We believe in a closed society."

"For a people who say they are an advanced race," Dorkin said, "you seem unwilling to grant freedom to your own people. How much advancement is there in that?"

Alt took a long swig of the Scotch, and that was when Scotty cast a glance at Spock. Spock merely nodded ever so slightly, and a slow smile spread across Scott's face.

Alt then lowered the bottle, wiping a sleeve across his mouth. "We cannot allow," he said, "indiscriminate distribution of our people hither and yon. We believe it contrary to the best long-term interests of the galactic society as a whole. There must be control. Don't you understand that? Our society, our environment, our thoughts must all be"—he interlaced his fingers—"like this. Try to pry this apart. You cannot. But if a finger is removed, then it becomes that much easier. Our society needs each and every individual to remain whole and strong. Everyone knows his position and place in that society, and his responsibilities. To shirk that responsibility is to damage the society."

"Laddy," said Scotty slowly, "do ye know that you're rambling on and on, and by and large not making a lot of sense?"

Alt giggled.

Scotty looked at Spock. "This," he said, "is promising."

Matters had gotten somewhat unpleasant—even nauseating—for a time in the *Enterprise* sick bay in the course of Ecma's weaning from whatever had a grip on her. But Kirk and McCoy had changed their uniforms and gotten cleaned up, and now they returned to the tortured Calligarian refugee.

"Heartbeat and respiration normal . . . well, normal for her, at any rate."

McCoy was studying the vital signs over Ecma's bed and nodding slowly. "All right, I admit it . . . I'm impressed," he continued. He turned to Kirk, who was standing nearby. "You have something of a knack, Captain—although I would have to say that lecturing patients is not something that generally produces results."

"Whatever works, Doctor." He stood over Ecma, whose eyes were still serenely closed. Her breathing was shallow but regular. "I don't think I'd care to make a habit out of that, though. I'm perfectly content to let you take care of the medical situations on this ship."

"What a relief. I was getting worried there for a second," said McCoy.

"So . . . so what happens now?" asked Tyler.

"Now we wait," said McCoy. "She's gone through the equivalent of what used to be called 'cold turkey.' That term was usually in reference to drugs in the system. Here it's not a drug, but instead something in her mind. It's having the same sort of effects on her just the same. I believe she's come through the worst of it, but still, I'm dealing with an alien physiognomy relating to some sort of societal compulsion so overwhelming that it's invaded her biology. There's no way I'm going to say she's completely clear until she sits up, looks at me lucidly, and asks what's for breakfast."

"And until we can talk with her and get a thorough grasp of what's going on, we can't do anything to alter the situation," said Kirk grimly. "Meanwhile, we lose precious time."

"Bridge to Captain," came Uhura's voice through the intercom.

"Never a dull moment around here, eh?" asked Tyler. Kirk didn't even bother to answer as he tapped the intercom.

"Kirk here."

"Captain, we've picked up private transmissions from within the ship."

"What? Localize."

"We already have. They originated from the cabins of the Tellarite and Andorian ambassadors."

Kirk and McCoy exchanged glances. "The aides. They've alerted their governments," said Kirk in sudden realization.

"Alerted them that their respective representatives are being held on the other side of the rift because we've given Ecma sanctuary. But how did they find out?"

And this time they spoke together: "Fox."

"I'll kill him," said Kirk.

Tyler nodded. "I'll help."

Chapter Nineteen

MACRO WAS STANDING on the edge of the water, looking out over the cool lake.

"This is where it began," he said slowly, unable and not needing to hide the resentment in his voice.

"Where what began, Father?"

Macro did not even bother to turn to see his son behind him. "Must you follow me everywhere?" he grumbled. "It's endless with you."

"Can I help it if I want to be near you? You are my father, after all." He paused. "What's going to happen to Mother?"

"I don't know, and I don't care."

"Are they going to make her come back?"

Macro turned on him. "Oh, you'd like it if they didn't, wouldn't you?"

Regger looked astounded. "Father, why do you keep saying that?"

"Because you know it's true! Because you welcome the opportunity to become the Master Builder!" He advanced on his son, waving a meaty finger. "Your scheming and your plotting. Acting to everyone as if you're pleasant and thoughtful and couldn't care less about advancement. Oh, but I know you, Regger! I do! I know what motivates you! I know how happy you'd be to have your mother gone, and don't think I don't know! Your plots and your schemes—"

Regger drew himself up and, eyes filled with hurt and defiance, said, "Who are you describing, Father? Me? Or yourself?"

Macro threw a quick right that caught Regger just under the chin and lifted him clear off his feet. He fell to the ground, nursing his injured jaw, and Macro stood over him, body quivering in indignation.

"You," he snarled at his son, "have got one hell of a nerve."

"I," shot back Regger, "am—at least for the moment—the Master Builder. I outrank you, Father, and that's what's really gnawing at you, isn't it? That you were passed over. That you just don't have the talent or the will. You can't accept that things aren't going your way, so you come up with these fabrications of plots and plans. So you can believe the whole Worldnet is against you, and poor, poor Macro the maligned is being schemed against. No one is plotting against you, Father, or plotting against my mother. And the greatest enemy that you have in this world is yourself, and that's the truth."

Macro's jaw shifted from side to side, and his muscles seemed to be tensing under his skin. "Sooner or later," he said, "everyone is going to see. Everyone is going to see who's right and who's wrong, and who's deserving . . . and who's not."

"Yes, Father," shot back Regger. "I have no doubt that they will."

Alt didn't so much sit down in the chair as pour his body into it. The bottle hung in his hand, and Scotty pulled it from his unresisting fingers. The engineer studied it in surprise. "He only drank about"—he appraised the remaining contents with a practiced eye—"about one and a half glasses. Now there's someone who can't hold his liquor."

"Yes, I am aware of that, Mr. Scott," said Spock. "Nor was he able to do so when we first encountered him. I surmised that his tolerance for such had not increased during the intervening years."

"So now what, oh great strategist?" asked Dorkin.

"Now," said Spock, crouching down next to Alt, "we get the information that we—and, in all likelihood, the captain—require. The nature of this situation that has Ecma refusing to return to her people."

"But why do you say the captain requires it?" asked Scott. "He said he knew it already."

"That was a bluff."

"How do ye know?"

Spock glanced back at Scotty. "The captain has never been known for his reticence. If he were fully cognizant of what was bothering the Master Builder, he would undoubtedly have delivered a lengthy argument on her behalf, based on the knowledge of what was concerning her. His failure to do so can only be interpreted as a lack of information on his part."

"So what are you going to do?" asked Thak.

It was Daystrom who answered. "The mind meld. Isn't that correct." It wasn't a question.

"Yes, sir," replied Spock. He stretched out a hand, and his fingers touched Alt's face.

"Why didn't you just overpower him and do that when he first got here?" demanded Dorkin. "It would have saved lots of time."

"Force is not the answer to everything," replied Spock. "For that matter, it is rarely the answer to anything. I sense that the Calligar have very strong minds—penetrating a mind under assault or on its guard would have been difficult, if not impossible.

This, however, is more feasible. Now, may I have silence please—as difficult as that may be for some?"

"Was that crack directed at me?" said Dorkin. "What, are you saying I don't know how to be silent? I can be silent. I can keep my mouth shut. I have as much self-control as anyone. And I resent the implication that—"

Thak moved so quickly that Dorkin never saw it coming. Considering the perpetual air of deference that Andorians projected, it was completely unexpected. That air also, however, served to cover the utter fierceness of Andorians when they were provoked.

All Dorkin knew was that suddenly there was an impact on the side of his head, and stars exploded behind his eyes. Then his face was on the floor, and he wasn't quite sure precisely how it had gotten there. That was the last thing he thought of before he slipped into unconsciousness.

No one else so much as budged from his position. Scotty, surveying the scene, said, "That was a wee bit drastic . . . but no less appreciated."

Spock didn't even seem to have noticed. His fingers strayed across Alt's face, working the upper part of his head as if physically drawing what he needed to know out through his fingers. His face was absolutely immobile; he wasn't even blinking. His mind probed deeper, deeper into Alt's consciousness.

And then he gasped, his head snapping one way and then the other as if someone were battering him. He grunted in the manner of someone shoving a boulder up a hill, and Scotty took a step toward him, uncertain of what to do. He didn't want to break the contact. He wasn't sure what would happen to Spock if he did.

"Worldnet," whispered Spock. "Worldmind. Thinning. Dying. So many people. So many minds. Dead and alive. Gone and here. Thinning. Culling. Separate the best. Best and brightest. Take them. Save them. Preserve them. Dead and alive. Gone and here."

Each word was more labored than the one before, the effort seeming greater and greater.

"Dead and alive," said Spock. "Dead and alive, gone and here, thinning, thinning," and his voice grew louder and louder, and then suddenly he shouted, *"Stop him! He's invading me! Stop him!"*

"Spock!" shouted Scotty, for the voice speaking was no longer the Vulcan's. He could hold back no more, and he grabbed Spock under the arms and yanked him away from Alt. The Calligarian slumped back, his eyes open but looking at nothing, his mouth moving but saying no words.

Spock seemed dazed, leaning his full weight on the sturdy shoulders of the engineer, and now Daystrom was on the other side, helping to support him. "Spock!" said Scotty, "what happened? What did you—"

That was when three Calligarians burst in. In their hands were small disks, no larger than their palms.

Scotty turned and demanded, "What's happening here? What are you people doing in—"

The closest one to Scotty flipped his disk almost casually, and it landed on the engineer's upper shoulder. And to Scotty's astonishment, he collapsed like a marionette with severed strings. He hit the floor hard, cracking his head, and his senses swam around him. He heard a grunt and a thud, and that was clearly Daystrom going down as well. Scotty tried to reach up to remove the disk, but his arm wouldn't budge. He had as much control over his limbs as if they'd been removed and affixed to someone else's body.

The Calligarians turned on Thak and, their arms at the ready with more disks, said, "Don't move."

"I've grown roots," replied Thak calmly. At his feet was the unmoving Tellarite.

Alt was beginning to haul himself to his feet, making every effort to shake off the effects of the alcohol. He regarded Spock lying on the ground. The Vulcan was trying to pull himself up but was not having tremendous success.

It was at that point that Macro ran in, looking around in momentary confusion before fully assessing the situation. He stared at Alt. "You've looked better," he said, in regard to Alt's complexion, which had taken on a distinctly greenish hue.

Alt, for his part, was focused entirely on Spock. "I thought," Alt said thickly, "that you had a better understanding of our point of view in this situation. We tried to associate with you and yours. We truly did."

And now Macro interrupted, saying disdainfully, "Zyo had a vision, and one man with a vision can bring an entire race into focus. But obviously that vision was flawed. We will have to do something about that . . . but first we will have to do something about you."

"Get away from him!" said Scotty.

Alt glared at him. "Now you express moral outrage? Try the indignity of having someone invade your mind, wresting from you the most personal aspects of your race's belief. Something that is important to us, virtually sacred, simply . . . ripped from within me by this butchering Vulcan mind technique. Well, he will not hold on to this information. Of that I can assure you. Take him," he said to two of the Calligarians who were nearby.

They reached down and hauled Spock up, draping his arms around their shoulders to be able to drag him to wherever they were bringing him.

Alt looked at the rest of them pityingly. "We had the best of intentions for you. You brought this on yourselves."

And that was when Spock's hands clamped down on the shoulders of his two supporters.

Their heads snapped around, and they went down immediately. Spock, on his feet, reached out for the third Calligarian.

Alt stepped back and shouted, "Stop him! Stop him!"

The third Calligarian moved like lightning, catching Spock's hands before they could reach his shoulders. In doing so, he dropped the neural disruption disk to the floor. They struggled, angling for position and leverage, and Macro tried to get in close while Alt shouted in consternation.

That was when Thak moved once more, like lightning, clearing the distance between himself and the others in one bound. He came in low, his shoulder slamming into Macro's midsection, and the larger Calligarian grunted with the contact. Thak straightened up and completely lifted the astonished Macro off the floor. And then Thak, with a quick twist of his deceptively slender upper torso, tossed Macro across the room to land with a crash on the far side.

Macro roared and leapt to his feet, and Thak turned to face him. Unfortunately, he turned his back on Alt, who grabbed the disk dropped by the Calligarian struggling with Spock and threw it.

His aim was lousy, but the result was formidable— the disk landed on the Andorian's antenna.

Thak shrieked, the neuro-paralyzing power of the disk ripping through his body due to its coming in contact with his sensitive antenna. It was as if his brain had exploded, and he went down, clawing at his head, his face; his limbs becoming useless to him. He trembled on the ground as if in an epileptic seizure.

Macro saw him, grinned, and started to step over the unmoving Tellarite to get to Thak.

That was precisely the moment that Shondar

Dorkin chose to wake up, and he did not wake in a particularly good mood.

Dorkin drove a furry fist straight up, directly into Macro's crotch. Macro gasped, and the Tellarite rolled, smashing a blow to the back of Macro's right knee. The Shondar did not get the satisfying crack he would have liked to hear, but the result was still gratifying as Macro collapsed.

Unfortunately, he collapsed right on top of Dorkin, but the Tellarite was not slowed by this. He rolled out from underneath, grabbed the moaning Macro, and threw him back across the room. Macro crashed right into Alt, and they went down in a tangle of arms and legs. Neither of them got up.

The impact momentarily distracted the last Calligarian enough for Spock to suddenly twist his arm free and fasten his hand onto his opponent's shoulder. The Calligarian's head turned so fast it seemed as if he'd gotten whiplash.

Spock quickly removed the disks that were holding the others immobile. The relief was gratefully felt and pretty much instantaneous. Scotty began flexing his muscles, Daystrom wiggled his fingers as if he were seeing them for the first time, and even Thak—the most devastated of the group—recovered quickly.

Shondar Dorkin was still snarling, pumped up by the fierceness of the battle that he'd woken up into. "Who hit me?" he demanded. "Who knocked me out? Who *dared*—"

Thak pointed at one of the unconscious Calligarians. "He did."

"Come, gentlemen," said Spock, and he headed for the door. The others followed, the Tellarite pausing only momentarily to give the Calligarian that Thak had fingered a good, swift kick.

They made their way out of the building and went quickly to the field where the shuttlecraft was waiting.

That was when they heard a roar behind them, and they didn't even have to turn to see that there were a number of Calligarians in pursuit. Spock immediately recognized one of the voices as belonging to Macro. It would have been the height of bad taste to apply the Vulcan nerve pinch to an opponent already apparently unconscious—such as Macro. In this instance, though, that breach of etiquette might have been acceptable.

They picked up the pace until they were loping across the open field, the shuttlecraft in view and getting closer. Daystrom staggered, his breath ragged in his chest, and at one point he almost stumbled. Spock caught him, however, and helped him limp to the shuttle.

The door opened, and they clambered in. Scott bellowed to Spock, "I thought ye said that we couldn't go anywhere! That we're sealed in!"

"That is correct," said Spock. "However, there is no reason we cannot become airborne while we send a message to the captain to inform him of what we've discovered. *Enterprise* is well beyond the range of our hand communicators, but not the subspace transmitter on the shuttle."

"You know what's going on?"

As the door shut behind them Spock looked at Scott with something akin to surprise. "Of course, Mr. Scott. That was the purpose of the mind meld."

"But you didn't say—"

"Why affirm something that should be self-evident?" he asked as he sat in front of the control panel.

Scott sighed. "Whatever you say, Mr. Spock." He dropped down to the pilot station next to Spock and quickly fired up the engines. Then he looked out the front window.

There they were, several dozen of the Calligarians,

205

and in the lead was Macro. Furious, pumping his fists, and holding some sort of an instrument that looked like a long steel rod.

Spock regarded the approaching onslaught calmly as he said, "Take us up, Mr. Scott."

The shuttlecraft rose into the air just as the Calligarians arrived on the scene. They hurled themselves against the small vessel, which lurched one way and then another, and Scotty increased the thrust by twenty percent. An instant later the shuttle lifted into the air, leaving the crowd of angry Calligarians far below.

"Proceed with caution, Mr. Scott," said Spock as he manipulated the controls for the subspace radio. "Excessive velocity would not be advisable—"

"Seeing as how we have nowhere to go."

"Quite correct." He patched in a channel. "Spock to *Enterprise*. Come in, *Enterprise*."

Chapter Twenty

"YOU HAVE GOT ONE hell of a nerve," said Kirk.

He was standing over Fox, fists clenched in barely controlled fury. Tyler was next to him, looking ready to watch Fox eat the chair that was holding him immobile.

Fox, in contrast, seemed utterly calm. "I don't see what your problem is, Captain."

"You don't see?" Kirk shook his head, which was not precisely the head he would have liked to be shaking at that moment. "You told the aides of the Tellarite and Andorian representatives that they were being held hostage!"

"They are," said Fox.

"But you didn't have to tell them that!" Tyler said. "That's just going to cause trouble."

"You're saying I should have participated in covering matters up? Is that it?" Fox made a disdainful face. "What's the matter, Captain? Done anything that you're ashamed of?"

"Of course not," said Kirk firmly. "But the last

thing I need is to have other governments breathing down my neck, watching every move I make."

"That is the price of leadership, Captain," Fox replied serenely. "To be under scrutiny."

Tyler leaned forward and said, "Let's get down to the real reason you did it. You did it to try and make Captain Kirk look bad, and to get back at him because he made you toe the line."

"Wrong," said Fox. "I did it because it was the right thing to do. I did it because their governments had a right to know about danger their representatives were thrust into, just as much as you have a right to know what's happening with your people. You speak to me, Captain, of the rightness of your actions. That being the case, you should have no problem about going public with them."

"There is a time and place," said Kirk patiently. "We are in a very delicate situation that you've made that much more difficult."

Fox stared at Kirk for a long moment. "When I was a boy," he said after a time, "I was very much interested in bugs. Insects. And one of the things I would do is go to my mother's garden and turn up rocks in order to watch the insects beneath them. And what I always thought was fascinating was the way, when you'd lift the rock up, the insects would react, exposed to the purity of the sunlight. They would try to scurry or crawl or in some other way hide from that exposure." He paused. "Are you perceiving the metaphor I'm drawing here, Captain?"

"I am," said Tyler. "You're saying you've got rocks in your head."

Fox smiled at that. "Very witty, Commodore. Now, if you'll excuse me, I wish to return to studying what information we have on the Calligar. Maybe I'll be able to discern something that will help us." He

208

turned the chair away from them and faced the computer screen.

Tyler and Kirk exchanged a look, and then Kirk, shaking his head, started for the door. Tyler followed him but stopped long enough to say to Fox, "You know, I once busted myself up pretty badly. Was stuck in one of those chairs for two weeks. Got all sorts of sores on my butt. Itched like hell."

Fox looked back at him and with thinned lips said, "I am *not* itching."

"You will be," smiled Tyler. And as they headed out Tyler was rewarded by the sight of Fox shifting uneasily in his chair.

Out in the corridor Tyler matched Kirk's stride and said, "It'll be like telling him not to think about pink elephants. Now he won't be able to get it out of his mind."

"And what I can't get out of my mind," said Kirk regretfully, "is that he might have a point. I should have enough confidence in my decisions to be able to stand up to scrutiny." He shook his head. "You'd think that age would bring more conviction, not less."

Tyler shrugged. "You have more of a chance to look back on all the decisions you've made in your life and see all the zigs when you should have zagged. When you're young, confidence in your own invincibility and belief in your own immortality carries you through situations that older, wiser men would look back on and say, 'Madness.' Do you look back on your life and see madness, Captain?"

Kirk's mouth twitched. "I look back on my life, Commodore, and see an asylum."

"You wouldn't like an asylum, James. Too quiet for you."

"I thought there was lots of screaming in an asylum."

209

"Only at the asylum known as Starfleet Headquarters."

"Ah. That would explain a great deal."

They stopped at the sick bay, where Ecma still lay unconscious. Her status had not changed, and Kirk looked down at her regretfully. "Damn," he said softly. "If only she'd come to. There's so much that she could tell us."

"Look, Jim, at least her life signs are steady," McCoy pointed out. "That's way ahead of where we were yesterday."

"Has it been that long?" sighed Kirk. He rubbed the bridge of his nose. "I don't think I've slept since this business began."

"I always know when I'm getting really tired," said Tyler. "Everything sounds very loud to me."

"Really?" asked Kirk.

"Yes, and stop shouting."

Kirk started to say that he wasn't shouting, but then he got the joke and forced a smile.

"No, actually," said Tyler, "I got some sleep a while back. You should get some, though. You look exhausted."

"I have too much to do. I've got people trapped over there—"

Now McCoy stepped up. "And you won't do them a damn bit of good if you're too fatigued to think straight."

Kirk sighed. "It used to be I could go forty-eight, seventy-two hours without a wink of sleep."

"Yeah, but now you're old," said McCoy tactlessly.

"Dr. McCoy, you seem to take extraordinary joy in pointing that out to me time and again."

"Someone has to. There's a gap between young and old that you don't seem to have grasped yet. Now get some rest."

"All right. I'll go back to my quarters for—"

"No," said McCoy firmly. "I know you, Jim. You'll lie there for five minutes, then head up to the bridge to try and come up with some new plan to get our people out. But if you're not at a hundred percent, you're just going to wind up getting us all in trouble, or worse. Give Spock a chance to work some of his Vulcan magic on the other side. I hate to remind you of this, but the fact is that he's got more experience under his belt than you do. And so does Scotty. Between the two of them they've got something like a million years of seasoning. Let them see what they can work out. I bet we hear from them within the next few hours. Until then"—he walked over and rapped one of the meditables—"you can lie down here, where I can keep an eye on you."

Kirk looked at Tyler, who shrugged, and then back to McCoy. "How would it look to a crew member if they walked in and I was sound asleep in sick bay?"

"Better than if it happened while you were in your command chair. Besides, how would it look if there was a call from the bridge and you were asleep in your cabin, snoring right through the comm summons? Lose valuable time that way."

Kirk sighed. "All right," he said. "I'll close my eyes for just a few minutes."

He eased himself up onto the medibed and remembered that once upon a time he would have just vaulted onto it. Every muscle in his body ached.

"Do you mind if I stay here?" Tyler asked McCoy. "Just for a bit. To keep an eye on Ecma."

"Sure," said McCoy. "It won't make any difference to her. Sit over there." He pointed to a chair in the corner. "And make sure to stay out of my way."

"Aye, *sir,*" said Tyler gamely, sitting in the chair.

Kirk closed his eyes, frustrated by his own fragility. Remembering how it used to be in the old days.

Not too long ago he'd tried to climb a mountain.

Once upon a time he'd felt as if he could leap over one.

And women. He smiled inwardly. Across the galaxy, and there had been wonders such as other men didn't dream of. He could taste them on his lips, smell their intoxicating aroma. Each name, each image set off an entire string of associations.

So much he had seen and done. And yet it all seemed now as if it had been a waking dream. Or as if it had happened to another man named James T. Kirk.

What had distanced him? What had pulled him away?

Was it the death of his son? Of all the hardships and losses he had endured, that had probably been the worst. He remembered years ago, years and years ago, making an offhand joke about the being called Nomad. A young voice, an amused voice. *You saw what it did for Scotty. What a doctor it would have made. My son, the doctor.*

His son. Dr. Marcus. And he was gone. Dead and gone.

It wasn't right. It wasn't fair. That there had been that separation between them for so long, and just when it seemed as if that open, festering wound had finally been cleansed and mending, David had been torn from him. His son was gone.

And Carol . . . God, her reaction had been . . .

He pushed it away from him, trying to find somewhere to escape. And he found it in the oblivion of sleep.

All of the thoughts and recollections had floated through his head in less than a few seconds. In point of fact, he was somnolent the moment his head was on the small headrest.

And then an instant later McCoy was shaking his shoulder, whispering urgently, *"Jim!"*

Kirk sat up immediately. "What?"

"Call from the bridge. Spock."

That was all Kirk needed to hear. He clambered immediately off the medibed. Across the room Tyler was asleep in the chair, hands folded and on his lap. "We both fell asleep for a minute?" asked Kirk, straightening his jacket.

"You've been out for five hours," replied McCoy.

Kirk blinked in surprise and headed for the door. "Tell them I'm on my way up."

"I told them," said McCoy, falling into step next to his captain, "and I'm coming with you."

They were out in the corridor, leaving the commodore sleeping and a medtech keeping an eye on both the senior officer and Ecma. Kirk started a quick jog toward the turbolift, and McCoy, huffing slightly, kept pace. "Why are you coming with me?" said Kirk. "Worried about Spock?"

"Of course not," grunted McCoy. "But if I don't, then you won't tell me what's going on. You never do."

"I always do," said Kirk. "But you're getting so old you forget things."

"Touché," admitted McCoy.

"Putting him on now, Captain," said Uhura.

"Spock," Kirk said, taking his chair. "What's happening?"

Spock's image was on the screen, and Kirk could see the others in the background. To his surprise, they were in the shuttlecraft. "I have discerned the nature of the problem with the Master Builder," said Spock. "It has to do with the Calligarian philosophy of nonexpansionism, coupled with a firm if somewhat extreme belief in the quality of life and being part of the society as a whole."

"Specify," said Kirk.

"The Calligarian belief," Spock said, sounding a bit pedantic, "is that one is only an acceptable member of the society as long as one continues to contribute to that society. Once the contribution ceases—or, more precisely, reaches its peak—the individual abrogates his right to continue being part of that society."

"In other words, if you're not part of the solution, you're part of the problem," said McCoy.

"Quite right, Doctor. The Calligar society is set up as follows: All members of the society are constantly monitored, and their activities appraised. The growth of their minds, their perceptions, ambitions, and potential accomplishments are in a perpetual state of assessment. In each individual's life, there is a point where it is decided that they have attained the peak of their existence. Any continuation beyond that point is perceived as stagnation, creatively and intellectually."

"What are you saying, Spock? That someone decides, for each and every Calligarian, that he's done enough for one lifetime, and then that lifetime just . . . just *ends?*" said Kirk.

"Yes, sir. It is seen as a needless drain on available resources—a particular consideration since the Calligar mind-set is geared toward nonexpansion."

"My God!" said McCoy. "That . . . that's inhuman!"

Spock actually looked surprised. "They are not human, Doctor," he said matter-of-factly.

"If they're so damned concerned about population growth, why the hell don't they practice birth control?" said McCoy. "The—"

"Not now, Bones," snapped Kirk. "Spock, this . . . 'forced retirement,' as it were . . . how does it happen? And who decides who goes when? And don't they object to being terminated that way? It's Eminiar all over again. Fox is going to have *déjà vu.*"

"It's quite different, Captain," said Spock. "The Calligar are very spiritual—"

"Spiritual!" bellowed McCoy. "They march into death—"

"Bones, shut up!" Kirk said in exasperation. "Spock—"

Spock, from long practice, seemed to pay no attention to McCoy at all. "They believe in continuing to exist as one with their surroundings long after their bodies have ceased, and they have put that belief into actual practice. A Calligarian does not die in the traditional sense. Once he or she is selected for 'thinning'—the term for being removed from the population pool and placed instead into the mind pool—his or her essence is removed and placed within a vast network, which they term the Worldmind. It is their equivalent of heaven, except while theologians argue over the nature of heaven, the Calligarians have fashioned it. Everything that the thinned individual knows, remembers, and has experienced becomes a part of the Worldmind, a vast computer network that is based in a satellite city at the Southern Pole of the planet. The living may access the Worldmind at any time, and indeed, according to what Dr. Daystrom has said, they can spend many hours simply communing with the minds and thoughts of their departed brethren."

"It's insane," said McCoy.

Spock raised an eyebrow. "No, Doctor. It is crossing the gap between living and dying. There is no end to the life of a Calligarian. He simply continues to serve society in a different manner. The Worldmind is linked with most facets of the Worldnet. After many centuries of its use, the Calligar even have a low-level telepathic sense of it when they're not in direct communion with it. From that sense of unity comes their philosophy of being part of a great whole. And it is the Worldmind that, as part of that perpetual communion, decides who has reached his or her peak and will be thinned."

"And Ecma was scheduled for thinning," said Kirk.

"So it would appear," Spock said. "And she, apparently, balked at the notion."

"I can't say I blame her," said McCoy.

"Spock," Kirk said, "here's what I want you to do—"

And suddenly Scotty shouted something in alarm, and Spock turned to him and then back to Kirk. "Captain," he said with his usual sangfroid, "I believe we are about to encounter some difficulty."

And then there was the sound of something being smashed, and Kirk could see the crew of the shuttlecraft reacting to something.

And then the image of the shuttlecraft interior vanished, leaving the mocking image of the rift, hanging as always in the depths of space.

Chapter Twenty-One

"So IT WOULD APPEAR," Spock said, "and she, apparently, balked at the notion."

Scott was only partially paying attention as he heard Dr. McCoy make some sort of sardonic reply. For his attention had been caught by an instrument reading that he should have noticed earlier, except that his attention was being distracted by the bickering of Thak and Dorkin toward the rear of the shuttlecraft.

According to the lift indicator, they were over two hundred pounds heavier now than when they had first taken off from the *Enterprise*. That made no sense, particularly since they had unloaded all their gear, which should have made them lighter, not . . .

And then Scott realized what was wrong. "Mr. Spock!" he shouted.

Kirk was just saying, "Here's what I want you to do," but Spock could not fully concentrate because Scotty was bellowing, "Someone must be hanging on to the hull! We're not clear!"

Spock digested this piece of information, turned back to Kirk, and said, "Captain, I believe we are about to encounter some difficulty."

And at that moment a pointed metal rod slammed into the front window from overhead.

Amazingly, the sturdy front view window ribboned with weblike cracks. Spock had a quick flash of Macro's face from overhead, on the roof of the shuttle, and then the rod smashed down once more. The window exploded inward, sending needle-sharp pieces hurtling through the interior of the shuttlecraft.

Scotty desperately angled the shuttlecraft steeply downward, and from overhead Macro started to slide off. But his hand snagged the underside of the frame, and he swung his legs through the now-empty screen. With one large foot he smashed the engineer in the face. The world spun around Scott, and he slumped forward onto the controls.

Spock rerouted the shuttle control to his own console, but now Macro had insinuated himself through the window completely, and he stood facing Spock, roaring. He swung the rod at Spock.

And without looking, Spock caught his arm at the wrist. "Shondar Dorkin," he called, his forearm trembling slightly at the strain but otherwise betraying no difficulty whatsoever, "if you wouldn't mind."

Dorkin unbelted himself from his seat in a heartbeat and lunged forward with a roar. Daystrom clung helplessly to his, and Thak's eyes widened in amusement as the Tellarite jumped into his element.

Dorkin, with an unrestrained howl, drove a furious roundhouse punch to Macro's chin, snapping his head back, and Spock released his grip on Macro's wrist so that he could concentrate on keeping them airborne. As he kept the shuttle on course with his left hand he started reconnecting the subspace communication

218

with his right, tossing off a quick glance at Scott to ascertain the extent of the engineer's injury.

And then there was a truncated roar, and Spock turned just in time to see Macro grabbing the Tellarite's throat, about to bring the rod slamming down on his head. But Thak was on his feet now, and he lunged toward the struggling pair as the shuttle took another sudden lurch. He stumbled forward, smashing into them from behind, and the three of them collided with Spock. Under the weight of the three bodies the Vulcan was almost shoved out of his chair. As it was, he lost his grip on the controls, and the shuttlecraft angled straight toward the ground.

Spock tried to bring his arms up to take Macro out with the Vulcan nerve pinch, but they were pinned beneath the crush of bodies. The Tellarite was bellowing Tellarian obscenities, the Andorian was hissing furiously, and Macro was shouting at the top of his lungs, almost drowning out Shondar Dorkin.

Arms and legs twisted and writhed, and Thak found himself staring down the business end of the rod. Its fierce, pointed end was directed right at his face, and he could see that the end was gleaming with hardened sharpness. It would go right through his head, and Macro, in the throes of the struggle, drove the rod toward his face.

And then a furry paw shot upward, deflecting the thrust just to the left of Thak's head. The rod went directly into the controls, circuitry blowing out and sparks flying.

The directional control shut down, and the shuttlecraft fell like a crippled sparrow. The air whistled around them, and the interior of the shuttle was filled with yelling and howling.

Spock, determined to make one final effort to avert disaster, gathered his strength and shoved at whatever body parts were available. The weight was suddenly off him, and he sat up, yanked the rod out of the controls, and tossed it aside. One look told him that it was hopeless. A second look told him that a crash was imminent, because the ground was screaming up at them.

There was no time for subtlety. "Crash positions!" he shouted, making himself heard over the hullaba-loo, and again "Crash positions!"

Down, down plunged the shuttlecraft, and still Macro was locked in battle with the Tellarite. "Shondar!" Spock called. "Macro! This is futile! We are about to strike the ground! You will both die unless you cease hostilities immediately!" Even as he spoke he buckled himself in.

Thak heard and tried to rip the combatants apart but received a fierce shove from Dorkin, who yelled, "This is between this arrogant fool and me!" and sent the Andorian stumbling back to his seat.

Spock was about to get to his feet again and then saw that there was no more time. He also saw that Mr. Scott, unconscious, was still not strapped in. He lunged over, pulling at his own restraint, and snapped Scott's in place. The belts were not standard issue but had been added to this shuttle when the warp sled was attached, in anticipation of possible hazardous condi-tions. Spock made a mental note to suggest that they be installed in all shuttlecraft, and then the ship hit the ground.

And to the horror of all in the shuttle, Dorkin and Macro were thrown right through the space in the front of the shuttle. Then they were gone, and sudden-ly the remaining crewmen found themselves taking a ride straight to hell.

The shuttle flipped over and over again, hurtling across the ground accompanied by a crash of metal and an earsplitting shriek of a human—specifically, Richard Daystrom. Sparks flew all around them, and Spock heard a rip and a snap that told him one of the warp sled nacelles had been shorn off.

The shuttlecraft barrel-rolled once more and then slowly, painfully creaked to a stop. It was sideways.

There was a moment of uneasy silence, and then Spock called, "Is everyone intact?"

"Dorkin!" the Andorian was shouting. "He was thrown out! At the speed we were going—"

"I am aware of that," said Spock as he quickly unbelted himself. After giving Scott a cursory glance he hurried to the Andorian, who was trying to pry loose his restraint. Spock pulled at it, found that it was jammed, and with a quick motion snapped the belt in half, freeing Thak.

Thak quickly made his way toward the front of the shuttle, for the exit door was on the side of the shuttle flattened against the ground. The front window was the only means of egress.

Thak shoved through the window and vanished around the other side of the shuttlecraft. Moments later Spock had freed Daystrom and had brought Scott to consciousness. Scotty looked around the shuttlecraft and, instead of inquiring as to the welfare of the other passengers, moaned softly, "Ach . . . muh poor ship."

Making sure that no one had broken bones or serious injuries, Spock, Scott, and Daystrom made their way out of the shuttlecraft.

Fortunately, the shuttlecraft had happened upon large, unoccupied area. Either that, or the thought-responsive city had managed to clear the way for them with no problem.

Macro was crouched on the field, shaking his head, apparently none the worse for wear. The physical endurance of the Calligarians was clearly far beyond anything that the Federation had previously suspected. They could be slowed, they could be hurt, they could even be stopped, but apparently their ability to bounce back from injury was unparalleled among any race that Spock had encountered before. Still, the wind was clearly knocked out of him, and Macro could do little but glare at Spock and the others as they ran past.

A significant number of Calligarians was approaching from the other direction. Apparently they were the same ones who had been pursuing them earlier, and Spock came to the unpleasant conclusion that they had, in fact, wound up flying in a tremendous circle.

All of that, however, was secondary to the unmoving form of Shondar Dorkin lying on the ground, Thak the Andorian crouched next to him. Spock, Scotty, and Daystrom slowed as they saw the hideous angle at which Dorkin's body was lying. His back was clearly broken.

Dorkin was gasping, his thick fur matted with black blood, and he was looking up at Thak. "Idiot," he murmured. "I had to hold up . . . your end and mine . . . in the fight."

"You stopped him from killing me," said Thak in wonderment. "You saved my life."

Dorkin coughed and spat out a thick glob of black, viscous fluid. "You were . . . in my way . . . that's all." Then he shivered. "It's . . . cold."

"Shhh . . . lie still. You're going to be all right," said Thak, but he looked hopelessly up at the others.

The Tellarite's body was trembling, and he murmured, "Look, Andorian . . . do one thing for me . . . and don't botch it."

"What, Shondar?"

"Tell my wives . . . and offspring . . . that I took

222

about . . . a dozen or so of these bastards . . . with me."

His piggish eyes seemed to recede for a moment, and then they rolled up into the top of his head. A soft breath escaped him that had an odd, singular rattle to it.

And then he was gone.

Chapter Twenty-Two

THE ATMOSPHERE IN THE briefing room of the *Enterprise* was extremely tense.

"Jim, you can't possibly be serious," said McCoy. "It's crazy. It's suicide!"

"If I were dead for every time that I ostensibly committed suicide, Doctor, I'd've died several hundred times by now," Kirk said patiently.

"The doctor is correct, sir," Sulu said. "It's far too great a risk for you to take. If anyone should go, then it should be me."

"As what?" Kirk said. "The most expedient of my junior officers?"

"Junior officers!" snorted McCoy. "For God's sake, Jim, get a grip on reality. Junior? Sulu there is in line for his own command, and he'll probably get one before you know it. So is Uhura. So is Chekov, a couple years down the line. We're not kids anymore, Jim. None of us is. And you going off to the rescue on some headstrong damned fool crusade is sheer lunacy."

"Suicidal. Lunatic." Kirk actually smiled slightly. "Why don't you just declare me unfit for command, Doctor?"

"How about if I just declare you unfit to have a sensible conversation with?"

"Captain, may I speak frankly?" asked Sulu. And when Kirk nodded slightly, Sulu continued with a slight edge to his voice. "You asked us here to solicit our opinions. Our opinions are unanimous in this respect. And yet I have the feeling that you're going to do what you've decided to do anyway. May I ask, sir, why you requested this conference in the first place, if you intended to ignore our advice all along?"

Kirk's eyes narrowed. "The doctor, it would seem, is correct. In the old days, Mr. Sulu, you would not have addressed me in that manner."

"It's only because I would like there to be new days to come," replied Sulu. "Captain, revised Starfleet procedures clearly state that the ship's captain is not to put him or herself into any unnecessary danger."

"And it is up to me to decide, Mr. Sulu, what is necessary." Kirk slowly surveyed the room. "The contact team, including two of our own, is being held on the other side. We are running out of time. The rift will seal itself off at a maximum of eighteen hours from now—and that's if nothing unexpected happens to disrupt the temporal waves. Also, we have been told repeatedly that the Calligar have tremendous respect for authority figures. Commanding officers. We have been trying to raise the Calligar for . . ." He looked questioningly at Uhura.

"The last hour, sir," she admitted.

"The last hour. And after the initial reply—'There will be no discussion until the Master Builder is returned to us'—we haven't heard from them. That does not sound promising. Therefore, it is my belief that the only way I'm going to be able to get our people out is to go in person."

"No," said McCoy fiercely. "You think you're some sort of knight, riding your white horse to save the day. There's a damsel in distress down in sick bay. There are fellow knights trapped by an evil wizard. And you're going to mount your proud white charger and gallop forward, your lance at the ready, prepared to smite down anyone who'll stand in the way of your completing your great and noble mission. Who cares about the danger or the wisdom of it? Sir Galahad, cloaked in righteousness, will triumph over them all!"

Kirk stared at McCoy and then nodded slowly. "That seems a fair assessment," he said. Then he reached over and tapped a comm button. "Shuttle Bay, prepare the remaining shuttle with warp sled."

"We'll have it prepped in ten minutes, Captain," came the reply.

"Good." Kirk started to rise.

McCoy, gesturing in frustration, said, "Didn't any of what I just said get through to you?"

"All of it, Doctor," replied Kirk. "And I can't deny any of it. And I can't deny my men, either. I can't separate myself from what and who I am . . . that's one rift that will never be created. See?" he added with a wink. "More irony."

McCoy grumbled as Chekov now said, "Keptin . . . you'll require someone to assist you in the piloting of the wessel . . ."

"You mean a squire," came a voice from the doorway.

They turned to find José Tyler standing there, smiling lopsidedly. He was studying his hands. "Navigator José Tyler reporting for duty, sir."

"Commodore," began Kirk.

"Consider it an order, Captain," said Tyler firmly.

"I've never been one to be obsessive about rank—indeed, that's probably an attitude that's held me back to some degree. But this time I give you no choice. I'm coming along with you, or I close up this little junket of yours and bust you so far down that you'll have to tunnel your way upward for three days just to see daylight. Do you read me, Captain?"

"Yes, sir," said Kirk without blinking an eye. He crossed to Tyler, turned to his subordinates, and said, "Mr. Sulu, you have the conn. Furthermore, in case you decide to emulate your crackbrained captain and his crazed heroics, I am giving you a direct order: No matter what happens, you are not to come after me. I will not have you putting this ship at risk."

"I'll keep her safe for you, sir."

Kirk nodded and then added, "Tallyho."

No one smiled.

Settling in at the controls of the shuttlecraft, Kirk and Tyler quickly and efficiently did the last-minute flight checks. Tyler whistled the 1812 Overture softly, and then he paused while continuing with the check procedures and said, "Your crew obviously thinks very highly of you and is extremely fond of you."

"Why do you say that?" asked Kirk.

"Because only a crew that feels that way about their commanding officer could get quite so pissed off with him."

Kirk nodded in embarrassed agreement. "I can be a very irritating individual. I'm amazed any of them has stuck with me for so long."

"You command loyalty among your people. You're very fortunate."

"It drives them crazy when I take it in my head to go running off to rescue one of them."

"Perhaps that's why they're loyal to you. Because

they know that you are the type of person who will risk everything for them. You are dedicated enough to them, and to your own ideals, that you will lay yourself on the line. As you have, time and time again."

"A cowboy," said Kirk.

"A knight."

Kirk nodded and informed the shuttle bay that they were ready to depart, and the shuttlecraft lifted off the hangar bay floor. A moment later the shuttle was sailing out of the hangar bay and angling toward the rift.

"Bring us around," said Kirk.

"Coming around, heading 103 mark 2," said Tyler, laying in the course. He smiled. "The old reflexes. It all comes right back to you."

Kirk surveyed Tyler's handling of the instruments and nodded approvingly. "Solid work. You'll go far."

"All the way to the other side of the rift," said Tyler. "Preparing for warp drive."

"Joe," said Kirk after a moment, "has it occurred to you that in order to pull this off I'm going to have to accomplish one of two things? Either I have to convince the Calligar to release the contact team out of the goodness of their hearts, or else I have to talk them out of thinning Ecma so that the threat to her is gone. And if that happens, she might not want to stay with you."

"That has occurred to me, yes," said Tyler evenly.

"Does that concern you?"

Tyler looked at him evenly. "Getting our people out of there without compromising our promises is what concerns me. That's all. The rest I'll gladly leave to the fates to decide."

"The fates," said Kirk, "can be singularly nasty. Life is often unfair."

"Of course it is," replied Tyler. "After all, no one gets out alive."

On the bridge of the *Enterprise* Sulu watched from the command chair, his face unreadable, as the shuttlecraft dwindled, kicked into warp drive, and vanished into the rift.

More than anything, despite whatever disciplinary actions might be taken later, Sulu would dearly have loved to send the *Enterprise* leaping through the rift as well. After all, the Calligar might very well change their tune with the full power of a starship staring down their throats.

But that, he knew, would be a singularly bad idea. The projected stability of a temporal rift was delicate enough. To disrupt the timestream flux with the power of the main warp engines—considerably larger and far more spatially distorting than the far smaller warp sled propulsion on the shuttlecraft—would risk having the entire ship and crew trapped light-years away from home. They would not make it back to earth in the crew's lifetime, if at all.

He could not take that chance.

And then he was immediately snapped out of his thoughts when Chekov suddenly said, "Commander Sulu, sensors are detecting a wessel entering the area."

He waited for the computer to feed through identification of the ship's design. "An Andorian class D-3 ship," he said after a moment.

"Open a frequency," said Sulu quickly. "We have to lay down the ground rules immediately. Andorian ship, come in please. This is Sulu, in command of the *Enterprise.*"

Subspace crackled for a moment as the Andorian vessel grew closer on the screen. Long and sleek, it was a nasty-looking piece of work. A moment later the

Andorian commander came on the screen. His chin was a bit more squared than Thak's, his eyes a bit more canny. "This is Vandar, commanding the *Stealth*. We have been alerted to difficulty in regard to our representative, Thak."

"There is a difficulty," said Sulu, "that is true. However, we have a negotiating team on the scene, and we anticipate all will be equitably worked out."

Vandar seemed to consider that a moment. "Very well, *Enterprise*," he said in that soft, sibilant hiss. "For the moment we will take no action. But we must be kept apprised of—"

"Another wessel, Commander!" said Sulu. "Coming in at—"

Before he could even get the full warning out a gruff and angry voice cut into the audio. "This is Khund of the Tellarite vessel *Belligerent*."

"They certainly believe in truth in advertising," observed Uhura drolly.

The viewscreen split in two, and the face of an irritated Tellarite—and it was becoming more and more evident that that was the only way that Tellarites ever appeared—came up on the screen. "We have learned," he said, "of the unprovoked, heinous attack upon one of our representatives. We demand to know what action is being taken."

Deciding to play matters safely, Sulu repeated virtually word for word what he had said to Vandar.

Khund's response was predictable.

"Some weak-kneed Federation peace-lover is negotiating for the release of our representative?" bellowed the Tellarite. "Who do these Calligar think they are? By what right do they make demands on us and hold one of our Shondars as prisoner? We're going to go in and put a stop to it!"

"We cannot allow that," said Sulu firmly.

"You cannot *allow!*" snarled Khund. "You puny Starfleet officer—"

That was when the turbolift opened and Ambassador Fox, wearing anti-gravity boots that came up to mid-thigh and relieved the pressure on his legs, appeared on the bridge. Sulu, maintaining his rapidly waning patience, said, "Ambassador, this is not the time—"

But Fox turned to him and said in no uncertain terms, "No, Commander, this is precisely the time. With your permission." And then, before Sulu could object, he faced the screen and said, "Khund—and Vandar, for that matter—you're not facing simply the capricious whims of a Starfleet officer. The *Enterprise* is the jurisdictional vessel here, assigned that status not only by Starfleet, but by the Federation. If you cross *Enterprise,* or provoke her, or in any way do anything to upset the delicate situation that has developed here, you'll have the full weight and discipline of the Federation Council brought down on you. I, as their official representative, can assure you of that. That includes the ire of your respective governments and their delegates, with whom I met just last week, and with whom I am on excellent terms. And if you give Commander Sulu any difficulty, I will personally prevail on those noble delegates to see to it that your next assignment will be commanding the lithium-cracking station on Delta Vega. Is that understood?"

Vandar, who knew the remarks were not really addressed to him, simply smiled and said, "Understood."

Khund, to whom the remarks *were* addressed, didn't realize it and assumed that they were being made in order to scare the craven Andorian. He simply said, "Understood."

231

"*Enterprise* out," said Sulu gratefully. The moment they vanished he turned to Fox and said, "Ambassador, that was much appreciated. Especially considering that your making public the situation is what brought them here in the first place."

"Captain Kirk mentioned that to you, did he?" said Fox. He shrugged. "I was doing my job then, Commander. And I was doing it now. That's a simple truth that your captain apparently finds difficult to comprehend. Perhaps you can explain it to him some time— assuming he returns in one piece from doing *his* job."

Chapter Twenty-Three

KIRK WALKED INTO the council chamber, Tyler directly behind him, and the captain felt as if he were under scrutiny from everyone on the planet. Even though there were only several dozen Calligar surrounding the perimeter, watching from high-backed chairs, he sensed that there were far more present, and far more at stake.

In a corner of the room were Spock, Scott, Daystrom, and Thak. Thak looked the most shaken; Spock had informed Kirk of the death of Shondar Dorkin and the profound effect it seemed to have had on the Andorian. A member of a race driven by an awareness of indebtedness, Thak was obviously at odds with his assessment of Dorkin's uselessness, which had been undercut by Dorkin's saving of Thak's life. For an Andorian, being indebted to someone whom you could never repay was a little piece of hell.

Alt was seated there, as was Macro, plus various other Calligarians that they didn't know. It didn't seem to matter particularly about the others—these two were clearly running the show.

"You are the commander?" asked Alt. "The leader?"

"Yes," said Kirk. He stepped forward. "And I'm here to—"

"He is not the leader," snarled Macro.

Kirk fixed a gaze on him and said slowly, "I cannot say I appreciate being interrupted."

But Macro was paying no attention. Instead he had risen from his place and come around to face Commodore José Tyler, who was standing thirty feet away. Macro stood, relaxed and ready, his arms at his side. "It has been a long time, Tyler."

Tyler looked to Kirk, for they had agreed that Kirk was to be spokesman. But Kirk merely nodded in Tyler's direction. Tyler shrugged. "Yes. It has." Tyler's manner showed polite interest, but nothing more.

"It is because of you," said Macro, "that this has happened. Because of you that Ecma left me."

"Me?" said Tyler in amusement. "I'm not the one who developed this philosophy of thinning."

A number of the Calligar visibly winced, and Macro said angrily, "It's obscene to hear the word spoken by other than a Calligar."

"That's fine," Thak interjected. His voice was laced with contempt. "We consider it an obscenity when spoken by anyone."

"The Master Builder is terrified of the fate that awaits her," Kirk said. "If you are a civilized people, you'll—"

"Don't hold us to your standards of civilized," snapped Macro. "How typical of your self-satisfaction that you presume to judge us. And you"—he was speaking again to Tyler—"you are the one who influenced Ecma to fear the honor of thinning."

"The *honor?*"

234

"The last and greatest reward that a Calligarian can aspire to," Alt now said.

"I had nothing to do with it," said Tyler. "Ecma wanted out entirely on her own."

"You *lie!*" said Macro fiercely. "You did something to her. What I would give to ram those lying words down your throat . . ."

Kirk saw it coming. "Commodore, careful," he warned.

But Tyler didn't care. "You want a piece of me, don't you, Macro? Ever since I beat you years ago. You've thought about it, dreamed about it." He struck a defensive posture, poised on the balls of his feet, the edges of his fists ready to strike. "Dreamed about getting your hands on me, settling this between the two of us. So that's what we'll do. You and me, right now. We settle it, one way or the other. What do you say?"

"Macro," cautioned Alt. "You can—"

But Macro wasn't paying attention. Years of jealousy, of hatred, of fury that had built up now came pouring out. The great hall was awash with outrage, as deep and as foul as an ocean of bile.

"*The two of us, then!*" shouted Macro. "*To the finish!*"

He charged straight toward Tyler, hands flexing, ready to dig his large fingers into Tyler's body and rip him apart.

And José Tyler calmly pulled out his phaser and shot Macro down while he was still twenty paces away.

The force of Macro's charge carried him a couple of extra feet, but he was unconscious during the skid. He wound up at Tyler's feet, and the commodore smiled down at him. "Works every time, *Pendejo*," he said. And then he looked up at Alt. "So can we leave now?"

"I began to say," Alt informed him, "before Macro

235

interrupted me, and I quote: Macro, you cannot speak for us on this. The decision of thinning is made by the Worldmind. It is irrevocable. If Ecma returns, she must submit to it. If she does not, we will not permit any of your people to leave."

"This is unacceptable," Kirk said.

"No, Captain. We are simply certain that you will not leave your friends and associates behind in favor of one woman. It is an inequitable situation and solution, and one for which we doubt you will settle."

Slowly Kirk turned and studied the assemblage.

"Is this what the proud Calligar come to, then?" he asked. "Bartering hostages for the life and freedom of a young woman? Is this what you represent?"

"No, Captain," said Alt quietly. "This is the type of behavior historically typical of your people. It would seem that you have had an unpleasant influence on us. We have had to descend to your level to deal with you."

"Deal with us?" said Kirk. "Why? Because we don't share your view about thinning? Because we find your attitude . . . distressing? Cavalier in its disregard for life?"

"Cavalier? We are a merciful people, Captain. We spare lives the pain of never matching their accomplishments. Our people accept that."

"How could they?" demanded Kirk. "Who could reasonably say that they'd want to die and give up hope of ever surpassing their previous accomplishments?"

"I would."

To Kirk's shock, the words had not come from a Calligarian.

They had been spoken by Dr. Richard Daystrom.

Daystrom stepped forward, looking even older than he had before. "They're right, Captain. They are."

"Doctor . . ."

But Daystrom continued to talk, and it didn't even seem as if he was aware that Kirk was standing there. That anyone was there. "It would have been a blessing," he said distantly. "If someone had come to me and shown me, after my first quarter of a century in this universe—if they'd come to me and said, 'Look. Look at the pointlessness of the rest of your life. Look at the tries and failures, the breakdown, the frustrations that will be yours—yours and no one else's. No one to share them. No one to care for you, or about you. A lifetime of feeble attempts to recreate the glory."

Not unkindly, aware of the man's personal grief— not to mention his precarious mental condition— Kirk said, "Please, Dr. Daystrom . . . you're not helping."

Daystrom looked at him for a moment, refocused, and then seemed to lock onto Kirk's presence. He sighed, his chest trembling, and said, "My . . . apologies, Captain."

"He has nothing to apologize for," Alt said softly. "He is simply elevated enough to understand what every Calligarian already does. What is the point of taking up society's resources for a life that has reached its point of anticlimax?"

"Because," said Kirk with firm authority, "you risk missing the unexpected twist towards the end of the second act."

He stepped over the unconscious body of Macro and raised his voice to address everyone rather than simply Alt. "With all due respect to all of you, we're going in circles here. We have reached a stalemate. And I see only one way to break it."

"And that would be . . ."

"I wish to commune directly with the Worldmind."

If Kirk had suddenly blown his brains out before the assemblage, he could not have gotten a more

237

surprised reaction. There was a rush of muttering that followed Kirk's request, and then Alt said loudly, "That would be . . . unwise."

"Perhaps," said Kirk. "But you've said that the Worldmind made the decision. Therefore, it seems that only the Worldmind can settle this matter. Ecma feels that she has more to do, that her life has not reached its peak. She wants more time to attain her accomplishments. She should have that right. And if the Worldmind is the entity that wants to deprive her of that right, then that's whom I have to address."

"You do not understand, Captain. You do not have the mental discipline that even Calligarian children have."

"And Calligarian children," replied Kirk, "do not have the years of experience I have."

"We cannot allow it, Captain. You have no idea what you would be facing. To let you go would be tantamount to allowing you to kill yourself."

"I see," said Kirk sardonically. "How thoughtful that you have more concern for an outsider than for the life of one of your own people."

But now Spock stepped forward. "Master of the Status," he said, "am I correct in assuming that I, as a Vulcan, would have the proper mental discipline to withstand communing with the Worldmind?"

Alt glanced at him appraisingly. "We have had many years to study what we gleaned of Vulcans from our first encounter, Mr. Spock. I believe that you would be able to cope with the mental demands. But that is—"

"Then, with the captain's permission, I wish to be the spokesman for the Master Builder."

Kirk quickly crossed to the Vulcan and spoke to him in a low voice. "Spock, you've been over here most of the time. You hardly even *know* Ecma."

238

Spock raised a sardonic eyebrow. "Knowing the individual in question is irrelevant, sir. What is important is the concept—the value of free will versus predestination. A gulf in ideological discussion that has separated philosphers for centuries. A rift, if you will, much like the one that brought us to this pass. Do you not find that ironic, Captain?"

At that Kirk actually had to smile. "No. Contrived."

"What is required here," continued Spock, "is an exercise in logic and debate. With all due respect, Captain, if debate and logic are required, sending a human to do a Vulcan's job would be—"

"Illogical," said Kirk.

"Totally," agreed Spock.

"I suppose you're old enough to know what you're doing."

"Indeed. In point of fact, I am old enough to know better. But I wish to do it nevertheless. It will be . . . fascinating."

McCoy entered sick bay and walked over to Ecma's bed. To his surprise, Ecma's eyes were open, and she was staring up at him in some confusion. He quickly glanced up at her bioreadings and was pleased to see that they were stable. He looked back down at her and said, "Welcome back."

She licked her lips. "Why does my mouth taste so bad?"

"The, uhm, contents of your stomach vacated rather forcefully some hours ago," said McCoy.

"Oh, dear," she said, sounding remote. "When? Where?"

"Right after the captain shouted at you about fighting. On myself and the captain."

"I'm—I'm so sorry."

"Don't worry about it," McCoy said gamely. "In my case it comes with the territory. In the captain's case . . . it looked good on him."

"You must hate him," said Ecma in wonderment. "He and Mr. Spock. You're always insulting them."

McCoy glanced right and left to make sure no one was listening and then, in a low voice, said, "Of course not. People that I hate, I just ignore. Kirk and Spock I . . . " His jaw flexed for a moment, and then he said, "I put up with their foolishness. After all, without me looking out for them, they'd have woken up dead a long time ago."

"I understand," she said softly. "For my mouth . . . could I . . ."

"Oh. Of course. Where are my manners?" He went to the food slot and punched in a quick code, and a glass of shimmering clear liquid was produced. "Here," he said, handing it to her. "Since I was wearing some genuine Calligarian food, I took the liberty of having the computer analyze it. Derived the basic building blocks of your nutrition from it, and I took the liberty of programming it into our food system. You can eat human food, but this should taste more like what you're accustomed to."

She took the glass gratefully and drained the contents in one gulp. Wiping her mouth, she held it up and said hopefully, "More?"

McCoy smiled. "Can't ask for a better review than that." He returned to the food dispenser and came back with two more glasses. She drank the second immediately and nursed the third. "How are you feeling?"

She stared off into space. "Empty," she said in puzzlement. "I feel . . . very empty. It's . . . it's a little frightening."

"I'm not surprised," said McCoy. "You were so
240

linked with your people—with their philosophies, with your society—that withdrawing made you physically and mentally ill. I believe you'll be all right now, though."

"I feel so . . . so alone." She trembled slightly. "How do you . . . how do you stand it?"

He put a comforting arm around her and said, "We seek out others, and we try to pull one another through. That's all any of us can do."

"Joe. Where is Joe? And Captain Kirk?"

McCoy hesitated, unsure of whether to tell her so soon after she had come to, but she sensed that he was holding something back and clutched his forearm agitatedly. "Tell me," she insisted.

"They've gone through the rift," said McCoy. "They're trying to convince the Calligar to let you go."

"They'll never do that," said Ecma. "Never."

"Well, your people have said that they won't release Spock, Scotty, and the others until such time as we return you."

Her eyes widened. "They can't!"

"Apparently they can."

"I"—her eyes were wide, her voice quavering—"I never thought that . . . I never realized what they might do."

"Chances are, neither did the captain, or he might not have been so quick to grant your request," said McCoy ruefully. "I don't think he counted on all of you being so attuned to one another that they would sense your sudden attempt to break away from them. How come they didn't know you were thinking of running off in the first place?"

"We're not mind readers," she said, "except in times when we're directly in communion with the Worldmind." She stopped, surprised that she had

241

mentioned it so casually, and whispered, "I—I really am separate from them now." Then, forcing herself back on track, she said, "Shifts of thought pattern, that sort of thing—those are our private thoughts. But when I made a decision to break away, that was a determination so profound that it got the attention of the Worldmind and caused—"

"Your withdrawal pains," said McCoy. "I understand."

"I cannot believe that they would resort to that," Ecma said.

"Well, what did you think they would do?" demanded McCoy.

"I don't know! I had not even truly decided that breaking away was what I was going to do! It's unprecedented, Doctor. You have to understand that. Part of it was desperation, and the rest was just pure spur of the moment."

McCoy sighed heavily. "Well, whatever it was, the captain gave his word, and he's not going to break it. He's there fighting for you now, charging on his horse."

"His horse?"

"Never mind."

"But—but what could he possibly do? How could he convince them of something about which they will never be convinced?"

McCoy thought a moment. "This Worldmind of yours makes the determinations about when you die?"

"Yes," she said in a small voice. "I am scheduled for thinning two days from now."

"All right, then. Knowing Jim as I do, the chances are he's going to want to talk directly to this Worldmind of yours."

"*No!*" she cried out in alarm. "No, he can't! This is too much! Your people being held prisoner, the captain risking himself—this can't go on! I have to go back!"

She tried to sit up, and McCoy grabbed her by the shoulders. "You can't!" he said. "We have no other shuttles that can withstand the rift!"

"My ship can! The one I came in!"

McCoy blinked. "I'll be damned. I forgot about that."

"Where is it?"

"Right where you left it, I presume. Next to the *Enterprise.*"

"Tell them I'm coming back."

"No," said McCoy. And before she could protest further he continued, "It's not up to me. We have to talk to Mr. Sulu about it. No one enters or exits a starship without permission from the commanding officer. You want to go back, no one's going to force you to stay—but we clear it through him. Now, just wait here. I'm going to get you your clothes, and then we'll get things sorted out."

He headed for the closet where Ecma's clothes had been hung, stopping only to tap on the comm unit. "Sick bay to bridge."

"Bridge," came Sulu's voice.

"Commander," said McCoy, feeling a little tired, "I have some interesting news for you. After all this brouhaha, you're going to love this."

The huge building was as cavernous as Daystrom remembered it. He glanced at the others and saw that they were impressed as well. In the dimness the ceiling of the communion center seemed so far away as to be nonexistent. The individual beams of light that shone down during communion, to a more fanciful individual than the scientific Daystrom, could have been rays directly from the eyes of God.

Unlike before, however, no one was standing in the

cones of light. In fact, there were no cones of light except one single, solitary beam. All of the other Calligar had been removed.

"A Calligarian," Alt had explained, "is capable of screening out, or allowing in, the thoughts of others as he or she chooses. Since you may lack that facility, we have endeavored to simplify matters by making sure that all our people are 'off line,' as you might put it. It will be you and the Worldmind, Mr. Spock."

"I thank you for your indulgence," Spock said graciously.

"I will admit," said Alt, "to a certain degree of curiosity as to what the Worldmind will say in response to you. I have been raised to accept and believe certain things. Only the most closed-minded of individuals will refuse even to speculate as to what might happen if another philosophy were to enter their sphere. This will be . . . interesting."

"I shall endeavor to be challenging," replied Spock.

He approached the beam of light, and Kirk followed closely until Alt said loudly, "Captain, have a care. The moment an individual steps into the light he is in communion. Best to keep a distance."

Kirk glanced back at Alt, and at the assemblage of Calligarians behind him. Then he looked back to Spock. "We're an interesting experiment for them, aren't we, Spock?"

"So it would appear," replied Spock. "But any experiment can yield surprising results."

Kirk put a hand on Spock's shoulder. "Be careful."

"Naturally."

Spock turned and faced the white light. The silence was that of a sunrise in a desert. There was no heat from the light. It was simply there, purity and truth, bridging the gap between the real world and the world of the mind.

For Spock, who was accustomed to striding multiple worlds every day in his continuing fusion of Vulcan and human influences, did not find it intimidating in the least.

Without another word he stepped into the light.

His back was to Kirk and the others, and the captain waited apprehensively for . . . what? He didn't know. Some sign. Some word from Spock. Some display. Something.

He sensed, directly behind him, Dr. Daystrom. In a very low voice, as if whispering in a church, Daystrom said, "Captain, I wish to apologize for earlier."

"No apology required, Doctor," said Kirk, his eyes never leaving his first officer and friend.

"I feel as if I weakened your arguments to the Calligar with my ill-timed outburst. If there is any way I can make it up to you—"

"I said it's all right, Doctor. Now, if you—"

And then Spock's back stiffened as if he'd been stabbed. His legs began to quiver, his fingers clenching into trembling fists.

There was a confused murmur from the Calligar, and Kirk shouted into the darkness, "What's happening?"

"I do not know!" called Alt. "He is encountering problems. It must be because he is not one of us."

And Spock suddenly twisted in place, his head snapping around, and to Kirk's horror, a trickle of green blood was running from Spock's mouth down over his chin. He had bitten clean through his lower lip.

"*Spock!*" shouted Kirk, and he lunged toward the Vulcan.

Daystrom dived at the captain, trying to stop his headlong rush. Now there was shouting from everyone, confused babbling.

The blood was pouring down Spock's face and onto his uniform shirt. His eyes were wide open and looked as though they were going to leap from his head.

"Let go of me!" shouted Kirk, and he shoved Daystrom away. And Daystrom tried to grab him again, throwing his full weight into the attempt.

Their legs became tangled up, and together Daystrom and Kirk fell headfirst into the beam.

Immediately their bodies stiffened, their faces frozen in a look of total surprise. And their minds leapt out of their bodies and flew away.

Chapter Twenty-four

SULU SAT IN THE COMMAND CHAIR, stroking his chin and regarding the shaken but nevertheless determined Calligarian woman in front of him. "After all this," he asked, trying to mask his annoyance, "after everything that's happened, now you've decided you want to go back?"

Ecma drew herself up. "I feel it's the only way to avoid further ill feelings and difficulties on my account."

"And if I send you back through the rift," said Sulu, "and while you're going through the captain returns with the contact team, how do you think he's going to feel about having gone through all of that for your sake, with you not even here?"

She glanced at McCoy, but the doctor simply shrugged. "I think," said Ecma, "that he will realize that I was trying to do what was best for all concerned, just as he was. I put it to you another way, Commander. How would *you* feel if the captain, and Joe and all the rest, never returned, and your letting me return to my people could have saved them?"

Now it was Sulu's turn to look at McCoy, but once again the *Enterprise* chief medical offer was silent. The message was clear: This was a command decision.

There was no reason to rush into things, though. There was still time, although it was dwindling rapidly. "Uhura, put me through to the Calligar," said Sulu. "Let's see if they'll talk to us now."

She nodded and sent out a subspace hail into the heart of the rift. Nearby, on the screen, were the waiting vessels of the Andorians and Tellarites. They had kept their counsel all this time, but their continued presence served to remind Sulu of exactly the amount of difficulty that they were in. This entire business was going to have to be handled with a great deal of tact.

In a low voice Uhura said, "You do realize that they'll probably be monitoring the conversation. Should I scramble—"

"No," said Sulu. "They'll know we're talking to the Calligar, and if we try and cover it, it will just irritate them further."

"Especially the Tellarites," noted McCoy. "They were born irritable."

"You're on, Mr. Sulu," said Uhura after a moment.

"This is Sulu, in command of the *Enterprise,*" he said.

The screen shifted, and a Calligarian appeared. To Sulu's surprise, he actually seemed to be upset about something. Well, this should cheer them up a bit, he thought. "This is Stanzia of the Calligar," he said.

"Your Master Builder has stated"—Sulu gave her a quick look, and she nodded, her jaw set—"that she has no wish for further difficulties between our peoples. She has stated that she is willing to return to the Calligar in exchange for the return of Commanders Spock and Scott, Shondar Dorkin, Dr. Daystrom, and Thak. Please relay this information to your leaders and to Captain Kirk and Commodore Tyler. We await your response."

"There may be a problem," said Stanzia uncertainly.

"What sort of problem?" asked Sulu.

"The problem being that it will not be possible to accommodate your request."

"I don't understand," Sulu said a trifle impatiently. "If we have agreed to your request for her return, there should be no prob—"

"The problem is," said Stanzia, "that Shondar Dorkin is dead, and Captain Kirk, Dr. Daystrom, and Commander Spock are trapped in communion and will, in all likelihood, die there. So you see, we cannot return them all. Will you settle for the survivors?"

"Oh, my God," whispered McCoy. Ecma was slack-jawed, and Sulu was cursing himself for not having scrambled the communication.

"Mister Sulu!" Chekov suddenly shouted in alarm. "The *Belligerent* is on course with the rift!"

"Uhura, cut the channel to the Calligar!" said Sulu. "Give me a line to the Tellarites! Chekov, move to intercept the *Belligerent*. All hands, red alert. Clear the bridge," he commanded McCoy and Ecma.

"I didn't mean—I didn't—" She was trying to get out, and then McCoy gently guided her into the turbolift.

"I've got the *Belligerent*," Uhura called over the alarm. "And Ambassador Fox wants to know if there's something he can do to help."

"Yes, he can sit on his thumb. *Enterprise* to *Belligerent*, come in, please."

The screen shifted, and there was the infuriated visage of Khund. "*Enterprise*, I will say this once: Get the hell out of our way."

"We cannot allow you to enter the rift. The fields of your warp drive will disrupt—"

"Why should we listen to you?" bellowed Khund. "You said you had everything in hand! That everything was under control! Well, it's not under control. The Shondar is dead, and every Tellarite aboard screams for vengeance!"

"Vengeance!" came the roars from behind Khund. "Vengeance!"

"I don't care if you're all screaming for ice cream," said Sulu sharply. "If you approach the rift, we will open fire."

Uhura turned and said, "Mr. Sulu, I have the *Stealth* on another channel. They are offering their support."

"And the Andorians will fire on you as well," Sulu said quickly.

"Their moral support," continued Uhura, "and they say they trust the *Enterprise* to be triumphant. They're moving out of range now."

"Give them our thanks for the vote of confidence," said Sulu.

"Commander, the *Belligerent* is on course for the rift. Estimate penetration in thirteen seconds."

"Fire a warning shot across their bow," said Sulu.

The *Enterprise* phasers lanced out, cutting just in front of the *Tellarite* ship and momentarily slowing its progress. In response the Tellarites suddenly changed course—more quickly than the larger and less maneuverable *Enterprise* could have—and banked hard around on the starship.

The phasers of the *Belligerent* roared to life, stabbing outward and striking the starship amidships. The *Enterprise* rocked under the assault.

The bridge shuddered as Sulu gripped the arms of the command chair. "Target their warp nacelles," he said grimly. "Photon torpedoes. Fire."

"Torpedoes fire," said Chekov.

The *Belligerent* came around fast, and the photon

torpedoes exploded against the shields just below the nacelles. The Tellarite ship was slowed for a moment, but then it regained strength and, with a daring U-turn, angled back across its tracks, dodging another set of phaser blasts as it screamed through the void toward the rift.

"Tractor beams!" shouted Sulu. "Grab them!"

The tractors pierced the darkness of space and momentarily snared the arcing Tellarite ship. But the tractors were designed for towing ships that, more often than not, were out of power—not for restraining vessels that were trying to escape. The tractors held on for barely a moment—enough time for Chekov to lock phasers on target—but by the time the mighty weapons of the *Enterprise* had fired, the *Belligerent* had ripped free of the tractor beams.

"Full phaser array!" shouted Sulu. "Fire!"

Phaser blasts bracketed the Tellarite ship, but Tellarites were nothing if not singleminded. The *Belligerent* sustained several vicious hits, and one of their rear deflector shields overloaded and burned out. But with Tellarites that was not enough. Not nearly enough.

And with a final, arrogant roar of engines notched up to warp five the *Belligerent* leaped into the rift and vanished.

There was dead silence on the bridge for a long moment, broken finally by two things. First was Lieutenant Newman, at the science station, reporting that sensors had detected a field disruption in the temporal structure of the rift, rendering it prematurely unstable. She estimated that, within ninety minutes if not sooner, it would collapse on itself.

The second was Uhura, reporting that the Andorians were calling to comment that they were sorely disappointed in the performance of the *Enterprise*. Sulu's response was not recorded.

Chapter Twenty-five

KIRK SAW NOTHING, and plenty of it.

And then everything came crashing down on him.

From everywhere, everywhere, sounds and images, millions of bits of information. It wasn't an attack. It was an assault. He didn't know where to look first, what to think first.

Logic. He needed to sort it out. He needed to process the information, sort through it, extract what he needed and discard the rest. But he couldn't; it was too much, like trying to pick out one snowflake in a blizzard.

Everything was twisting around and back on him, and he was a philosopher, and he was a healer, and he was an explorer, and he was a grunt, and an architect, sculptor, singer, writer, scientist, failure, success. Everything, everything and nothing, and oh God oh God oh God stop it *stop it stop it stopit**stopitstopit**. . . .*

Tears were rolling down Kirk's face, except he had no face, he felt it melting away, and his left leg was floating away, and he was literally coming apart, and there went his right arm, and it was waving to him. . . .

And the fields were waving to him, home, home in Iowa. . . .

Home, he had come home, after hiding on Vulcan for months, and there had been Carol Marcus waiting for him, and she was coming at him now, shrieking as she never had in reality, "You let him die you let him die you saved so many you saved Spock and McCoy and all of them over and over and over again and you let your son die you let him you let him you bastard you son of a bitch you don't deserve to live you don't you don't you don'tyoudon'tyoudon't. . . .

And Carol was screaming at him, and he heard the screams of all who had died under his command, all the security guards, all the crewmen who had placed their trust in him, and he was looking at a pile of bodies in the engine room of the *Enterprise,* the bodies piled like wood, phaser-burned or fried or sucked dry of blood or their red blood cells gone or crushed beneath the heel into powdered fragments, so many ways, and they were all equally dead, and they were being shoveled into the gaping maw of the engines, burning hotter than the flames of hell, but no, as hot as hell, because this was hell, and then he saw David's arm sticking out from the pile of bodies, he saw David's face staring lifelessly at him in its final twisted expression of pain, and he ran toward David, screaming into the soundlessness, and yanked on David's hand, and the hand came off, and it upset the pile of bodies, and they tumbled down on Kirk, down on Kirk, burying him, and the stink of death was everywhere, all the deaths upon him, upon him as they always had been and always would be, and hadn't he done it all? Hadn't he accomplished everything? What was the point, what was the goddamn point, there would just be endless repetition now, nothing new, nothing different, nothing that was remotely evocative of the days when it was all fresh and exciting and the adventure was out there calling to him, now it was just death and death and it was everywhere, in his eyes and up his nostrils, suffocating in it, and in his mouth, and he could taste it, and death tasted sweet, much sweeter than he thought, and the starship engines roared louder and hotter, powered and fueled by death, his lover, his all-consuming lover that had killed so many, killed his crewmen, killed his son, killed itself, but it kept coming back for more, and so did he, and they deserved each other, my God, it was so clear, just end it end it *God please,* and the end was going to be so good, as a shovel dug deep and lifted Kirk and the bodies up high, up over the engines, the flames licking at them, and he would finally be part of the ship, finally and completely consumed in body as he had been consumed his entire life in mind, and—

And a hand intertwined with his, pulling at him, pulling him free, and just like that the charnel house stench was gone. . . .

And he was surrounded by stars.

His arms and legs were back, and his face, and all of him. He turned, and there was Daystrom, Richard Daystrom, staring at him with a concerned look on his face. "Almost lost you there," rumbled Daystrom.

There was still the pounding feeling, the sense of being assaulted from all around, but it was subsiding, it was controllable now, and Kirk looked in wonder at Daystrom. "What is . . ." he managed to get out.

"We're inside the Worldmind mainframe," said Daystrom, "in its data base. All of the information stored in it is just that: random bits of information. And if you are unable to distill the data, then I'm afraid it's not—as the saying used to go—'user friendly.'"

"How . . . are you managing it?" Kirk put his hand to his head, trying to screen out the fierce pounding.

"It's a computer," Daystrom replied. "I'm in my element. I saw . . . all manner of things . . . but nothing as horrible as what I've faced in my life with my nervous breakdown."

"I was—I was almost immobilized," said Kirk. "I—"

"The further you bury your unhappiness, the more it hurts when the Worldmind gets at it," said Daystrom. "Now, me, I wear my misery on my sleeve. It's not nearly as strenuous."

"An argument for mental balance if I ever heard one."

"Furthermore," said Daystrom, "if we just concentrate, we can draw strength from each other. Singly it's harder, but knowing the other is here, we can pool our defenses."

Kirk looked around, fighting to keep his rationality. "Before we defend anything, we've got to find Spock."

They were standing on nothing, and suddenly Spock appeared to their right, or perhaps it was to their left. It was difficult to tell.

A vicious-looking knife—something distinctly Vulcan in design—was lodged in his back. He was vaguely waving at it, trying to pry it from between his shoulder blades.

Kirk gasped. "Spock!"

He ran toward him, and it took him a full thirty seconds to realize that, no matter how fast he ran, he wasn't getting any closer. Daystrom was right behind him, and when they came to the realization, they stopped and tried to catch their breath.

"It's like any other data base," said Daystrom. "You just have to manipulate the data that's at hand. And it comes from all around you, and from in you. It responds to what you think, what's on your mind."

And then there was a low laugh from everywhere. It grew louder and louder, filling Kirk's head, and he clapped his hands to his ears to try and block it out. But that was impossible because it seemed to be working its way from the inside of his brain outward.

"I'm calling on the Worldmind!" shouted Kirk. "I'm here on behalf of Ecma! "I'm here on behalf of Spock! If you're so blasted benevolent, why are you doing this? Why are you trying to destroy us? Why are you trying to destroy your own people?"

And the laugh grew louder, and suddenly a Calligarian melted into existence some feet away from Kirk. "The Worldmind is benevolent," cried out the Calligarian. "In fact, to the rest of Calligar, nothing has changed. But there's just one small pocket of it that's been . . . fixed. Calligar doesn't know it. And the Worldmind doesn't know it. I've hidden the existence of this little subsystem far too well. And that's where you are, and that's where I am, and you will not leave this place. And you have only yourself to blame."

"Who *are* you?"

"I'm Regger, you Federation idiot!" snarled Regger, his face twisted in fury. "I'm the son of Ecma! I'm the next Master Builder. And you've come so close to ruining everything, it's not even mildly amusing. I've planned this for so long, and you, in your blundering, have almost brought it crashing down. I'll give you this: I never thought you would survive this far. But you'll go no further."

"What did you do to Spock?"

"He wasn't expecting an attack," said Regger simply. "He was anticipating interaction on a plane of intellectualism. He was easily disposable the moment he arrived. I couldn't let him probe too deeply into the order for the thinning of my dear mother."

256

"Of course!" said Kirk. "You didn't want him to, because the order wasn't legitimate. It's not her time. But you wormed your way into the Worldmind and had it issue the order."

"Took years of my life to accomplish it," Regger said proudly. "Making my inroads, hiding my progress, bit by bit."

"It was perfect," Kirk realized. "Arrange for your mother to be slated for thinning at the time when you knew she would be meeting with us. She felt that it wasn't her time, but she respected the Worldmind too much for it to occur to her that there was outside interference. She'd never question it. So you knew that one of two things would happen. Either she would flee her fate and beg for sanctuary, and you would be made Master Builder. Or she would accept the decree, march to her death, and you would still become Master Builder."

"I was giving her an opportunity for happiness," said Regger. "How much fairer could a son be than that?" And then he was holding a phaser in his hand. "Recognize this? It's from your mind. You'll die here, and no one will suspect what really happened. You gave it a fair shot, Captain, I'll grant you that. But you can't be the hero every time."

He brought the phaser up, aimed, and fired.

And Kirk, literally with the speed of thought, ordered, "Shields up!"

The shield came up.

It was round and large and had a spike in the middle. Lettering forming Latin words surrounded the edge of it, and in the middle was a large representation of an eagle. The shield was on Kirk's arm, and the phaser beam bounced harmlessly off it.

He looked at Daystrom in surprise.

"It's all subjective," said Daystrom. "All of it. This

257

isn't physical against physical. It's mind against mind. I'm with you. Get him."

Kirk gave it no conscious thought at all. Just that quickly he was astride a magnificent white horse. The horse's eyes were glowing red, and it reared back, neighing so loudly that it seemed to fill the skies. The horse had armor covering the upper portion of its head and its mane, and on the fitted metal piece, as naturally as if they should always be there, were the letters NCC-1701A. And then Kirk realized that he was armored as well. It glistened and glittered, and his lance was secured under his arm.

"Yaaah!" he shouted, and the horse charged forward.

The horse thundered across the nonexistence of the Worldmind, and Regger fired again with the phaser. Kirk angled his shield down, and it deflected the phaser blast once more, and then with a roar Regger metamorphosed.

He grew larger and larger, his maw as wide as space, his eyes as hot as the sun, losing all resemblance to anything humanoid.

The horse reared up, whinnying in fear, and Kirk fought to control it. The monster took a step forward, the nothingness shaking beneath his step, and then another step forward, and Kirk suddenly took command because, dammit, he was the commander, he would not lose control, he would save the day, he would save everything and everyone. And there were McCoy's acid comments about being a knight, about being Galahad, and he had said it so disdainfully, but it had been true, all true.

He charged forward, the flag of the UFP a fluttering standard at the end of his lance. The monster swiped at him with its vicious claws, and Kirk ducked under, barely missing having his head lopped off, and spurred the horse forward, shouting in defiance as the lance slammed straight into the monster's chest.

The lance snapped, and the monster roared, staggering back, clawing at its chest. Kirk brought the horse around, pulled his sword from its sheath, and charged forward again.

The sword whooshed just over the monster's head as it ducked and lashed out once more with its claws. It ripped across the belly of the horse, and the magnificent animal screamed once and went down, its entrails spilling out. Kirk threw his sword away as he rolled across the ground to avoid falling on his own blade.

He rolled to a stop and got to his feet, and David Marcus was coming toward him, desperation on his young face. Kirk froze in place as David called out, "Father—let me help you!"

"You're not real!" shouted Kirk. The sword was a couple of feet to his right, just beyond reach.

"Yes, I am! Don't you see? I was pulled out of your mind. Your subconscious! I want to help you. I want to forgive you. Let me, please! Don't turn away again. Don't let me die again. Please! I want to help you so much!"

Everything in his voice, in his appearance, was sincere, and for a moment Kirk hesitated. David came toward him, reached out for him . . .

Kirk leapt to his right, grabbed the sword, and in one quick motion brought it swinging upward just as David grabbed for him, the scientist's face twisted in disdain. The sword cleaved David Marcus from just under his rib cage up and through to his opposite shoulder, bisecting his torso.

David shrieked, loud and long, his face transposing back into Regger's.

(And somewhere, in Regger's home at that very

259

moment, in a very private, very personal communion center that he had constructed for private access to the Worldmind, Regger slumped forward, his mind gone before his head hit the ground.)

And then all of it began to melt away, the nonground beneath Kirk's feet. He heard a shout from Daystrom, and then he was falling, falling, stretching out his hands to try to grab something, but there was nothing, nothing at all. . . .

Nothing
   at
      all
         and
            he
               fell
                  and
                     fell
                       and

Stopped.

He sat up.

He was in his quarters.

Daystrom was there. So was Spock, looking extremely puzzled.

Kirk looked up. The top of his quarters was gone. Instead there was a sparkling blue sky, and the earth's sun shining down on him.

And a Calligarian whom Kirk did not recognize, but he could tell from Spock's expression that the Vulcan did.

Before Kirk could say anything the doors to his quarters hissed open, and his mother walked in to offer them brownies. There was a Tribble perched serenely on her shoulder. Kirk politely refused the offer, and she smiled, told him how nice his friends looked and said they should get along well together, and then left.

Spock watched her go and then looked back at Kirk. "Your mother seems quite pleasant, Captain," he said.

"You'd've liked her," Kirk replied, still a bit baffled.

"I would tend to agree. Captain . . . this is Zyo. It was his determination to open Federation-Calligar relations that—"

"Started all the trouble," said Zyo gamely. "I'm also Ecma's father. A pleasure to meet you. Your efforts on her behalf have been most gratifying."

He extended a hand, and Kirk shook it firmly. "You are aware of what just happened?" asked Kirk.

"Oh, yes," affirmed Zyo. "As much as I find it replusive, by the same token I must admit a certain degree of admiration for my grandson. Imagine altering our base perceptions without our even being able to tell. He deserved to be the next Master Builder. He really did. His intellect was quite formidable. A pity you destroyed his mind, Captain."

"You mean he's . . . he's dead?"

"Oh, yes. Quite. And worst of all, there's nothing left of his mind, his spiritual aspect, to salvage. He will be forever denied the privilege of joining us."

"The privilege he tried to bestow prematurely on Ecma."

"It would have been nice to see her," said Zyo. "But I understand now that that would be selfish of me. Her time will come, however."

"What do you mean, her time will come?" Daystrom asked. "After everything that's happened, you still intend to demand that she be returned?"

"Well, of course," said Zyo, sounding surprised that the question should even be broached. "She's still one of us. She's still of the Calligar. She can't be permitted to leave."

"You're not being fair. Why can't she leave?"

261

"Because then she will never be part of the honor, of the beauty, of the Harmony of the Worldmind," said Zyo. "Don't you see? Where is the fairness of depriving her of that? If she lives a normal life span and simply dies, then that is the end for her. She will be forever gone from us. She will live alone and die alone. The misery, the torture of that . . . we cannot permit that for one of our own. We love our people too much for that."

"If you truly love her," said Kirk quietly, "then you will let her go."

Zyo laughed softly. "That old human saying. A rationalization by humans who allow a relationship to dissolve rather than fight to maintain it."

"There is a time for fighting," said Kirk, "and a time for giving in. A time for realizing the difference between true love and selfish love. Just because you have believed this for however many centuries doesn't mean that you are right."

"And simply because humans have believed otherwise doesn't mean they are right."

"True enough," said Kirk. "But doesn't Ecma deserve the opportunity to decide for herself?"

"But she won't be able to," said Zyo. "If we let her go, and she decides she detests it . . . she can never come back to us. By the time the rift opens once more she will very likely be dead."

"That is possible," said Kirk. "But it is her decision."

"We have made plans for her."

"She has made other plans."

Zyo leaned back. "I must say I'm not totally convinced. Our way is—"

"Is not living," said Kirk.

"We have access to every aspect of living!" Zyo protested.

262

"Every aspect but one," Kirk told him. "The chance to go on living. To experience something new. You've forgotten already what it was like to be alive. To breathe in air, to feel the press of a woman's lips against yours. To hold a newborn child in your arms, or even—even, God help us—to bury a child who has died. To stand on the bridge of a starship and wonder what's out there, what's next? What will we find? The value of that can never be diminished, and the glory of the adventure cannot, must not, be forgotten. To feel happiness and unhappiness, joy and misery, and have the right to choose to feel those things—that's what she wants. That's what you must give her."

Zyo seemed to pause, and now Spock said, "You began this, Zyo. You started events in motion. Now they've gone in a way you didn't anticipate. But you must allow these events to happen. Your ideas were good ideas. Now let new ones take their place."

"Let her go," said Kirk. "Please."

Zyo stared at Kirk. "I must consult with the rest of the Worldmind. This will be a very long, exhaustive discussion, I am certain. Please wait here." And he vanished.

"Wait!" said Kirk. "We don't have time for long and exhaustive—"

And Zyo reappeared. He sighed deeply. "I was correct. That was exhausting."

Kirk looked at Spock and Daystrom, and then back at Zyo. "You're done?"

"Yes."

"You said it was going to take a long time."

"Captain," said Zyo smiling, "when you're part of a mind that is capable of making decisions within periods of time so brief that there isn't even a measurement for them, a discussion of more than a second is considered an eternity."

263

"And the decision?"

He smiled, and it looked like a smile filled with pain. "Take her, Captain. Tell Commodore Tyler to be good to her. And tell her her father loves her."

"You will not regret this, sir," said Spock gravely.

Zyo looked at him sadly. "I regret it already. When you leave, please tell Alt that he should commune immediately so that I can relate the Worldmind's feelings on this."

"That will be fine," said Kirk. "May I ask how we leave?"

And then he felt the hard floor beneath him.

The light had vanished.

Suddenly it was hard to breathe, but almost immediately he knew why. Spock and Daystrom were lying on top of him. "Somebody want to help me out here?" he called.

Immediately he was being pulled to his feet, and he found himself looking into the relieved face of Montgomery Scott. The engineer dusted him off as Kirk said, "How long were we out?"

"About forty-five seconds, sir."

"Seemed like an eternity." He looked around to see Daystrom and Spock on their feet. Spock was stretching his limbs slightly as if to rid himself of a backache, and Daystrom was shaking out his arms and legs.

And now Alt was there, saying urgently, "Well, Captain?"

"The Worldmind would like to speak with you. And Zyo says hello," he added as an afterthought.

Alt's eyes widened in surprise, and then he nodded and took a step back. The light immediately projected down from heaven, and Alt's face went slack.

"Alt's being given our marching orders. We're free and clear to leave."

"Two problems with that, sir."

264

"What?"

"We've just been informed by the Calligar that a Tellarite ship has come through the rift and is attacking us, and the rift is going to cycle closed prematurely. If we're not out of here within the hour, we're going to be permanent guests."

Chapter Twenty-six

As McCoy and Ecma passed the transporter room Ecma stopped, turned to McCoy, and said, "I am very sorry, Doctor."

"Sorry for what?" asked McCoy.

He never seen saw the uppercut that knocked him cold.

Ecma left him where he lay and walked into the transporter room. At the transporter console Tooch was just confirming that the red alert had been removed and shields were no longer up, and she looked at Ecma in surprise. "Can I help you?"

"I am very sorry, young woman," said Ecma.

"Sorry for what?" asked Tooch.

The *Belligerent* soared over the Worldnet, firing in fury at the domed cities and getting absolutely nowhere. Whatever the domes were made of, they were clearly impervious to the weaponry of the Tellarites.

Khund pounded the arms of his command chair in fury. "We must destroy them!" he snarled. "There must be revenge for the Shondar! And if we cannot

266

destroy them from space, then we'll beam down through their domes and destroy them one to one!"

"Sir!" called the communications officer. "Getting a hail from the Callig—No, wait! It's over a frequency from a Starfleet communicator!"

"Put it on audio," growled the Tellarite.

"This is Captain James Kirk of the *Enterprise*," came the voice over the comm unit. "Calling the Tellarite vessel currently firing upon the Calligar."

"This is Khund of the *Belligerent!* We cry for vengeance on behalf of Shondar Dorkin!"

"Vengeance!" shouted the crew on cue. "Vengeance!"

"You won't find it here," said Kirk. "You can shoot until your phaser banks are exhausted, and it won't make a bit of difference to the Calligar."

"We're prepared to fight a ground war, city by city!"

"And are you prepared to live out here? Scan the rift. It's closing."

"You lie!" snarled Khund. "Another lying—"

"Sir, he's right," said the science officer in alarm. "The temporal fluctuations are increasing. Within the hour it will close, and perhaps sooner than that."

Bubbling with ire, Khund shouted, "This is *your* fault, Kirk. Shondar Dorkin is dead, and you're responsib—"

"He's not responsible," came a new voice, the voice of an Andorian. "I was there when Dorkin died. He died bravely, nobly. He died with two dozen of his enemies crushed beneath his fists, and one in each hand at the moment he breathed his last. He died saving us, and we would not be alive if not for his brave and noble sacrifice."

Khund looked around at his officers. They were visibly impressed. Andorians and Tellarites historically did not get on. For the Andorian to speak so highly of the departed Shondar . . .

267

"He may be lying," said Khund slowly.

His first officer stared at him. "He says one of our own died in brave combat, and you're going to say he lies about it?"

"Good point," Khund admitted.

Now Kirk's voice came back on. "Don't let his sacrifice be in vain," he said. "His body is right here, at these coordinates. Beam us all up there, and let's go before we're trapped here."

Slowly Khund nodded. "We've got your coordinates," he said. "Stand by." And then he tapped a comm button and said, with great satisfaction, "Transporter room . . ."

On the surface, Kirk and company stood there for a moment, Kirk with the communicator in hand. Alt was there as well. "They'll bring us up," he said confidently. "It's a surer bet than the shuttle. The trip through was tougher than expected, and if I can avoid having to depend on the warp sled—"

"Aye," said Scotty. "Before all this started I was going to let you know about that. But now we'll—"

Then they heard the telltale hum of a transporter. Kirk prepared himself to materialize aboard the Tellarite ship.

It took him a few moments to realize that his concern was moot. The body of Shondar Dorkin dematerialized, but the rest of them stayed right where they were.

"Khund!" shouted Kirk. "You said—"

"No," came Khund's voice. "You said. I never said. Furthermore, I now understand—the flowery words and praise were simply so that we would bring you up. Well, I'm afraid not, my friends. Enjoy the Calligar. You're going to be with them for a very long time."

The channel was cut off, and Kirk immediately turned and said, "Let's get to the shuttle and get the hell out of here. Once they go through the rift again it'll close in minutes."

"That," said Spock, "is a very great likelihood."

They ran like hell.

"Mister Sulu!" called out Chekov. "Someone has just used the transporter!"

"What?" Sulu was astounded. "Where would they go?"

Chekov glanced at the coordinates that had been set. "Ecma's ship," he said.

"Send a security team to the transporter room and open a channel to that ship. *Enterprise* to Ecma. Have you boarded your ship?"

"Yes," her voice came back. "I apologize for the means by which I did it. Your sensors must be telling you the same thing mine are. The rift is closing. I'm their only hope of getting back. And besides, I don't know if I'm ready to leave my people. I thought I was, but now I—I don't know. I'm not sure, and until I'm sure, I can't turn my back on them. I just can't."

Everyone on the bridge looked to Sulu as he was quiet for a time, and then he said, very softly, "Do what you have to do. Godspeed. *Enterprise* out."

And that was when the Tellarite ship hurtled out of the rift into normal space. Without answering any hails or even slowing down, the good ship *Belligerent* leapt into warp six and was gone in an eyeblink.

Leaving behind a temporal anomaly known informally as Pike's Rift, which—thanks to all the warp activity passing through—was now going to close in less than five minutes.

The shuttlecraft howled through the temporal battering at warp three and pushing it. The battering was intense, and it seemed as if the universe around them had gone mad.

The ride in had been strenuous enough, but in the moments before the rift was preparing to cycle closed it seemed as if the bizarre distortion was doing everything it could to prevent the last refugees from getting out. Time twisted and turned back on itself, and Kirk, seated just behind Spock and Scotty, saw things spinning back and away that didn't seem to make sense.

"Captain, we're running out of power!" shouted Scotty. "We've got two minutes at warp three left!"

"Full ahead, Mr. Scott. Be the little shuttle that could."

Around them space was on fire, flaming images dancing around them, and two minutes ticked down to one.

"Estimating exit time in one minute, ten seconds," said Spock.

"We've only got a minute of warp left!" shouted Thak from the rear. "We're not going to make it! We'll be crushed at impulse power!"

"Even when warp power ceases," said Spock calmly, "it will still take approximately fifteen seconds for the warp field to disintegrate around us."

"You mean we have a five-second margin for error!" said Thak.

"I would say 'error' is too strong a word," observed Spock.

Time ticked down, down, and the gauge measuring warp power dropped down, down . . . and then out.

The rift roared around them, howling its fury, and Spock said, "Warp field disintegrating. On my mark and ten, nine, eight, seven . . ."

The shuttlecraft staggered into normal space and out.

In front of them, big as life, eminently welcome, was the *Enterprise*. Thak also noticed the Andorian ship many kilometers away.

"Five," Spock said serenely.

And then they saw Ecma's ship hurtling toward them and then angling away, toward the rift. "What the hell?" came a shout from Tyler.

"Attention Calligarian vessel." Spock opened a link to it. Tyler had unbelted and was right behind him, and now Tyler shouted, "Ecma!"

Her surprised voice came over the comm. "Joe?"

"Ecma, we're here! We're fine!"

"They—they let you go? But what about my being thinned?"

"That was an elaborate ruse on the part of your son," said Spock. "You are not scheduled for termina—"

"SPOCK!" said Tyler, horrified.

"I—I don't have to die?" came her voice.

Tyler looked daggers at the Vulcan and then said, "No . . . you don't. But . . . you can stay with me."

"But I can live with my people now! I don't have to run away from them!"

"You wouldn't be running away from them," said Tyler desperately. "You'd be running to me! Ecma! Listen to me—"

"Twenty seconds until closure of the rift," said Spock, glancing at his instruments.

"Ecma! Stay with me!" shouted Tyler. "Please! After all this, please don't—"

And Ecma's craft vanished into the rift. There was a little spark where it went in, and then it disappeared.

There was silence in the shuttlecraft for a long moment, and then Tyler said darkly, "That bitch."

"Joe," said Kirk softly. "Come on, now . . ."

"She used me, James. Don't you see? You all must see it. She used me until she didn't need me anymore, until we cleared the way for her return, and then back she goes. She didn't love me. She never loved me. It was all a game to her!" As the rift grew smaller, shrinking into nonexistence, his anger grew greater. "That's all she ever was! Some—some link to a great moment in our youths! That's all. A memory of a moment when we seemed to connect but didn't. We never did, not really. Well, she never meant anything to me! I felt sorry for her, and she used me, so fine! We're quit of each other, and—"

And the rift closed.

And a split instant before it did, something emerged.

And a voice crackled over the comm. "Joe?"

He lunged for the comm, elbowing Spock aside. "Ecma?"

Her voice sounded thick, choked with emotion. "What you did for me—what all of you did for me—I thought I would be alone. And I was scared, but I . . . it won't be alone. It'll be together. A different kind of together."

"It'll be great," said Tyler, grinning. "You and me. I never doubted it for a moment. I knew it was going to be us. It was destiny. I love you, Ecma."

"I love you, Joe."

Spock looked at Kirk. "He never doubted it for a moment?" asked Spock.

"Doubted what, Mr. Spock?" asked Kirk. "I don't recall the commodore doubting anything. Do you?"

Spock stared at Tyler, back at Kirk, and then said, "Considering the vast number of emotional flipflops humans make in their lifetimes, it's amazing you do not all come equipped with trampolines as standard issue."

Epilogue

THE MARRIAGE OF Commodore José Tyler and former Master Builder Ecma was performed by Captain James T. Kirk while the *Enterprise* was en route to Vega for rest and debriefing.

James Kirk, in his arguments and fight for survival with the Calligar, settled a number of uncertainties and doubts in his own mind. He found this ironic but never had the nerve to tell anyone.

The Tellarite government lodged a formal complaint with the Federation and declared war on the Calligar. This declaration lasted ten years, during which time not a thing was done and the Tellarites eventually declared victory in absentia, since the Calligar were clearly not brave enough to show up and fight. Shondar Dorkin was enshrined in the hall of heros on Tellar, and a minor holiday was named for him.

The Federation Intergalactic Studies Council thoroughly debriefed all members of the contact team and made a recommendation that the Calligar be contacted again upon the next opening of the rift.

273

However, when the time came for the rift to reopen once more the Federation was engaged in major hostilities as part of the Klingon-Romulan war and unable to dispatch a research team. The rift opened and closed undisturbed.

Thak the Andorian wrote a popular musical play based on the Calligar and won the Zankar-Bowles Prize for creative fiction that year.

Dr. Richard Daystrom, combining elements of a thought-responsive environment with his previously discarded M-5 research, developed a theoretical computer program that would create images with the ability to think and respond in a human manner. Hailed as "Daystrom's Comback," this was the groundwork from which holodeck technology was derived.

Macro awoke from Tyler's phaser stun blast to be informed that he was the new Master Builder. He was also told that the reason he had acquired this high honor was that his sister was gone forever, and his son was dead.

Upon learning of this, Macro began crying.

And he never stopped until the day he died.

STAR TREK
THE NEXT GENERATION

A ROCK AND A HARD PLACE

Under the best circumstances, terraforming is a tough, dangerous task that pits the hardiest of pioneers against an unforgiving environment. When the terraformers on the planet Paradise fall behind the schedule, Commander Riker is given temporary leave from the *Enterprise* and sent to assist.

Riker's replacement on the *Enterprise* is a volatile officer named Stone whose behaviour soon raises questions about his ability and his judgement. Meanwhile, Commander Riker has become enmeshed in a life and death struggle with Paradise's brutal landscape. However, he soon learns that not all of the planet's dangers are natural in origin - as he comes face to face with Paradise's greatest danger and most hideous secret...

STRIKE ZONE

Deep in the uncharted regions of our galaxy, a
primitive, warlike race - the Cantovs - have stumbled
upon weapons powerful beyond their wildest
imaginings. The Cantovs have used those weapons to
attack their most bitter enemies - the Klingons.

Now Captain Jean-Luc Picard and the crew of the
U.S.S. *Enterprise* have been called in to mediate the
dispute. The *Enterprise* will ferry diplomatic teams
from the two warring races to the source of their
conflict - the mysterious planet where the weapons
were discovered - in an attempt to find a peaceful
solution to the conflict, and discover the origins of the
super-powerful weapons. Before the entire galaxy
erupts into full-scale war.

STAR TREK
THE NEXT GENERATION
VENDETTA

The Borg - half organic being and half machine, they
are the most feared race in the known galaxy. In their
relentless quest for technological perfection, they have
destroyed entire star systems, enslaved countless
peoples, and, in a single brutal attack, decimated
Starfleet's mightiest vessels. Only a final desperate
gambit by Captain Picard and the *Enterprise* crew
stopped the Borg from conquering the entire
Federation. And now they have returned...

Answering a distress call from a planet under attack by
the Borg, the *Enterprise* meets Declara, the lone
survivor of an alien race the Borg obliterated. Blinded
by hatred, Declara seeks the ultimate revenge - the
complete destruction of her race's executioners. But
the *Enterprise* crew learns that Declara's vengeance
carries a terrible price, for once unleashed, the
destructive force she commands will annihilate not
only the Borg, but countless innocents as well...

THE STAR FLEET
TECHNICAL MANUAL
by Franz Joseph

The classic handbook every Star Fleet cadet must have! Illustrated throughout with diagrams, charts, pennants, badges and flags, and packed with detailed information on every aspect of Federation life imaginable, the manual includes sections on the following:

- Federation flags, seals and uniforms

- navigational charts and equipment

- statutes and regulations of the Federation

- Federation codes

- interstellar space weaponry, equipment and technology

- alien life forms, communications, uniforms and insignia

- and much, much more.

For a complete list of Star Trek publications, please send a large stamped SAE to Titan Books Mail Order, 42–44 Dolben Street, London, SE1 0UP. Please quote reference ST52 on both envelopes.

MJB